Dark Destiny

Kamal Kant studied engineering in India and then went to the US in search of work opportunities. He has since been associated with some of the top corporates there. He lives in Florida with his wife, two daughters, Tia and Sam, and a dog. This is his first book.

Reach him at:
Twitter: KamalKantWriter@KamalKa13475386
Facebook: https://www.facebook.com/RealDealK2
Email: Kam2kant@gmail.com

Dark Destiny

Kamal Kant

RUPA

Published by
Rupa Publications India Pvt. Ltd 2019
7/16, Ansari Road, Daryaganj
New Delhi 110002

Sales centres:
Allahabad Bengaluru Chennai
Hyderabad Jaipur Kathmandu
Kolkata Mumbai

ISBN: 978-93-5333-561-8

First impression 2019

10 9 8 7 6 5 4 3 2 1

The moral right of the author has been asserted.

Contents

Prologue

Blood oozed sluggishly from her lifeless arm into a small pool on the glistening wooden floor. Soleil slept peacefully. No sound except a few scrapes of footsteps on the wooden stairs and a passing train's receding trundles and screeches in the early morning hours. In her inebriated state, thoughts flashed through her mind—she was an artist, she loved to dance, she wanted to have kids and move back to Paris. None of these will ever happen as she felt her life slipping away...

The dance floor is full of unknown silhouettes, a known face glows in the midst, and brings tranquillity to the chaos. I am drawn by Naina's hypnotic eyes. As I reach out to touch her, dark shadows grab her, she screams and is taken away. I struggle to grab her, scream for help, but words don't form. Naina's face disappears in the darkness, I follow her into the abyss. I open my eyes, breathless in cold sweat.

Vincent heaved a lifeless body behind Goa's old fort near the abandoned train tracks. He wiped the beads of sweat off his face to catch his breath before getting to the work, work of burying his father, the person he had admired all his life. He became collateral damage in a son's war against his father.

a quarter million dollars

My gleaming eyes didn't blink for the longest duration of time and my heart pounded against my chest as I stared at the pile of neatly stacked dollar bills in the middle of my work table.

I fixed my expensive kurta around the neck and let out a nervous, triumphant smile. My face gleamed under the reflection of the computer screen glare in my home-office. It was my home-office but in reality it was my family's dumping ground. Old stacks of books and Arjun's roughed-up, used toys took one corner of the room, old computers and printers took the far side of the room, a pile of freshly washed clothes sat in a basket near my chair, the mild fragrance of detergent emanating from it.

Chicago's short and depressing winter day had come to an end promising another cool crisp night and a snowstorm. Wind howled outside and spattered against the snow-covered window panes making trumpet sounds

I made decent money as a technology manager at a large investment firm. However it was not enough, I still lived pay cheque to pay cheque and usually fell short at the end of the month. But here I had two hundred and fifty thousand dollars staring at me. I never seen that much cash in my life. Sadly, none of it belonged to me, even though I had worked hard and played with fire for it. The cash had the stamp of Terrence, a ruthless African-American gangster in South Chicago.

I got sudden chills in my body, I did a few bad things to

get this money. But what I did seemed right at that time. It bought safety for my family. For the first time in months I sat without fear in my heart. I had to risk everything to win it all. I had taken a chance and played against all odds, but I had come out a winner.

A pleasant warmth began to exude from my body—I felt intoxicated even though I had had nothing to drink.

Money is a scintillating stimulus, but hope is the biggest stimulant in life. I could now hope to have left dangerous roads behind me.

Finally, we would be safe.

I got up leaving the chair rocking and squeaking. It was time to go downstairs. They were all waiting for me. I bent down under the table and moved the footstool away. With the tip of my fingers, I located a long cut in the carpet. I pulled it back and pried open a rectangular wood piece from the floor with my nails. I swiftly scooped up all the cash in my arms and shoved it into the hollow space in the floor. I placed back the footstool and stood up, looking at it for the last time before walking out of the room to the deafening chaos of guests and the screams of kids running around. Shahrukh's 'Aaj ki Raat' thundered in the backdrop.

Energized, I strode down the stairs searching for my family. A scrawny Indian teen was at the helm of the crowd, playing the role of a DJ. He was wearing a Lakers oversized jersey and big headphones. Koyal had probably promised him free food to convince him to perform and showcase his talent. Anyway, he was rocking it.

I scanned the entire floor, from the living room to the foyer and finally saw Koyal in that packed place. I ached for her touch and caught a quick glimpse of her. She was wearing a thin, low-cut blouse which revealed her graceful back.

I snaked through the crowd until I was a few inches away from her.

My perfect romantic scene shattered when Nick's head popped up between me and Koyal. *I have done so much for him! Moron! Works in TSA* (Transportation Security Administration for America) *safety but was stupid enough to get himself surrounded with gangsters like Terrence.*

Six feet tall, Nick looked like a young band member of One Direction or the Jonas Brothers. Cute and handsome. He was wasted and had a huge grin on his face. He cupped my face and kissed my cheeks. He hugged me and shouted in my ear, 'Aditya, thank you Bro! You saved my life...saved Maggie! I apologize for being an asshole. You are my man. I owe you so much!'

I was a bit annoyed, but I said loudly in his ear, 'Nick! Don't fuck up your life again, this is your second chance—earn it! You have a huge responsibility now.'

Overwhelmed, Nick nodded in appreciation. 'I've got to talk to you about Vincent, something real important,' he muttered.

I pulled myself apart from his embrace and said, 'Can it wait? Kind of in the middle of something really important of my own, buddy.'

Understanding my need, he stepped aside with a drunken smile and gestured towards Koyal. I looked at her again, the heat in my body shot up and I wanted to kiss her right there. But I couldn't have the kiss I wanted in front of the conservative crowd. I wanted to kiss her deeply, softly and passionately. As if there was a psychic connection between us, she sensed my presence behind her.

She turned around, brushing her silky skin on my arms. She pulled me down by my neck and locked her lips on mine with authority. I swear the touch was electrifying like never before.

Being bad isn't all that bad, definitely worth it, I got my family back.

The crowd roared in appreciation. It was unexpected but very encouraging. The DJ changed the music—something meant for Indian Punjabi parties, our feet started moving and hands clapped to Bollywood beats. Koyal was happy. I thought that smile on her face was worth any crime I had committed.

'Thanks, Adi! You made this happen. Maggie is so happy. I'm happier. You saved this family,' she whispered into my ear. Her eyes showed admiration for me and for what I had done for the family. I felt a knot in my stomach due to guilt.

The damn guilt...why does it ruin the good moments?

I simply smiled back at her. We continued looking at each other. I was falling in love with my wife for the first time. It was a moment of pure bliss. Everything was going great for the first time in years. We were celebrating the glorious occasion of Maggie's baby shower with family and friends. There were smiles and laughter all around. That happy moment hadn't come easily to me, it had eluded me for a long time, but today it had arrived.

Sadly, luck and I do not share a very friendly relationship. Nothing comes easy to me and when it does, it doesn't last very long. It was about to come to a screeching and embarrassing halt in the next five seconds.

In the next few seconds, I was about to get embarrassed in front of my whole Indian community when the Drug Enforcement Administration's (DEA's) SRT—Special Response Team would drag me out from my own house in the freezing cold and throw me into their van.

In the distance, I heard unexpected noises—someone screamed. I looked in the direction of the pandemonium in front of the house.

Fear exploded in my heart, and I stood frozen for several terrifying moments, trying to process what could have happened outside. I trotted towards the main door, and as I drew closer, I got the first glimpse of the SRT police. A phalanx of specialized law enforcement personnel swarmed all over the place. Scared and confused, people made way for them. The DJ quickly killed the music.

I froze. Many thoughts ran through my mind while I watched the SRT police raiding my house. *Are they here for me or Nick? Fuck! Can't be Nick! Although this whole shitstorm started because of him, they weren't here for him.*

I heard my name being shouted, 'ADITYA... ADITYA MALHOTRA.' So that's official. They were here for me. I had no idea I would go down like that. I knew I was doing wrong on several moral grounds, but I never thought I was doing something which would bring the SRT at my doorsteps.

I quickly pulled Nick closer and told him about the hidden money in the floor. Nick looked at me with bewildered eyes. Two of the SRT cops charged at me. All I remembered before going down was looking at their black hard helmets with visors covering their faces, assault rifles clutched in their hands. I was shoved down onto the floor while my guests looked at me in shock. My hammering heartbeats reverberated in my ears. Trained cops handcuffed me instantly. I whined with pain. I wasn't sure what hurt more, a broken jaw or twisted arms. I struggled a bit but the other cop put his knee on my face, the house suddenly filled with screams.

Everything was chaotic and noisy, but in the midst of all that I heard sounds of Koyal's screams. She grabbed me as the cops dragged me away.

I was no longer resisting. Things started to slow down. I was being lifted, hauled and pulled from my shoulders. I caught a glimpse of Koyal's and Maggie's scared faces. As soon as I stepped outside the door, I saw that my house was bathed bright in flood lights by the law enforcement people. I was blinded by the light. Several cops waited outside with guns drawn, a K-9 unit stood on the standby. The vehicles bore the logo of the DEA. *All this for an Indian engineer. Seriously, what the hell did I do?*

It had started snowing. It was a gloriously beautiful night. I was dragged in front of a lean, muscular, tall, white American man with a heavy moustache and a long grey beard. He was wearing a black trench coat and looked like he was in charge of this operation. I had never seen him before.

We looked at each other quietly, breathing deeply. He studied my bloodied face, ruffled hair and shivering body. I was struggling and breathing hard due to shock, pain and sudden exposure to cold.

Koyal came out running in a thin saree, her voice trembling as she screamed at the man. 'What is going on, officer? Where are you taking my husband? This is a mistake.'

The man in charge paused dramatically and said in a stern voice, 'It's not a mistake, Ma'am. We have been watching him for weeks. Your husband is involved in a very bad business with international drug cartels.'

He signalled his men to take me away. My heart sank after I heard his accusation. I had no idea what was going on. My body was dragged again, pushed and dropped on the flat cold surface of a van which smelled like the worst fucking luck. A strong overhead white light made me feel like I was dying.

The cop inside the vehicle stared at me and scoffed, 'Who did you fuck with to deserve such a grand reception, asshole?'

Soon the van started to roll, and my body and mind drifted away.

I fucked up! Plain and simple! My mother always said, 'Help others—it's the noblest thing you can do.' But what would you do if the others you help turn out to be a bunch of assholes?

Maya—the first love

Seventeen years ago, Mrs Rukhsar, my favourite teacher of the eleventh grade, yelled, 'If I catch any of you passing any note, it better be a love note. You have the immunity to pass notes on just about anything for the next two hours—it could be about solving global warming, or a plea to bring the World Cup back, or a storyline for DDLJ 2, or you can ask Rohan to stop flexing his non-existent biceps. But if I see the note is about the tests you are doing today—you will be thrown out, and I will fail you.'

Mrs Rukhsar always announced in a commanding voice. When she talked, we listened.

She continued, 'Now you are randomly selected for different tests. Students doing the titration exam, move to the far left corner. Obviously, students not doing titration stay right where you are and pick up your test instruction sheets. If you have paid attention throughout the year, this should be easy for you. If you were like Rohan, who focused more on his looks, you are out of luck.'

Everyone looked at the most popular boy of the class, Rohan, and laughed at him even though there were many guilty folks as charged. Rohan was my good friend and lived nearby. We did everything together except study. He was cut out for a different path—he was to join the Indian Army. I was his fan.

I picked up my backpack, moved to the far left and stood behind a stained white-tiled lab counter where all the apparatus was already arranged. I was excited because I had prepared well for the exam. Across me, Maya stood nervous as hell but pretty as heaven. She looked ravishing as usual in the school uniform of white shirt, grey and yellow argyle tie with a matching skirt and dark blue blazer fitted on her curved body. I never understood how anyone could pull off sexy in a school uniform like Britney Spears from 1998 until Maya joined. She looked way out of my league from day one, not that I was praying for a chance to score with her. I was focused on the most important goal of my life, the IIT examinations just like Mahabharat's Prince Arjun was on his aim.

The most important grade of a student's career. It makes or breaks your life. I heard that almost on a daily basis from my father who like every Indian father was encouraging me to get into IIT. I was like every obedient son from a middle class family. But my life wasn't a complete disaster. I had some fun. I had the liberty to play cricket and was really good at it, which compensated for my pimpled face and made me popular whenever school houses competed. I always lead my house in sports, math club or science/geography quizzes. *Yes! I was a nerd.*

As I said, on the surface Aditya and Maya were no match made anywhere but pretty girls know their game well. There was no social media, Facebook, Instagram back then to scheme plots and subplots among friends, but the girls used their beauty and charm to fool simpletons like me.

Maya moved from Bombay to Delhi because her father was sent to expand a struggling bank in north India. We both lived in Vasant Vihar, two streets apart, and I could see her house if I risked climbing to the top of the water tank on the roof. Her single-storeyed yellow house sat among the tall and green cedar trees which dotted our colony. On a lucky day, I would catch her going from one room to another or sitting in the cute little backyard of her house. I was a nerd and a stalker—all signs of a serial killer, but it seemed an innocent and romantic thing to do at that time.

I wouldn't be lying if I said that my heart started singing *Kuch Kuch Hota Hai* the day she walked into the lives of Modernites at Modern School. She reminded me of Rani Mukherjee in the film, with her bambaiya attitude, her walk and her skirt just inches above the knees—everything was killer. I also wouldn't be lying if I say that before the year was over Aditya and Maya eventually became a thing in the eleventh grade.

It all started when Maya won the hearts of whole school by rescuing an abandoned injured puppy in the school stadium. She asked everyone in the class for help but the girls didn't offer her any because they hated her for coming in and stealing their scene in school. The rich boys, on the other hand, felt they were too cool to touch a street dog.

'Hi, Aditya, is it?' She caught me coming out of the math club.

'Oh. Hi. Yes, it's Aditya, yes you can call me Adi. I was here for a friend. I don't do math…' I rambled while changing my voice to sound mature. It just ended up sounding awkward and raspy.

'Nothing wrong with it. Math is good. I wish I could be better at it. Anyway, I found this injured cute puppy. Can you help me otherwise he will die?' She made a droopy face.

How could I have resisted those teary eyes? I ended up volunteering and took the puppy home when she told me she couldn't adopt him because of her dad. I had the similar dad-hate-dogs situation, but I carefully decided to not disclose that when she mentioned she would visit to see little Jackie, as in

Michael Jackson—her favourite pop star. How could I have ever passed such an opportunity to get close with her? By the way, it was because of Jackie that my love for dogs began.

Maya and I eventually started seeing each other more often at my home. She was very scared of her old-fashioned father. We would talk for hours on the phone and write each other long emails about Jackie, school, movies and random stuff. She was a dreamer and a sort of rebel she was not a normal kid, she was aiming high to do something different.

'A fashion designer! To walk on ramps like models?' I asked while we lay in my bed, heads touching each other's, looking up at the ceiling. My ceiling was covered with posters of cricket gods like Sachin Tendulkar, Kapil Dev, Yuvraj Singh and Steve Waugh. My desk wall had formulae of math, physics and chemistry pinned to it. It looked like Aamir Khan's timeline wall of crimes in *Ghajini*.

'Stupid! I want to be a designer who designs those colourful innovative, provocative, sexy clothes which models flaunt on the ramp. Wait and watch!' She clicked her tongue. I could see a glint in her eyes.

'But that's not close to engineering, or becoming a doctor or a lawyer, heck even a CA. How will you convince your parents?' I got up shocked, looked at her and took Jackie from her arms.

'CA! Do I look like a stupid CA or an engineer? Although, I will look very hot as a doctor!'

I thought the girl was crazy. I couldn't even imagine going to my dad to discuss career options outside those mentioned above.

'Adi! You are set though, you are an engineer—it's in your blood and you are destined to be an IITian and then a big shot in the US,' she declared with a sparkle in her eyes.

I enjoyed talking about her big dreams. I also dreaded that one day, she would go out of my life in the pursuit of her passion. And I would get left behind.

The rest of the year flew by quickly. We agreed that I would help her in math and science. That was the best time of my life. I had fallen head over heels for her. Everyone at school knew about us.

Mrs Rukhsar yelled again, 'You have to perform the experiment, choose your type of indicator/titrand, quantity of titrant, write down your entry colour/end colour, record your data on the sheet—do the whole experiment. In front of you there are options of beakers and flasks. Choose the right equipment and chemicals—I'll be watching you all.'

Maya couldn't tell the difference in the colourless liquids even though they were labelled. Poor Maya had prepared for other projects. I was more upset than her. Like a loyal, evergreen reliable boyfriend, I took it as a challenge to help her out. It was not a matter of me and her, we were now one. I signalled to her to copy my moves and do exactly as I did. She copied my moves brilliantly. I noted all the readings along as I did my test but she had no idea what we just did. I lifted my head up and saw her adorable face. I was love-struck.

Looking at me, she bent forward on the lab table and slid her sexy arm towards me. Nerdy classmates were busy with their test and Mrs Rukhsar had finally taken a seat after she got tired of walking.

She moved her fingers on the lab table until she reached my exam sheet. In a swift move, she pulled my sheet back to her space and with the other hand replaced it with her empty sheet. I looked at her in horror. *For a nerd this was as bad as it gets.*

She tapped on the top left corner of the sheet. I stared at the sheet until it made sense. The blank sheet had my roll number on it. I craned my neck to look at her sheet. She blew a soft kiss to me. She had switched our sheets before we even started, and I just finished her exam on her sheet without caring to look at the roll number. *Sneaky girl.*

I had twenty minutes left to write my test again. It had taken me an hour to complete it the first time. She made a pout and air-kissed me as if to apologize. I melted again. When nobody was looking, I also switched my conical flask with hers so it matched with the results written in the sheet.

She pulled me aside as we exited the lab after turning in our answer sheets to the teacher. We pulled away from the crowd of students leading to the hallway and entered an empty classroom. We walked through the maze of desks and chairs to the farthest corner. She sat me down behind the last chair and desk. Someone had inscribed, 'I hate physics, physics sucks!' on the back of the chair. Somebody concurred with me on that horrendous subject.

I looked at her face which glowed from the soothing sunrays which channelled in from the window. Without hesitation, she put her soft tender strawberry-flavoured lips on mine. I had Vaseline smeared on my lips to prevent cold sores in the winter. I wondered what she thought of me at that moment. In the next moment, all tensions, inhibitions smoked away. I was in a blissful moment of my life. I had wished for this moment, this kiss with her, but it was nothing like what I had dreamt it would be. It was even better—pure magic, unexpected and special. She skewed her head and we locked our lips deeply. My hands, as always programmed in a high testosterone teen, automatically started caressing her back, and quickly found their way to her boobs. *Too soon.* I cringed in fear that I had made a mistake, but she understood my dilemma. She held my hand and put it on her left breast.

I snaked my hand through the inside of her shirt and cupped it. It was on fire. I felt her heart throbbing in a pulsating rhythm against my palm.

'I love you, Maya. I have always loved you, ever since you came in to the school.' Overwhelmed, I let my heart out in front of her.

A few kids scurried in the hallway noisily. We broke apart immediately before she could say anything. I took a long breath. She bolted right up and fixed her shirt and blazer. I waited until my teen sensations subsided and cursed myself for not wearing snuggly fit underwear and had to think ugly thoughts to normalize the sensual effects.

I had no idea what she was going to say to my proposal. I also didn't know that was the last time I would see her.

The best day of my life was followed by days of agony, anguish, pain, despair and every hurtful emotion in the world. Maya was gone. A big brass lock on their house gate waited for me when, breathless, I reached her house. It brought back the dreadful fear of losing her. She was gone in a daze. I heard a neighbour lady telling me that the family had left in haste.

I had no idea why she left. Her emails bounced, undelivered on her closed account. I camped outside her house in the rain and sunshine, anxiously, and waited. But she never came back.

I went into a shell for months. I cried out my pain and didn't share anything with anyone. I analysed every single moment I had shared with her, wondering if she really, actually ever loved me. Was it all just to befriend me to pass the eleventh grade? I realized how much I missed her. Jackie missed her too. I went back to her empty house several times to see if she had left me anything—a message—a hint or a memento of something that we both shared. But she hadn't left a trace.

First love is always the purest and the first break-up is always the hardest. It was not good for my young heart. I was broken inside. I still think about Maya. I thought I had moved on from that chapter, but she still lingers and sneaks into my thoughts.

the fugitive

I woke up with a sprain in my neck. Disoriented, I stared down for a few seconds until it dawned on me why I was in such a scary place.

I sprung up and immediately fell back in the chair. My hands had been shackled in a chain to the centre of the table. The rattling noise of the chain echoed in the room, and I flinched in pain. The enormous room was ominously lit with just enough light to see the walled area. I narrowed my eyes and realized that the front facing wall was a big two-way mirror—the one I had seen many times in movies, through which cops study the criminal's interrogation. *Holy shit, this is serious.*

A chill ran down my body, and I felt the walls boxing me tightly making it hard for me to breathe. My mouth was dry and throat was parched.

I had a lot of questions on my mind about why I was in that situation, but before I could ponder on them, the only door in the room flung open, filling the room with a bright dazzling light.

Two men walked inside. One was wearing a neat blue suit with a business shirt and a dark tie, and the other was a balding Caucasian in jeans and a loose sweatshirt with a large print of the famous American symbol of a bald eagle and the large letters—DEA underneath. He was huge, barrel-chested and overweight. He wore hideous big, brown 70s-style plastic glasses. *If he was a cop I could escape ten times before he even blinked.*

The guy in the suit was the same officer I had met earlier at the house. He spoke my name in a commanding and clear voice, and he pronounced it perfectly, a rarity in the US. 'Mr Aditya Malhotra! I'm Nelson…Richard Nelson. You can call me Dick.'

Dead serious, he stared at me, expecting some reaction like a chuckle or smile at his nickname. I was too intimidated to say anything. I froze, and I prayed to God to get me out of there. He took the only available chair in the room in front of me, throwing the file he brought on the table. It made a crisp splat sound.

The bald guy walked around the table and sat his big American ass on the corner edge of the table a few feet away from me. He crossed his arms on his chest and stared at me.

I immediately thought Richard may be the good cop in this routine.

'What's the meaning of this?' I mustered enough courage to sputter those words.

'Why am I brought down here like this? I'm a law-abiding immigrant.' My voice grew stronger as I continued to speak and I liked the sound of my confident voice. 'You know that you've got the wrong guy. I'm 100 per cent sure that this is a case of mistaken identity. I didn't do anything wrong. I am just a common Indian family man. If you let me go, I will pretend it never happened and I will not press any charges against you folks,' I finished my little speech like a parrot.

'I'm the deputy director of the DEA. This is Officer Jack Sullivan—Strategic Intelligence Detective of the DEA. We have been monitoring you for a few weeks. The charges against you are very serious and with special circumstances. Do you know what that means, Mr Aditya—that means NO BAIL!' Richard chose his words carefully, not only spelling out the meaning of me being there but also killing my hopes of ever getting out of there in years.

I asked, 'DEA?' to which Richard calmly responded, 'Drug Enforcement Administration.' My eyes squinted.

'Do you want to google it?' Sullivan offered his phone to me. I stared at him trying to seem as if I was not interested in talking to him, but deep down I was scared shitless.

He continued, 'Yeah the DEA baby—Drug Enforcement Administration. Nothing major but a little federal law enforcement agency for combating trafficking of cocaine, heroin, ganja and opium. You must have heard of us in the movies. We are the motherfuckers who control drug proliferation and bust assholes in this very ugly business! And guess what! You are one of those assholes!'

I was about to crap in my pants—that was a hell of an opening statement. I froze again.

Richard snapped his fingers in my face and brought me back.

He said, 'Mr Aditya. Let me apprise you of the seriousness of the situation here so there's no doubt in your mind. Your arrest is accurate, and by the time we leave this room you will be facing the dilemma of such a magnitude that it will rock your life as you know it. So let's wipe the slate and restart the dialogue by pretending that you have not said anything yet.'

Mr Nelson fanned his hand in front of my face to get my attention. He was stylish and of an average build. He was in his mid-forties and his white teeth glistened while he talked.

'Hello, Mr Nelson. Umm, Mr Dick, what's this really about? Am I being arrested for being a terrorist?' I asked slowly.

Sullivan giggled and I felt the table shaking like an earthquake with readings of 9 on the Richter scale.

He apologized to Richard. 'I'm sorry, Dick. The guy is funny. Who is this guy?'

From their reaction I was relieved that I was not mistaken

as a terrorist. I leaned towards Richard and said, 'Sir, you are wasting your time. I've got nothing to do with the drugs business. I'm not the guy you want.'

Richard slammed his fist on the table and screamed at me, 'You are EXACTLY THE GUY we want, Mr Aditya Malhotra, don't fuck with us and shut up and listen.' Shaken, I retracted into the chair.

He's not a good cop either.

'I'd like my phone call to a lawyer I feel like I need to exercise my rights,' I said in a low voice.

Sullivan replied, 'Your phone call is no good here, pretty boy.'

'C'mon Sullivan! Who talks like that?' Richard cleared his throat and loosened his neck tie. He took a deep breath to calm his nerves. He didn't look like he was the bad cop from the lot of those two. He had just lost his cool. Richard opened his arms straight on the table and brought his compassionate tone back.

'My suggestion: hear us out, Mr Aditya, and then make an informed decision.' He looked back at me.

For some reasons I decided to listen to him.

For the next 20-25 minutes I sat in my chair in one position listening to what he had to say. With each word coming from his mouth, my hope of walking away free from this room was subsiding away like a sailorless boat drifting away lost in an open ocean.

Richard signalled to Sullivan, who reached over and unlocked the shackles off my wrists. My eyes fell on the open file. In it were pictures of a woman. I felt stung and didn't move. Richard slid another picture of a man in front of me.

'From your reaction, I see you know them.'

I was scared and confused.

'Son! I want you to stay with me, we have not started the worst part yet. This is gonna take the whole night if you keep going in flashbacks. I'd suggest you start talking,' he said.

I came out of my trance. 'No, I don't know the man. I know this woman—she's Soleil. She's French. I met her only once.'

'Are you sure?' he pressed. I nodded, my eyes fixated on the pictures.

'Chicago Police found her dead in her house. This man in the picture is her boyfriend, François—goes by the name Franky. He's dead too. What do you know about him? Who did you tell about him?' Sullivan demanded.

Richard closed the file with a splat, stood up and pushed his chair back.

My head was spinning like a blender in a coffee shop. Richard put his hand on my shoulder and said, 'Look alive, Mr Aditya— you need to fight through this. The DEA was watching Franky in order to reach a high value target—Mexico's number two drug cartel leader—Don Carlos. Somehow your actions got Franky killed and that dented the DEA's operation, and we lost two of our agents. A lot of people in the DEA are mad at you. You have hurt this great country. Your actions will be proven in the court of law as obstruction of justice and treasonous acts against America, and for that I promise—you will pay...big.'

He paused and studied my face again.

He added, 'Unless...you help us. We need Carlos. You get us to him.'

Like a bad actor with bad lines Sullivan chimed in again. 'Still want RIGHTS? A lawyer? You can bring in your Indian friend Maya Varma or whoever, but get this: the minute a lawyer walks in here—this deal will be off the table. The amount of evidence we have against you—oh boy! Your ass is going to go into a prison for a long time. And you know what happens in prisons to pretty boys like you.' *He's racist and prison-sex obsessed!* I felt like complaining, but to whom?

Richard heard my emotional wordless plea. He gave Sullivan a sharp look and said, 'The DNA evidence shows you at Soleil's house before she was murdered. You are deeply involved in this dangerous game, Aditya—intentional or unintentional, I couldn't care less at this time because lives are ruined and somebody needs to go to prison. Now it's up to you if that somebody is going to be you or Carlos.'

I tried to speak but could only mumble, 'It doesn't make any sense. I knew Soleil and I heard Franky's name from her, but who's this Carlos? I don't know what to tell you.'

'You ever heard of Franklin Roosevelt?' Sullivan asked me randomly. I stared at his face trying to think of the relevance of what he had said. 'The president of the US?' I answered.

'He died in office in 1945. Do you know how?' He paused and then answered, 'You don't know. You can't know—most of the world doesn't know how he died because his medical records were erased a few hours after his death. Who made that possible? The federal agencies, guys like us made that possible. If we are capable of erasing secrets of that magnitude, imagine what we can do with a nobody like you! So now think again!' He gritted his teeth.

My legs got stiff and my body went numb. *That was the mother of all threats.*

'Maybe this will help you!' Richard leaned in and took Soleil's picture from my shaky hands, replacing it with another picture.

It was a picture of the money I had stashed in my office. The carpet, wooden plank and dollar bills were clearly visible. *Fuck me, they found my safety nest.*

'Yeah, we have your money. Try explaining the presence of 250,000 dollars in your rented house. We know you make 120K dollars a year with which you practically support a family of five in a pricey Chicago neighbourhood. There's no way you saved all that money with monthly savings. Like I said, you have a lot to think about.' He paused and threw another picture in front of me. It was of another woman.

'Asshole, you are America's most wanted criminal right now, and I'll personally make sure you die in a closed cell. You've got thirty minutes to think over your choice before we tell your wife to forget you,' Sullivan threatened me again on the way out.

The door closed. My eyes were still glued on the new picture Richard had left on the table. My eyes widened as I realized that the woman in the picture was Naina! My long-lost college love-interest.

My head truly began to spin. They had presented so much information in so little time. The things that they had accused me of were:

- I was the accused murderer of Soleil and her boyfriend.
- I had committed treason against the US, abetting a conspiracy to put national stakes at risk.
- I aided in foiling a live DEA operation to capture an Escobar-type Don, and finally, was responsible for the death of two US federal agents.

What the fuck was going on? Only Vincent knew about Soleil. Why would he deceive me? He was an old friend who was more than a brother to me. He was my support system from the college days when I was falling apart in India. He couldn't deceive me.

The DEA, Mexican mafia, murders and drug cartels. None of the words Richard told me made any sense.

Why was Naina back in my life and what is her relevance in all this?

My thoughts jumped hysterically from Soleil to Naina to the DEA. I sat in turmoil for minutes which felt like hours. My eyes burnt and my bladder was about to explode.

I patted my jeans pocket and found that I still had my cell phone in it. I secretly pushed it up out of my pocket until the screen popped up in sight.

No signal! Must have been jammed. I had to do something.

I couldn't focus. I looked at the glass window and at the camera in the right corner. 'Hey, anybody watching me here? I have to go to restroom. I can't think straight. Hello? Anybody there?'

After about a minute, Sullivan pushed open the door and signalled me to come with him. He wasn't happy.

We walked through the well-lit hallway which led to an office with multiple cubicles and desks.

I was uncomfortable because of my numbed legs from hours of sitting plus I was holding a substantial amount of urine in my bladder.

I noticed three tired officers on the late night shift, busy on computers. No one looked up at us. I saw Richard in one of the offices busy talking over the phone.

We walked past an elevator to a restroom. Sullivan opened the door and allowed me in. I entered the empty small restroom which had two urinals and two stalls. There was an incongruously placed yellow cone bearing the word CAUTION in the middle of the restroom. The floor was wet. I went straight to the last urinal next to the large window. Chicago's skyscrapers looked majestic through falling snow. The blizzard was at its extreme making the sky look like a white canvas.

I unzipped and waited. Sullivan moved the cone aside and blocked the door. I started my business, and felt relieved. I stole a glance at my phone. The signal bars on my cell phone had sprung to life.

I quickly sent a text message to Vincent. 'Meet me at Navy

Pier.' I pocketed the phone and glanced through the window. I saw the snow-covered rooftop of a smaller tower of the same building at least three storeys down. Big HVAC units were blowing smoke clouds. *That's where I escape.*

My heart started pounding as I thought of a plan that was so stupid that it may just work. *I'm going to make a run for it. I can't believe it, too dangerous. I don't have any choice. I need to speak to Vincent. He will know what to do. I have nothing to offer to Richard.*

Sullivan was observing my every move. He caught me looking outside the window and said, 'Yeah that's right, Babu! Look at the sky for the last time from a civilized place. Next time you will see the sky from a big-ass prison with someone riding on your ass.'

I was irritated with his hurtful racial and sexual insults. I moved to the sink and opened the tap. I soaped my hands and froth started to form. To activate my plan, I had to buy some time.

I asked, 'Why are you obsessed with prison sex, Mr Sullivan? You know those remarks are not only hurtful but also meaningless.'

'Shut the fuck up, Babu, you can't win your way out with your perfect grammar.' He gestured me to hurry up. I looked at the water. It was filling up, but I needed a bit more. I stepped towards him quickly.

'You've got to believe me. I don't know what to give to you and Richard. I've got no clue about Don Carlos. I don't know how Soleil or Franky sabotaged a DEA operation. I think you guys are setting me up and scaring me with your stupid racial tactics,' I said, feigning confidence.

That talk worked. It agitated Sullivan who pulled out his pistol and yelled, 'Wash your fucking hands right now or get the fuck out!' I complied by showing him my hands quickly and stepped back to the sink. I filled the frothy soapy water in my palms and splashed it on Sullivan's face. It stung his eyes. I threw more water on his feet and on the floor. He rubbed his eyes with his shoulders, gun pointing at me. I got scared that my plan hadn't worked. I had expected him to fall on that slippery floor.

As if God had finally heard me, in the next moment Sullivan took a step forward and then another, and his foot skidded. He lost his balance, fell face first towards the washbasin counter. Instinctively he got his gun arm in between his face and the counter, but it slipped due to his weight, crunching his bones. His other leg also folded and he was falling now head first on to the tiled floor. I quickly grabbed him from the chest and saved him from getting a fatal head injury. I just saved his life.

I rolled him down on his back. He looked at me in surprise and tried to raise his gun, but he couldn't with his broken arm. With his left hand he reached for his baton and quickly unbuttoned it from his belt. He hit me hard on my leg, causing it to buckle. I let out a soundless cry, and he hit me again on my back, making me fall on the floor.

I managed to snatch the baton from him and swiftly stood up, kicking the gun away from his other hand. Frantically I climbed over his body, picked up the heavy loaded gun and, as soon as it touched my palm, I felt sheer power in hand.

'I'm sorry, Jack. This is unintentional and you know that I've been set up. I'm innocent, and I need to prove that myself,' I said while shoving the gun in my jeans waistband and covering it with the kurta. I jumped on my feet and rushed to the door, slid the baton stick up my right sleeve. Suddenly, I felt blessed to be wearing a loose kurta with loose sleeves.

My head craned out of the open door. Business as usual

on the floor. I placed the yellow caution cone in front of the door. All I needed to do was to walk unnoticed in the midst of those armed agents to the elevator which was about twenty metres away.

I walked down briskly towards the elevator, my head down. My feet picked up speed and, from a distance, I saw Richard in his office busy on his computer with his back to me. I turned my head away and quickly pressed the elevator button and kept pressing it. I noticed we were on the fifteenth floor. *Come on… Come on… Three floors down. I'm on the fifteenth floor, the roof from toilet appeared three floors down. That's it, the twelfth floor.*

The hand that was holding up the baton started shaking in panic. It went lifeless and I lost the grip on the baton, causing it to slide towards the floor. I glanced over my shoulders at the office and saw Richard coming out.

The baton hit the concrete floor and the loud bang attracted everybody's attention, including Richard's. He immediately ran towards me.

I pushed the button frantically. Another loud bang and the restroom door swung open. Sullivan lunged out and entrapped himself in the yellow cone. His heavy body hit the opposite wall.

He yelled, 'Someone stop that bastard.'

Suddenly, the elevator made a ding sound, the doors opened and I threw myself in. I started pounding on the door close button frantically. The doors closed just in time. Elevator music was playing. I stared at the changing numbers until I reached the twelfth floor and the doors opened. The hallway ahead had dimmed lights. I peeked out quickly. No one was there. I quickly made a run to the restroom on the right. Finally, luck was on my side. The lazy architect built the restroom at the right place, as expected. I burst opened the door. My eyes lit up when I saw the big window. I pulled the gun out, aimed at the window. My hand shook and I was sweating profusely. I stuck a finger in my left ear and fired at the window. No fire. The gun was on safety. I couldn't believe it and stared at the gun like I was going to melt it with my gaze. I looked around. There was nothing else to use. I had no time to waste and desperation had kicked in. I positioned myself in front of the glass and kicked it with all the strength in me. But I didn't make any impact on the glass. I kicked the glass again and again. It moved a bit. Adrenaline was kicking in. I took the gun and used its heavy base to hit the glass. Soon it started to show cracks.

A ray of hope.

I shattered all the glass. A loud gush of cold freezing air blew in. The wind pressure was so high that I struggled to keep my eyes open. Cold air froze sweat on my back which stabbed me like a million knives. I should have been in front of a fireplace, cosied up with a brandy in my hand, but nothing was normal now. I was about to leap into an abyss of snow in a thin kurta. I looked out and realized that the rooftop of a smaller building was not attached to the same building, it was about six feet away. *You can't jump that far, who are you, Tom Cruise?*

A ray of despair.

I mouthed *fuck* countless times and went back into the restroom. I took a deep long breath, positioned myself and charged to the window, crunching the glass beneath my feet, and leaped out the window. I flew momentarily in cold air, kissed the beautiful snowflakes and barely made the distance. I landed with one foot hitting the edge of the roof and tripped. I rolled myself as soon as my feet touched the slippery iced rooftop to avoid a deadly fall.

I ducked my body and leaned forward, rolling on the cold icy rooftop fiercely before coming to a halt when my body hit the big aluminum HVAC ducts. It was a miracle I didn't hit my head.

I immediately felt pain in my back, but I had to keep moving. I looked up at the window. Richard's silhouette appeared. I shook off the disorientation and sprinted to a singular door at the far end of the roof.

My plan was to get away as far possible in the next sixty seconds—it was my only window of opportunity to lose Richard and his men. Richard hadn't gone down to the ground floor to catch me, following standard protocol but had somehow understood my plan. He had come directly to the twelfth floor and then into the restroom from where I had jumped. I ran, quickly. I must have gained a hundred metres when a bullet whizzed by me. I looked back and saw Richard flying through the same window and landing effortlessly behind me. *That was a Tom Cruise-style landing. I could learn from him. Shit!*

He fired two more shots at me which busted the AC ducts causing a huge escape of smoke clouds from them. I kept running. Wind howled as it passed between the buildings.

I reached the door and quickly swiped the badge I had stolen from Sullivan in the restroom. I thought it might come handy. *It did.*

I covered the stairs in long strides. I galloped faster and faster and was three floors down when the door upstairs flung open loudly and Richard burst in. He peered over the railing and fired two more shots at me. Bullets zoomed past me again and found their place in the wall behind me.

'Stop,' he shouted. I heard a change of clips in the gun. He was still behind me.

'Stop or I'll shoot you, Aditya,' he shouted. *Really! You are already shooting at me, asshole.* I kept running, covering another three floors, Richard was covering the distance faster and was gaining on me. I knew I couldn't outpace that fit monster. I burst through a door which opened outwards to another office floor. Not knowing what was ahead, I entangled myself in long hanging plastic tarps. The floor was under construction. I fell and slid on the dusty floor, hitting cans of paint, pipes and other boxes. I stood up quickly and my knee buckled due to sheer pain. I rolled on the floor.

I dragged my leg up and scanned the room. I heard Richard's footsteps coming closer and getting louder. A big gush of wind blew in from the open unfinished windows. The white dust from the floor swirled in the air, forming white clouds inside. Outside the window I saw another ray of hope. There was a metal gantry—a scaffold platform attached to the outside walls of the building which connected to the metal stairs. It looked antique, rusted and unsafe. *Just like I wanted it.* I jumped on it, and it shook violently under my feet.

I ran down the frail and risky stairs. Cold metal stabbed my palm and after a few seconds, I didn't feel my palms and fingers.

The endless stairs creaked and trembled with my weight. I looked up and saw Richard jumping onto the gantry. His eyes met mine. His face glistened with the reflection of lights. I stopped and looked at him for a second. I thought maybe we could talk. He didn't care and fired two shots back to back. They hit the metal near my hand, causing sparks to fly. I cursed, ran again, pounding down on the frail stairs until they started to come loose from the deadbolts in the wall. The staircase reeled uncontrollably. I kept running. I saw Richard losing his balance and slipping down the cold stairway until his fallen body stopped at the end turn. Finally, I heard him scream. *So he does get hurt. Phew!*

I stopped short on the second floor, realizing that the staircase ended there. My eyes widened with fear again. *No time to waste.*

My struggling shadow appeared on the dirty alley underneath. It grew longer as I hung from the end of the staircase while looking for a sweet spot to land. The landing had to be perfect and away from the ladder in case it did get unjammed and rushed down in a split second to crush my skull like in the movie *Final Destination*. *This can't be my final destination yet.* I let myself go and landed on my toes with bent knees and instantly rolled on my back away from the giant iron structure. The gravel on the street stung my back. I lay on the freezing street for a few moments to catch my breath until my nostrils were hit with the stench of urine and garbage. The shabby alley was empty. I was amazed that I had made it that far, like a fugitive.

How crazy is that? Stupid plan which worked!

I looked up, through the falling snow, and saw Richard's enraged, wounded and helpless face. I got up slowly and ran into the dark alley disappearing in it.

The alley opened into a busy street. Chicago never sleeps, even in a fucking blizzard. I walked briskly towards the sounds of cars, snow-plough trucks and, buses. Chicago Police cars were at every corner. I wondered if they had been alerted about me by now. I hoped not. I'm sure they wanted to stay inside in this cold. I kept my head down and raised my arm to stop a cab.

'Navy Pier please and turn the heat up in the back.'

The unconcerned tired Indian driver turned the heat to max and quietly put his cab on route to Navy Pier. I sat in the back with my head down. My hands were shaking and my heart was pounding. I did the unthinkable. I was definitely in deep shit now. Megaton of deep shit.

Why were they watching me? Why is Naina back in my life? Who killed Soleil?

I needed that money to save my family, but I didn't hurt anyone.

All the money I made is gone. That money was our ticket to safety, now it's gone.

We all will die one way or the other, but I couldn't save my family? Fuck!

I started panicking and mouthed fuck countless times. I needed to get my head straight, find my strength, and I did what I always do. I closed my eyes and pictured the girl who mattered most in my life—Naina. She's been my therapy my whole life. Whenever I'm helpless, I go to her.

Like a flashback, Naina's beautiful young, smiling face appeared before my eyes. Her hair, smooth as silk, danced under the colourful lights. That's where I saw her last, in Bangalore—when we were both nineteen-year-olds. We ran through the empty hallways, we were both happy that night.

I snapped out of my reverie as the car shook violently due to a pothole. *Focus, Aditya, focus! Why is the DEA after you?*

I had a lot to think about on the way to Navy Pier.

dark destiny begins—six weeks ago

There are close to three million Indians who have made America their home. Why? Because in this land of opportunity, talented Indians are prized based on their capabilities. Here they can fulfil the clichéd promise of the American dream. A nice life, a white picket-fenced house, an adorable family with kids and a pet. Indians make roughly 1 per cent of the total population in America, but their numbers are astounding when it comes to education and wealth by any immigrant community. Indians are in every prestigious industry be it medicine, engineering, IT. Heck! NASA's workforce is 36 per cent Indian. Why am I telling you this? Because at one point in my life I wanted to touch the sky and enjoy the meteoric rise my fellow Indians achieved. But some incidents in my life altered my destiny and I ended up where I am today. Living an average life.

I live in a suburb of Chicago in a rented house with Koyal. I married her because I was broken in my life and so was she. She has a ten-year-old son, Karan, from her previous marriage. He's now my stepson. We also have a dog, Romeo.

Here's the reality—I didn't turn out to be a specialist doctor or a NASA scientist. I am not a fucking CEO of any tech company either. I have no Cinderella or rags-to-riches story because it's not a fucking movie where everything ends well in the end. Sure, most Indians have done well because they knew what they wanted to do, and their hearts were in the right place. They applied themselves to a cause. I couldn't make it because I lost my way and would have wasted away my life had I not found the support of Koyal and her family. She gave my life a purpose.

I met her three years ago. She ran a flower shop, from where I used to buy flowers for my sick mother during my hospital visits. (My mom went back to India after getting better but she left me with a lifelong message to help others as it is the noblest thing to do.) She made me look at Koyal in a different way. She found Koyal's aura as pure as an angel's and told me to marry her. She said Koyal would give direction to my lost and wayward life.

Fast forward the sob story, clichéd dramatic sequences with her ex and I married Koyal six months later.

So if I say that all this madness with Soleil and the DEA happened because of my love and loyalty for this family it will not be a lie, and I have compelling reasons to justify what I did.

Was it stupid? Yes!

Will I do it again if I needed to save my family? Yes!

I have a vivid memory of the day when it all began. The day started with my normal routine and ended with death threats from Terrence and his gang.

A few weeks ago, I got out of the bed at precisely 5.55 a.m. with the usual sadness in my heart, took out Romeo for a run on Lake Shore Drive and admired the expansive mansions in my neighbourhood with wanting eyes. I came back, got ready for work, dropped Karan at school and Koyal at her flower shop and went to the daily grind of work. At the end of the day, I was supposed to pick up Karan from his baseball practice session. I was on my way to the school when I got the dreadful call.

This is when it all started.

'Adi Bro, it's Nick... I need your help. I need you to come get me,' Nick's frightened voice crackled on my phone.

Before I could understand anything another voice echoed on the phone. 'You better hurry, asshole, if you want to see your boy alive and better yet, bring me my money, brown boy!' I didn't know who it was but it sounded like death.

'He doesn't know anything about money!' Nick interrupted. I heard some scuffling before the line went dead.

I looked at the dead screen and suddenly two back to back text messages arrived. The first was an address and the second said, 'No COPS! Twenty Minutes'. I was stunned, not sure what to do. I texted the next best person in my life, Vincent, to meet me at the address. I called Koyal, apologized and asked her to pick up Karan.

After a few minutes, I was gunning my Honda CRV down the streets of downtown Chicago through the traffic. I searched for a sign of US-41.

I made it to the front of the Chicago Center Tower. It was a forty-two-storey glass tower which sparkled with the rays of the setting sun. I rolled my car to the curb and looked around for any suspicious activity. My heart was racing. Nick, my brother-in-law is Maggie's husband and Maggie is Koyal's little sister. Maggie is Koyal's life. Nick and Maggie are practically kids—in their early twenties. Nick usually never gets into trouble, so when I received that call, I was definitely worried.

I checked my phone, nothing there. Moments later a BMW blinded me from behind with its lights. I exited my vehicle and walked up to the other car.

'What is going on, Bhai? All okay?' said Vincent. My friend, my brother showed up. I felt better already.

'I don't know. We will find out soon. Do you have any weapon?' I asked. That surprised him, he looked at me in disbelief.

'What happened, Bhai? Weapon? What are you talking about?'

'I don't know. That's why I called you because of your expertise in such matters. You being an ex-criminal, drug lord and shit,' I said.

He hushed me quickly, 'I left that life behind in Goa and why are you risking your life for your brother-in-law?'

Annoyed, I gave him a stern look. 'He's family, I'm going up there with or without you. But if you come with me, I'll feel much better, you know, with your experience and all,' I chuckled. I felt at home with Vincent. We go a long way back. We spent two years in college together before he dropped out to join his family business. Vincent belonged to a long lineage of a Portuguese family who settled centuries ago in Goa and had spent most of his life there. He helped me during my tough break-up with Naina. We spent many hours at Delhi's disco clubs and nights sharing bottles of whisky.

We lost touch after he dropped off until he moved to America.

Vincent rolled his eyes grudgingly while getting out of his car, which shook violently because of his weight.

'You are going to get a Nobel Prize for this noble deed for sure! A posthumous award!' he said sarcastically.

Vincent had changed dramatically since college. I couldn't believe it was him when I first saw him after all those years. He was no longer a skinny boy and looked older than his age. Being of Portuguese descent he looked like a Latino. Five feet ten inches tall, Vincent was now almost a hundred kilograms. His skin tone was much more tanned from what I remembered, and he looked like the successful rapper 50 Cent, always dressed in a fitted three-piece suit with a tie and gel-soaked curly short hair. Round big face. The double chin. Arms twice my arms size.

His voice was even heavier due to excessive drinking, smoking and late night activities.

We headed into the building and then into the elevator.

'Weapon! Did you bring any?' I whispered to him.

'For the last time, Bhai, no gun! No weapon. These are multimillion dollar apartments. No one is going to mess up these designer homes by killing people. These are entertainment homes, if you know what I mean.'

I didn't know what he meant, 'So you are going to do gangster talk with them?'

'Man! What the hell is a gangster talk? You are so naïve, I wonder how you made it this far without the world eating you alive.'

'No need to get worked up, Vincent! Relax and talk, do your magic. Let's just take our boy home safely.'

'This is what I do. Don't tell me to relax. You got me in this, I'll handle this. Most probably it's only a typical threat-based rattling-the-confidence type meet-up. Nobody dying here in this clean model home,' he proclaimed with confidence.

The elevator door opened in front of a door that led to an open hall which was filled with expensive and luxurious furniture and vintage artwork. I did feel better thinking that nobody would make a mess by breaking the bones of people in such a spotless and elegant place.

As we crossed the living hall and stepped into the kitchen area, two nicely dressed African-American guys appeared. They were dressed in sleek black and signalled us to keep walking. My eyes widened as soon as I saw Nick sitting in the middle of the floor. His hands were tied and his face was bloodied. I rushed to him and suddenly realized that the entire living area was covered in thick, plastic sheets. There was fresh blood on it, possibly Nick's.

The men shoved us from behind and we fell on the sheets. Terrified Vincent, gulped air. I shook my head in disbelief—all our theories from the elevator went out of the window. This was our end. The henchmen straightened us up and made us sit on the two empty bar stools next to Nick.

A handsome African-American man came towards us. He was dressed in white tight pants and a blue blazer with a bowtie. Terrence, the man behind all my problems. He was a well-groomed gangster. He looked at our dreary faces and laughed.

'Well! Look at the diversity of races in this room. Shit! Is the United Nations in town or something? A white boy gets in trouble, he calls someone and here comes an Indian and a Latino!' he chuckled.

He stopped in front of me and looked at me dead in my eye.

'Are you his saviour? He called you?'

Before I could say anything, Vincent opened his mouth to negotiate. Terrence backslapped him hard, jolting all three of us. I quickly held Vincent's hand.

'Motherfucker! Did I talk to you or did I talk to this gentleman in the middle?' Terrence raged.

'Now, I'm a man of reason. I've a business to run, a business which I started with these hands and it's very dear to me. In my business, I care a lot about people. They are my strength. The right people with potential can help take a business to unimaginable heights.'

He paused and took a good look of Nick. 'I thought Nick had that raw potential. I gave him a chance, but he blew it bad, and now he got you two mixed up in this. Tell me how can you help me? Like I said, I'm a reasonable guy and open to ideas.'

He finished his monologue, but none of us spoke.

'That's great, lots of productive ideas at once. I like the enthusiasm,' Terrence laughed sarcastically.

I cleared my throat, 'I… We…don't even know what we are talking about here. Can you give us a hint?'

'My bad, gents, how can I expect a solution when you guys don't have any clue about the problem?' Terrence put his hands on his chest sarcastically and signalled to one of his men.

The guy behind Nick grabbed Nick's neck in a chokehold and started squeezing. Nick struggled, gagged and kicked his feet on the sheet. Vincent and I instinctively stood up. Terrence waved his .44 magnum steel revolver in front of us and signalled us to sit down.

I felt helpless. I clapped my hands and shouted, 'Okay, I get it. This is your scare tactic. We are in the game now. Full mode! You have our attention, leave the kid. Let's talk. It's about money, right? It's always money. What are we talking about here? You said you are a man of reason, let's reason. Shall we? Let the kid breathe. If he dies, you don't get anything right! I don't think you are that kind of businessman.'

'Wrong! If he dies I will still get my money—from you! You are right—I'm a man of reason and a man of my word.' He pointed the gun at me and signalled his man to let Nick off. Nick fell on the floor coughing, wheezing and struggling for air. Terrence hunkered in front of the tortured Nick and, gently touched the steel of his gun on his face.

'We get it! Reason, threat, motivation, money—what is the bottom line? What do you need?' Vincent spoke.

Terrence, like a 90s villain, stood up and scratched his chest with his gun and smiled. 'I'm in awe of your love for each other. Three Musketeers! I'm ecstatic to work with people who have so much camaraderie. This will be so much fun—killing you all one by one and then your families, loved ones, friends.'

My heart sank. He was right—we were fucked.

'If I want, I can milk you guys for years, but my conscience won't allow me that. All I want is my money and some penalty for doing wrong to me. Your boy, Nick, lost about 75k dollars in my casino in an effort to fulfil his dream to get rich fast. Now that's a lot of dough, Bro! So I offered your boy a deal since he works in the TSA! I proposed that he let one of my men carry a certain non-explosive packet internationally—help a brother through the security and shit, and that's it—we are even. Should be fucking easy for him right! But hell no! He fucked up—he managed to get my packet confiscated—it was worth 100k dollars, Bro!'

He paused again to see our reaction.

'So now that you are all caught up with today's top news— tell me which one of you motherfuckers is going to give me 250k dollars?'

'250k dollars… No, it will be 175k dollars,' I said quickly.

'Don't go Asian math whiz on me, homie! The sticker price went up. Call it my hassle fee, to put me through all this grief. I had date plans tonight. I was all dressed up to woo a girl I've been working for a week.'

Silence ensued. I looked at Vincent, Terrence looked at us.

'Nobody died yet so don't sulk here. Get the fuck out of here and work on the plan to get me my money. You have eight weeks.'

On the way back, as my car careened on the highway back to Edgewater, Nick and I sat quietly in the car. We both carried the 'You are fucked' look.

I broke the silence, 'Can you borrow any money from your dad?'

Nick replied in a heartbeat. 'I already did, the first 25k dollars I lost was his.'

I mouthed 'beautiful'. There was nothing else to say or hear for the rest of the trip back to home. I pulled the car into my garage with a heavy heart and a lot on my mind. Nick quietly walked to his house which was in the same lane.

For the next week, we planned how to come up with the money.

green light—Weeks 1 and 2

For the next week, our state of mind was beyond any expression. I read all there was about drug trafficking—best and safe ways to do it and what to avoid, drug mules, how they smuggle drugs across borders. All three of us met daily and brainstormed on ideas to come up with the money. Nick couldn't sell his house, it wasn't in his name and it was worth nothing because his dad took out massive loans to live his retired life lavishly.

I didn't own a house and have a measly 17,857 dollars in the bank, which I couldn't touch without risking Koyal knowing about it. My 401(k) retirement plan had about 75,000 dollars, but Koyal would know if I touched that. Vincent had left his old life behind, so he didn't have much cash on him.

Next, we started thinking out-of-the-box ideas—some crappy ideas discarded outright were rob a bank, abduct a rich person, go to Vegas and try our luck in poker. I liked the poker idea. I was good at it. Foolishly, I took out ten grand from my savings and drove to Rivers Casino in Des Plaines. It did not start well, I lost 8,500 dollars in the first two hours, and it took me a whole lot of stress, and all weekend to recover my lost money. I slept two days straight to catch up on all my lost sleep. We had to lie to our wives to make matters worse.

A week passed, and we had no money and no plan. We met at a bar and sat in the back table where we could talk privately.

Vincent suggested, 'Nick! I hate this idea, but you got to

be the Easter bunny!'

We looked at him as if he had sniffed drugs. He explained, 'Like an Easter Bunny delivers eggs to kids, you be the bunny, as in the drug mule and drop the packets wherever Terrence says. Three to four rounds and you are done. Everyone will be safe.'

'Vincent! You have gone mad, tell me you are not serious,' I protested.

'Nick, if we all want to live, this is what you gotta do! I'm sorry this is your mess—you've got to man up and clean this shit up,' Vincent shrugged his shoulders and looked at me.

Nick pondered for a few seconds, then nodded his head in agreement and said, 'Let's talk more on this tomorrow, only way I can do is by practising it. I need to take Maggie for a doctor's appointment today. We are finding out the sex of the baby.'

When he left, Vincent pulled me aside. We ordered another round of beer. He asked me, 'Bhai, why are you risking your American life? Look it's none of my business, but I'm your friend and as a friend I've to advise you.'

'Vincent—there's no choice, we have to do something. The poor kid is having a child, have a heart! Also I don't know if you noticed, it's not Nick's problem any more. Terrence knows us—our whole family is a target now.'

'Yeah, but why you? You and Koyal do not have exactly a perfect marriage. And as far as I know, it's more like an agreement for your American citizenship.'

I smiled and put my hand on his shoulder, 'Yeah, it's not perfect, but it's my family now. I won't abandon them. We can't go to the cops, they'll throw him in prison as soon as they sniff his TSA stunt. And you know Nick can't do this drug mule shit. He thinks he can, but tomorrow he will know it fucking hurts.'

'How do you know?' He gave me a sharp look.

'Because I fucking read everything about smuggling drugs

in your body. I already tried for a day—I tried to swallow grapes and tried to keep them down. I puked ten times that day.' I laughed as I admitted my stupidity. It made Vincent laugh too, and then we laughed so hard that tears started to build in our eyes.

'I've realized that I cannot have a future in the drug mule world. I cannot smuggle drugs or any other object by swallowing. I can't put that on my resume,' I spluttered. I had not laughed like that in years.

Vincent and I gave each other a high five. I was blessed to have him there in that difficult time. I have no other friend.

I sighed, 'I'm a common man. I don't know what else to do to arrange this amount of money in such a short time.'

Vincent nodded in disagreement to my last statement.

'There's a way, but I'm afraid you are too swallowed in your daily life to notice that. How old are you? Thirty-five? You are still fucking sexy! You have forgotten your playboy charm. I have not. I still remember the day in Goa when you saved my ass by getting some information from a girl in five minutes with your charm.'

I looked at him in disbelief, 'What are you talking about, Vincent? What charm? What playboy? What's the connection here?'

'All I'm saying is, I left my criminal world but I have made some connections where "information" is pure gold. All you need to do is get some information and pass it along. There are several interested parties in such transactions. No one gets hurt, one party never knows what the other party does with that information. I've already asked a few folks, and they have some jobs lined up if you are interested.'

I got curious when he mentioned that no one gets hurt. 'C'mon it sounds too good to be true. What do you mean?'

'It means steal some information from a vetted source. The source is always a person. However, the sources of the transactions I have in the pipeline are women.'

I finished my beer, staring at him. I knew there was more to it and waited for him to spill the rest of the proposal.

'The way it works is you will have to befriend the source, gain their trust and steal the information the buyer needs. And then you walk out—no mess. The source may or may not even know that you tricked them, even if they do, for their privacy and safety, they will not reveal what happened.'

'Then?' I asked.

'Then nothing—you give me that information, and I will pass that along to the buyer. Then we get paid homie! A handsome amount for my handsome bhai. Buyers decide the value of the information. It can be thirty grand or half a million dollars. The bigger the amount the bigger the risk.' He finished his beer and knocked his bottle with mine.

'Cheat, steal, flirt, sleep with people—is that what you are proposing?' I looked at him suspiciously.

He nodded and smacked his lips. 'James Bond does it. To save the world. You will be saving your family. If that makes you feel any better.'

'He's a fucking fictional character, you lunatic. Plus he has been single for the last thirty fucking five years.'

'In Russia, the KGB trains their agents to get intimate with people of interest all over the world in order to steal classified information. That shit is real and that happens at all levels— bureaucrats, politicians or CEOs. You can look it up, google it. That's all I'm saying, Bhai. Do your research.'

'Russia, Russia… Are we in Russia, Vincent? You are a fucking moron to even come up with such ideas.' I shook my head in disbelief laughing at his ludicrous reasons.

'And you are legitimizing your unethical idea as well! Kudos to you, Vincent.'

Clearly Vincent was annoyed. He took out two twenty-dollar bills and threw them on the table.

'This is the deal, my friend. I have nothing else to offer you. You want to be a hero to other people, this is the only way you get to be one and walk out unhurt. My advice, think about it. You don't have to sleep with anyone. Just use your boyish charm and your smooth tongue. If I could do it myself, I would have done it, but I don't look like you. I'm not a six feet two inches, dimpled-cheeked, fit man with seductive eyes. I mean look at you—you don't even have a belly, no fat anywhere—how's that possible? And look at me—years of drug abuse made me soft. Plus, I still have no balls to talk to a woman confidently, let alone seduce her. This is the only option on the table which gets us paid.'

He slid out of the booth, fist bumped me, put on his jacket and walked away. He paused, walked back and said, 'I'm not mad. Do what your heart tells you. Try the grapes with your moron Nick and see how that goes.'

The next day, Nick sat with a plate full of grapes in my garage. I sat in front of him. He took a grape and looked at it.

I said softly, 'You have to be gentle, think of this grape as a small package of drugs. You can't bite it or it will explode in your body. It is lethal enough to kill you in seconds, so carefully swallow it because your life really depends on it.'

'Bro! Never before in my life have I looked at grapes like this,' he whispered. He placed the grape at the end of his mouth and swallowed it. It came right out. He tried it again with a big gulp of air, it worked. His eyes gleamed.

'Man, I'm born to do this,' he exclaimed and picked up another grape. As soon as he opened his mouth, his body shuddered, face cringed and out came everything. I jumped out of his way and handed him the bucket.

After two hours of trying, Nick gave up. 'Adi, Bro! I'm not meant to do this. Nothing left in my body, yet I can't keep it down. It hurts—how do people do it?'

I was out of all ideas.

That night, I couldn't sleep in my bed. I walked by Koyal's room many times to check on her, hoping to talk to her. She had a way of resolving things, but this situation was different, there were lives at stake, gangsters were involved. She had no idea what kind of danger our family was in.

I sat staring at the clock. I got up and took Romeo out for a morning run. It was still dark outside. Other joggers, cyclists passed us. Chicago's beautiful fall season was coming to an end. The enormous Lake Michigan looked like a large canyon of blackness in the dark and drew a parallel to my dark destiny.

I stopped running to catch my breath. Chicago's downtown skyline looked glorious. I took out my phone and called to an Vincent. As soon as he picked it up, I said, 'I'm in. Tell me what I have to do? One more thing—this stays between you and me. No one needs to know, not even Nick.'

Nikki—first 75k dollars, Week 3

With a pounding heart, I leaned forward and put my lips on her soft lips, my hands trembling. It was an awkward kiss. I pulled apart after a few seconds and looked at her. I hoped to see some feeling in her eyes, but there was none. Instead, she looked uninterested. My heart sank. Everything was wrong about this.

'Are you sure, Nikki? This is blackmail!' I protested.

'There ain't no doubt about it!' Nikki said.

'But why?'

'I'll tell you when you show me the money.'

'I trusted you, Nikki. You broke the unwritten, unsaid pact...'

'Excuse me! What pact?'

'The unspoken pact... You keep my secret, I keep yours... that's how it works right? Isn't it?'

I was so unconvincing even she knew that I was trapped in my own web of lies.

'Okay Eddy or Adi whatever... You are wasting my time now... Are you going to get me the money or not?' she said, irritated.

'Why do you need money? You seem to be doing quite all right,' I inquired.

She pointed her thumbs at her breasts and looked at me.

'I don't like them... I mean, I don't hate them, but I want to love them. Your money will help me love my breasts. You know! I need that wow factor. Round and pointy!'

Suddenly, I felt like a jackass. I would pay for her bodily augmentation so her boyfriend could be the delighted beneficiary of those perfect round assets.

Way to go, Aditya.

Nikki was a financial consultant in my firm. She was also my first assignment. Yeah, assignment! A client of Vincent was interested in finding out account numbers of five clients in the firm I worked for. My firm is like Charles Schwab but not that big, I work in the IT section of the firm.

Those five people are private clients of Nikki Williams' boss. She managed their communication, handled their meetings, lunches and events. She was a young, sexy and confident black woman, and Vincent thought she was an easy target to seduce and get the account information. 'Piece of cake for you, Bhai'—those were his words.

Here I was getting blackmailed in my car, after putting in two weeks of effort and fighting with the guilt of doing wrong to Koyal. *Piece of cake, my ass.*

Since we worked in the same firm, I arranged a work meeting with her and some of her colleagues under the pretence of an IT management outreach programme. In the firm, I led the team which supported the applications and platforms which our financial brokers and advisors used. My responsibility was to make sure those applications perform. The security of these applications was obviously of paramount importance to the company. Only authorized users were given access to specific parts of the portal. One advisor wouldn't be able to see another advisor's clientele, and that's why the firm had two-person teams—in case one person was unavailable, his partner would be able to provide the necessary customer service to their clients. Nikki and her boss were a team.

In the meeting, she arrived dressed in capri pants, a white

shirt with a matching grey vest buttoned under her breasts.

Her toned arms had a variety of black and golden coloured bangles and bracelets. I realized that she was the queen bee in her department. Everybody drooled over her sexy figure and flawless smooth bronze-coloured skin. I tried to not stare at the middle button of her vest which sat just a tad above where her breasts met. I knew the others were wishing for the button to give up, in the name of the god. *Perverts*.

After the meeting ended, I stayed to see how I could meet with her again, so I could steal the information which would get me 75k dollars as promised by Vincent.

She said, 'So you think your team can help us, Mr Eddy?' That's how my name is pronounced in the US.

'I'm sorry, did I get that right?' she asked concerned that she had messed it up for sure. I was touched. Most Americans don't even care.

'Absolutely...' I said and paused to see her face muscles relaxing.

'Not... But thanks for at least trying... Most just call us Babu or Appu behind our backs. Thanks to *Seinfeld* and *The Simpsons*.' I finished my sentence with a smile, I had to work my so-called charm on her. I had no idea what I was doing. I felt so old in front of her even though there wasn't that much of an age gap between us.

'Oh, I'm sorry... I was told by someone and I really did practise a couple of times to say it right before I came in,' she blushed.

'By the way, it's AA-DI-TT-YAA.'

'Oh... that's easy... AAAAADIAAA,' she tried again.

'Hmm... Too much AAAA and I don't remember saying T is silent. Did D eat T?' I gave a fake laugh and leaned in a bit. Her eyes gleamed.

I looked into her eyes straight and wondered if I still had that magical charm after all these years of hibernation. Was I still a ladies' man? Vincent believed so. There was only one way to find out—a subtle touch. My heartbeat took off.

'Ouu is there a T in it.. I'm so SORRRY!'

I laughed, put my hand on her shoulder and told her, 'Don't worry, I was just messing with you, but I'm really impressed and touched by your diligence.'

She didn't mind the touch at all.

'So… It seems like we need to get together again to discuss this because we really need your inputs on this project. Can we meet tomorrow?' she said. I was delighted that she was doing exactly what I wanted her to.

I removed my hand from her shoulder and nodded.

'I'm sorry. Is that a yes or a no?' she asked with a confused look.

I said, 'Yeah… I see you have been fed the usual dose of Indian head bobbing. Yes, tomorrow is good,' I finished my sentence nodding my head both horizontally and vertically, sending her out of the conference room, laughing.

I had a smile on my face, but I noticed that one of her admirers from the meeting was eyeing me in front of the elevator. He was a big man and was pressing the button hard as if he was pounding on my head in his imagination. I had no right to come in and swoop their girl.

'There's an ATM in that intersection, you can get the cash from there.' Nikki's demand for money snapped me out of memory lane.

I shifted in my seat and asked reluctantly, 'How much are we talking here?' I needed to solve my problems, but my fate was finding ways to multiply them.

'Give me ten grand, and I will be out of your way forever!'

'Holy crap! I don't have ten grand!' I shifted in my seat.

'Not my problem,' she said while looking at the evening traffic. I needed to make some progress with the account information, but now that seemed mission impossible.

'I really don't have that kind of money lying around to give you for a kiss,' I almost pleaded.

'This is not negotiable, Eddy!' she remained unfazed. 'You remind me of my sister. She thinks she's above everyone just because she's got the perfect natural boobs and butt. You both think you got it all, but on the street, you both are zero. You did no research before embarking on this dangerous extramarital journey with me.'

'What do you mean? You spied on me?' There was no more space left for me to shift in the seat, but I noticed that my tolerance to getting insulted was faint. *Maybe I should plan better next time I need to master the art of disappearing from such ugly situations.*

'What did you think, Eddy! You think you charmed me? I was playing you since the first time you put your hand on my shoulders. I need this money, and I don't care how you get it.' She scoffed at me. *Man, she was on fire!*

'There lies your problem, Eddy... You think you are slick... You are a rookie. You've got no experience and you are playing with fire and failing miserably... I mean, didn't you plan at all? When you and I started talking to each other, did you right away think of us getting cosy? Or did you have any back-up plans?'

I shook my head dumbfounded. *Those were valid questions and no I didn't want to get cosy at all.* She continued, 'I went along because I researched about you. That you were married, maybe even happy with the little wife of yours; and you've got a son—don't ya? So you had everything to lose, and I had everything to win from this. Even though we kissed once, the paper trail you left on WhatsApp and Skype—that's all good enough to create havoc in your life, man!'

Nikki was killing me and winning all rounds of soul-stirring discussion unanimously. *I felt like a guest on the Dr Phil show, being judged and not in good way.*

'Nikki, I know I fucked up really bad. I made a huge mistake—please forgive me. I'll get you your money from the ATM, please wait here.' I decided to end it because the more she talked, the more I felt belittled. I had guilt painted on my face like a tattoo and she was showing me how wrong I was to even think of doing something like this, given I was married.

I opened the door to go out, but she put her hand on mine and said, 'I don't know why you are doing this. You may have had some good reason, but ask yourself again if it's worth it.'

She ran her fingers through my hair and said softly, 'For what it's worth, you should know that you are a nice guy, and I liked you. If you weren't in this complicated mess, I'd have gone out with you and maybe had a relationship too. You are kind of my type—tall and hot. I like your dimples when you smile.'

And at that moment, something in my mind sparked, and I thought I should try once before giving up. *Worth a try! Being a little cheesy never hurts.*

I closed the door and looked straight into her eyes. 'Nikki—I think you should know that you are perfect the way you are, and I'm telling you the truth—your body is awesome. I know you are not going to believe me, but think of it like this. I'm an outsider, not your friend, not your family or even your co-worker.'

She nodded, a bit astonished but she was following me.

'So whatever I say wouldn't be biased or fake, right? Just to make you feel good. I think your perfect sister is gone in your head. Forget about sibling rivalry; she's got a bigger butt;

she has full lips. Who cares? Why would you want to go under the knife and risk it all? You have got it all, you are killing with your body—you have no idea how much people in your team adore you. They'd die to go out with you You are the sexiest black woman I've ever met. You work in a fancy investment firm, so you are a role model not an erotic model.'

I spoke so fast that I didn't even breathe the whole time. Her eyes were wide open.

Silence ensued in the car. I had shaken her soul and planted the seed of self-esteem in her mind.

She was speechless. *Did I just win this match in a knockout? I can't believe it. Vincent is right—I still have some mojo left in me.*

She needed some think time, so I decided to get the money as a back-up in case she changed her mind.

As I stepped out on the curb, a cold Chicago breeze hit my face and reminded me to zip up my jacket. I walked towards the ATM location at the intersection.

The evening of disappointments continued when I tried withdrawing the money from the ATM machine. The machine had a limit of 500 dollars per transaction and my card allowed only five transactions in a day, so all I could manage was 2,500 dollars, 25 per cent of her demand. I shuddered. *She would kill me in a heartbeat. I should kill myself for being born with such a destiny.*

I exited the ATM branch with a disappointed look on my face. A dog was barking nearby ferociously, and I saw a few Latinos harassing a homeless man. They were laughing and pushing the old man around and were trying to steal his dog. The old man seemed gutsy and was putting up a good fight. I thought of walking away. There were four of them and one of me with money in my pocket. They may have had weapons. All I had was a chapstick and a chewing gum stick in my pocket. What can I say—I came to love, not to fight.

I stepped away, but my foolish heart stopped my feet. *Do the noble thing, Adi!*

I walked back to the four guys and pushed one of the guys hard. He fell and the old man's dog grabbed his leg. The other three guys turned on me quickly. One of them took out a sharp knife. I almost crapped.

'Mr Malhotra!' said one of them. I looked at the goon who said it. I recognized him right away. He was the brother of the analyst in my company.

'Miguel! Is that you? What the fuck are you doing beating up this helpless old man?' I shouted at him as I found my lost voice.

Terrified, Miguel signalled to his gang to bounce.

'Kids are assholes these days, if you want a dog get a dog from the shelter—you will save a dog's life. Why are they snatching my dog, that beats me!' he yelled, looking at them.

I asked concerned, 'Are you okay, Sir?'

The old man quickly turned to me with a big grin, 'Krishna, man! It's aite. You seem like a nice fella. Thanks for saving my Cubby, he's my life. My name is Fred. Frederick Smith Junior Vietnam War Veteran. I fought against Nazis for this country.' He was wearing a torn, weathered army fatigue and was holding Cubby by leash.

I gave him a confused look. 'Nazis? In Vietnam? Sir, I believe you got your wars mixed up!'

'Really... I'm in extreme hurry. If you are okay then I will take your leave.'

I pulled out my wallet and took out a 10-dollar bill and gave it to him. He looked at me in surprise. I turned to leave when I heard, 'Don't do it, Krishna.'

I turned back and gave the homeless person a confused look. He was staring at me with his shiny blue eyes. Suddenly, his thin strands of long white straight hair started flowing, giving him a God-like illusion like Morgan Freeman from *Bruce Almighty*. Bewildered, I realized quickly that it was due to the breeze.

I sighed—he was no God. *Shit, I could use some godly intervention though!* He was just a crazy old man.

'Don't do it, my Indian friend. Don't throw away what you have in your life for nothing.' His dog was sniffing me—he reminded me of Romeo. I patted his head, but I needed to go and face Nikki. I ran back to the car and Fredrick yelled from behind, 'I'll pray to Ganesh and Shiva, they will protect you my friend.'

How the hell does he know so much about the Indian gods?

a narrow escape

Nikki waited for me outside the car, the street lights made her face sparkle. She looked at me as I stopped in front of her. My heartbeat jumped and my legs weakened, expecting the worst.

It looked like she was ready to open her heart out. Her mannerism had changed from a few minutes ago. She hugged herself crossing her arms to fight the cold as her hair blew in the breeze. She said softly, 'I'm best the way I am. I love myself and you were right that I'm perfect and these are perfect. Skinny and fat bitches would kill to have a rack like this. You showed me the way. Thanks, Aditya. I don't need your money. You gave me the best lesson of life.'

Tears formed in her eyes and trickled down her cheeks, she wiped them off and smiled. 'You are like the big brother I never had. Don't worry about the WhatsApp and Skype messages—I was just threatening you. I didn't save any. However, we should not meet each other any more.' She leaned forward and hugged me lightly and then walked away to her car. I was stunned.

She turned around and yelled, 'I'll pray for you like a real sister and will send you a rakhee this year.' I lowered my head in embarrassment. However, I was relieved at how it had turned out. I took a deep sigh, looked up at the sky and smiled. *Brother! Rakhee! I came out to score an affair and I'm going home with a newly found sister. Nevertheless. Thank you, God! You saved me. I guess you are looking out for me for doing a good deed for the homeless old man.*

I looked in the direction of the ATM and saw Frederick walking away with his dog.

On the way back home, I had a lot of thinking to do. I had escaped narrowly, nobody was hurt in the end. Meanwhile, I still had no money and three of the eight weeks I had were already passed. My cell phone chimed with the arrival of a new text message from Vincent. It read, 'Did you get what we need?' I ignored it.

I would have to steal the account information on my own. Risking my job and inviting jail time.

I called Nick while driving and asked, 'In your line of work have you come across any devices which are like hidden cameras, but they don't get detected through metal detectors?'

Nick paused to think for a moment and gave me a few options. I didn't like any and asked him to keep thinking and let me know by tomorrow.

Koyal

As soon as I turned on to my street, I noticed a beaten-up Ford F-150 parked in my driveway. It belonged to Himesh, Koyal's ex-husband. I hurriedly got out of my car. His presence in the house was not a good sign. They got divorced a couple of years ago and the bastard had blamed me for their divorce, completely overlooking the fact that he was a complete asshole.

I opened the door, got in and scanned the house quickly. He was in the kitchen. Koyal was on the other side of the island counter and had a phone in her hand.

She screamed, 'Himesh! You have no right to be in the house, leave or I'll call the cops right now.'

Karan sat in the corner, scared. I understood the whole story.

Koyal's threat didn't work on Himesh. He walked around the counter to get near her and said, 'All I want is to see my son whenever I feel like it. Is it too much to ask for? I can't be with him this weekend due to work, so I dropped in to see him. He's my son, Koyal! Understand my situation.'

I hated the situation too, but Himesh has not been a good father or husband. I already had too many things on my mind and was not in the state of mind to have a scuffle with Himesh. I took my phone out and dialled 9-1-1 and started speaking, 'Yes, 9-1-1, we have an intruder in our house. He's not leaving and is threatening me and my family. Could you please send someone quickly to my residence?' My voice got his attention. He looked at me with hate-filled eyes. He kicked the floor in despair and tried to curse me but stopped due to Karan's presence.

He turned to leave, Koyal came after him and gave him the Lego toy box which he had brought with him.

She said firmly, 'Stop trying to buy my son! Be a father. If you can't do that, then don't pretend. Walk away from our lives so he won't grow up hating you. Next time you pull this kind of a stunt, I will file for a restraining order against you.'

Himesh, angry as hell, didn't say anything. He took the box, looked at me and said, 'It's because of him! He's driving us apart. We had a good life until he came.' He paused.

'How do you even sleep at night, home wrecker?' he said while getting really close to my face.

'I sleep fine, Himesh. I suggest if you want to sleep fine then keep moving before the cops throw you in the lock-up for the night.'

I walked towards Karan and picked him up from the corner. Himesh exited. Koyal followed him to the doorstep to make sure he would leave. I heard her saying, 'Himesh, we were never fine. You were abusive. Your son was too little to comprehend what you did to both of us, but I will never forget that, and if you want to maintain your "nice" image in front of your son then don't violate the custody terms. Otherwise, I'll tell him everything. How you used to beat me, wasted with drugs and alcohol. How you physically tortured his mom for not making enough money and for not allowing Aunt Maggie to marry your stupid useless cousin so he could get a Green Card.'

'Green Card! Green Card! Why do you think Aditya married you? Doesn't he want a Green Card also?' he yelled.

'Lower your voice, Himesh. Don't worry about Aditya, you will never be half a man as good as he is. He saved your son, he saved me and never asked for anything back. So you mind your own life and let us live ours.' She slammed the door on him.

I heard her and immediately felt guilty about cheating on her with Nikki. I wished I could talk to her. She came inside, tears rolling down her face. She went straight into the kitchen to finish whatever she was doing earlier.

We have been married for over two years, but we are not like regular married couples. We fell into each other's world coincidentally. We both had broken lives and found comfort in each other.

When my mother was in the hospital three years ago, Koyal helped me through my difficult time with her presence and her flowers. We got to know each other and soon there was no secret between us. She knew a few things about my past which even Mom didn't know. I told her about my break-ups with Maya and Naina and how they both left me without saying a word, and how I had lost my trust in women. She shared the horrific story of how her love marriage with Himesh had gone horribly wrong.

There was nothing wrong with Himesh in the beginning. He belonged to a respectable Gujarati family. His parents settled in the US a long time ago and started a Mom & Pop shoes store. They made a good name and money until the big corporate stores and shoe chains put them out of business.

Himesh, being the only son, grew up with easy access to money and never understood the importance of it, until they lost it all.

He was called HH, Handsome Himesh in the Gujarati community. Himesh and Koyal studied in the same high school. He was the only guy Koyal ever loved, Himesh, however, had a few affairs before he finally settled down with Koyal.

They were young and stupid. If only Koyal didn't believe in fairy tales and happy endings, life would have been different. She would have been prepared for the harsh realities of life.

It was a big deal when Koyal went against her parents and married Himesh. They wanted her to focus on education and make a career. They didn't like Himesh due to his playboy reputation and eventually, they broke their ties with Koyal.

Koyal and Himesh tied the knot at a very young age. She believed that her love would turn Himesh around, and that she would prove her parents wrong.

The pressure of married life gradually got to Himesh. He became frustrated and when his business failed, he turned bitter, jealous, abusive and violent.

Koyal asked me to marry her so Karan could be around a fatherly figure, but I knew she just did that to help my lost soul. Before I met her, I was a traveller, always changing jobs, travelling through different states. After I met her, I made Chicago my home. She saved me.

As I said earlier, I'm a sad man because I'm a traveller without a destination. Deep down I know that my journey is not over yet because I'm still looking for some closure.

I asked Karan if he needed help with his homework. He replied he was already done. I went upstairs and took a long shower, trying to wash away my guilt and sin. I cried in the shower because I felt helpless and wanted to live a normal life with Koyal and Karan, and leave my past behind.

I lay awake in my bed. We always slept in different rooms.

I moved on from my life's sob story to thinking about what to do next after the Nikki debacle. I had made up my mind to steal the accounts information in a heist style from my own company. It was almost impossible, but I hoped that I could pull it off. There were many risks involved. To make matters worse, it looked like I would need additional manpower—at least two more men. The plan in my mind called for a team.

I heard footsteps approaching. It was Koyal. She came in

the frame of the door and stood there, as I got up slowly and turned on the light.

Thinking something else might have happened, I quickly asked, 'Koyal, are you guys okay? What happened?'

Overwhelmed, she walked towards me with quick steps. Her face looked puffy as if she was crying; she smiled and cried at the same time. She came closer, and sat down on the edge of the bed and looked at me.

She said, 'This may sound weird, but I think we are our own worst enemies. We have everything we need to be happy, our small world has so many hopes which remain unfulfilled yet.' She paused fighting for words, almost choking with emotions. I knew this was very hard for her.

She slid her hand on my chest and said, 'I'm ready to trust in life again. I am moving on from my past. I want to laugh freely. If you are ready to move on then take me through this journey with you.'

I wanted to say something, but I was speechless. She had said everything. I was ready to move on. Koyal leaned forward slowly and touched my lips with hers. I wrapped my arm around her and pulled her slowly into the bed, hugging her tightly. Soon our tops came off. She lay on me, pressing her bare breasts on my chest, it was sensational. We kissed for a long time—deep passionate kisses. I pulled the covers on top of us. My hands caressed her slender, curved body. Her bronze skin glowed under the lamp light. We had waited for a long time, and finally, it had happened unexpectedly. She moaned with pleasure and kissed my neck and mouth intensely. My hands found their way to her butt, and I slowly squeezed it. She moaned again and guided my hands to her shorts. I swiftly pushed those down and wiggled my body to get mine off too. We lay on each other naked. She opened her eyes, looked at me and said, 'I don't know why we waited so long!' And then she kissed me again.

We made love four times that night. I slept in till 7.15 a.m., for the first time in years. Romeo woke me up because he had to go out for poop. He was certainly not happy with the change in his schedule. I on the other hand was optimistic about everything. God was definitely looking out for me. Though this new-found love between Koyal and I was great, I was still mortified thinking about Nikki.

I was running outside with Romeo when my cell phone buzzed. It was Vincent asking. 'Bhai, status? Buyer impatient.'

I replied, 'Change of plan. Meet at 6 p.m. in Berkshire Room, downtown.'

hacking games—Week 4

We sat discreetly in the posh Berkshire Room whisky bar. Vincent and I had straight Scotch in our hands. Nick was working on his local IPA beer.

I started 'Guys! We are at Week 4 and have no money. Terrence's men have started watching our houses every night.'

Vincent folded his hands on the table and said, 'This is a standard threat to show who's in power.'

I gave him an angry look, 'How's that helpful, Vincent?'

He backed off in his chair and showed his palms, 'Just saying, Bhai! Hate the game, don't hate the player.'

Nick jumped in, changing the topic and pleaded, 'Adi Bro! Please let me help you. I've got you all dragged in this mess. I want to help.'

'You are helping, Nick. Get me those anti-glare spy glasses with HD photo capability. Anything more than that will not be in your best interest,' I insisted.

Vincent asked, 'What is the full plan, Adi? Then we can decided if the kid is useful or not.'

I nodded in agreement. 'Nick I promise—you will play a big part in this, but I'm sorry I can't tell you whole plan, trust me. Why don't you finish your beer and then buy us another round? Pay cash only.' Nick grudgingly left the table. Vincent gave him two hundred-dollar bills.

I took a sip of my Scotch. I was getting into the zone. I was a different man this morning. A lot happened in the past three weeks, but what happened last night gave me hope and renewed my desire to go as far as possible to save my family. I came up with a stupid and dangerous plan that just might work.

Vincent jumped at me. 'What the fuck happened? You got her in the car, I saw you guys made out. But then why did you go to the ATM?'

I looked at him embarrassed, contemplating if I should tell him the truth now or later and whispered, 'Long story, for now this is our plan which will get us the information your client needs. I've thought through all of it and it's not easy but may work.'

I paused for any questions, but Vincent blinked his eyes and signalled to me to go on. 'So here's the situation. The information about the five clients you need can only be accessed by special laptops which are encrypted and authorized by the information security team. They take three weeks to secure and authorize new devices. We don't have three weeks. Do we? So that option is out.'

'We could steal Nikki's laptop, but we will also need to know her ID and password, *and* when she logs in she gets a random generated eight-character security token texted to her cell phone. If we steal her laptop, we would also want her cell phone. As a policy if she loses her cell phone or laptop, she must notify our 24×7 security operations team immediately so they could disable those lost devices.'

Vincent said, 'That's fucked up, *amigo*. The security is like what you see in the movies. It's like the *Mission Impossible* and those fuckers show Pentagon or CIA buildings and here you are talking about a civilian company. This shit is crazy!'

My legs were shaking under the table. I exhaled and said, 'I know. So here's the plan on how we are going to do this. If everything goes according to the plan, we should be out of there in fifteen minutes.'

'I knew you'd come around. This dimpled-cheeked boy is resourceful.' Vincent jumped in his seat in excitement without even listening to my plan.

I explained my plan for the next twenty minutes and by the time I finished, my heart was throbbing and sweat formed on my forehead. I exhaled and had a nervous smile on my face. My eyes looked for Vincent's approval but he was dead serious. Biting his lips, he leaned over and whispered, 'Are you fucking out of your mind, Aditya? Getting information from Nikki was okay because it would have been mostly on her if anyone were to find out, but this! This hacking is a crime, and it implicates you and only you!'

I took a deep breath and said, 'That's why we need to execute this super tightly. There's no margin of error, trust me and we will get paid!'

'I don't know, Bhai, I liked the plan with Nikki better, but if you are in it then I'm with you all the way,' he assured me. 'When do we do this?' he asked.

I looked at him dead in the eyes and said, 'Tomorrow.'

We signalled for Nick to join us.

Next morning was mission day. I couldn't sleep all night. I reached my office wearing my new spy glasses, parked my car at my usual spot and entered the elevator. I looked at myself in the mirror. I looked like Clark and Kent and I wished I had some superpowers like his alter ego Superman. The elevator stopped at the tenth floor and I dropped off my bag in my office. My team usually arrived late. I carefully avoided contact with people and went to the stairs because I knew that they didn't have CCTV cameras. With enthused energy, I climbed down to the level where the company had a fitness club.

'How's the weather?' I said while running down. It was

the code to check the tiny microphone which I had in my ear.

Nick's clear voice crackled in my ear. 'Perfect conditions for the sun to shine.' Nick was sitting in the coffee shop at the main concourse level of the building. He had finally got to play a bigger role in the mission.

I was relieved to hear his voice. I needed the audio communication to work because cell phones were not allowed where I was going.

I opened the door and walked through the hallway to the fitness club's glass door. There were no cameras in the hallway. Many fitness conscious employees worked out in the mornings and evenings, taking advantage of the free facility. I went straight to the locker and shower area. It was humid, which meant people were in the hot showers. I checked a few lockers, found an opened one which had an employee's clothes. I unhooked a security badge belonging to Jake Barnes, a handsome white man with a smile as big as the Grand Canyon. I pocketed it and walked out of the club in brisk steps. I jumped in the elevator with other people. This elevator dance was necessary to show my movement at legitimate access points in case my access card reads were investigated later. Corporate security personnel have ways to track an employee's movements by checking which door he or she accessed and at what time.

At the tenth floor, my floor, I swiped my card again and pushed L for Lobby. I went past the turnstiles, exited the building and walked past a trash can. I dropped a roughed-up envelope in the trash can. I had placed the stolen ID card in the envelope and Vincent was supposed to pick it up from the trash can and enter the building using the card at the turnstiles. Vincent didn't look like happy Jake Barnes at all. I just hoped that no one would match the face card on his entry.

I went back into the building and this time took the elevator to the sixth floor, the on-site data centre of my company. This was where big racks of hundreds of computers were housed. It was a sophisticated, state-of-the-art data centre facility. Due to high risk security measures, every entry door was monitored. Since I was in charge of the infrastructure and application availability, I visited the data centre once a week for inspection and maintenance. I'd also perform some command level operations on the computers to ensure the health of the systems and to check for any data-breach threats.

After entering the data centre's main door, there was another door to get in the main floor where servers were housed. Two guards stood in front of the internal door, ensuring that no smart device entered the room inside. There was also a metal detector.

I was expected, according to the schedule. The guards knew me, but according to protocol, we never exchanged any pleasantries. We simply nodded. I deposited my phone, car keys and loose chains from my pocket into a clear plastic box. I closed the lid on the box and handed it to one of the guards. I took off my belt and put it in the bin to run through the X-ray scanner, and I walked through the metal detector. My heart was racing all this time. Nothing beeped. I exhaled in relief.

I looked at my watch. It was 9 a.m. In five minutes Vincent was going to create a diversion to buy me time. I put on my belt and fixed my eye glasses. One of the guards gave me a checklist to cover the key activities I needed to perform during my visit.

I entered into the cold, glass room and found myself between several rows of ten-feet high racks containing the multimillion dollar equipment which ran the company's business. These servers tracked millions of transactions worth billions of dollars on a daily basis. The machines enabled clients wire money, buy and sell stocks, and maintain funds every minute of the day. They are a virtual bank with unlimited money. People's lives were saved in these machines.

I checked on the guards through the corner of my eyes. I walked through the long lanes at my usual speed and opened a cabinet which had the equipment needed for inspection.

I started doing my regular business. I inspected the cables and fan speed. I touched the equipment with digital sensors to feel the temperature. I took notes and checked sections on the paper I brought in.

I looked at my watch. It was 9.03 a.m. I went to the last rack of the servers and stopped in front of one with a keyboard. I usually did a health check on the servers from here. This was the failsafe rack which I had access to in case the main website was attacked by hackers and disaster recovery plans took longer to recover the website. This rack was fully capable of providing service and peace of mind to customers about the safety of their money.

Since I had no user ID, password or device ID which stockbrokers use, I had no way to look up customer data. From this rack, I only had access to run the application portal in the safe mode. Even though I was there, I was still nowhere close to the data Vincent needed which was stored encrypted in the database. The database was also safeguarded against direct querying. I needed a code which would act as a regular broker on my behalf. I needed a computer code to run in this contained environment capturing the device ID on the fly. The code would call the databases for the five accounts I needed and if there was no other hidden security then it would return the results back on the screen.

I had worked on that ghost code for the last two days. But I had not tested it, so I had no way of knowing if it would even work.

With trembling hands, I logged in. Sweat beads formed on

my forehead in that ice-cold place. Since I was in the internal network, I pulled my code from a shared secured mounted drive and executed it by pressing ENTER on the keyboard. Nothing happened. I prayed to God.

I looked at the watch. It was 9.05. *Any second now*, I thought.

Suddenly, the fire alarms went off. It was very loud and jolted me even though I knew it was coming. By protocol everybody on the floor where the alarm goes off must evacuate the building. The guards banged on the glass door and waved their arms for me to leave. I signalled for them to go, conveying I would follow them.

Since they knew me they left the area hurriedly.

The cursor on the screen was still blinking. There was no activity. My mind was racing, trying to think where the code may be in its execution cycle. *Oh God—I don't even know if it's even working. I never tested it. What if it takes forever to find these five records amidst millions of records? Shit, all this for nothing!*

My heart was racing, palms started to sweat, I was losing hope. I looked at the watch, 9.06—only one minute had passed, but it felt like an hour. One minute changed into two, and suddenly the screen flickered and data started scrolling. My heart jumped in excitement—the code worked. *Phew! I'm an evil genius!*

I spoke, 'Weatherman, stand by for the report.'

Silence on the other side. The fire alarm was blaring at ear-deafening level. Nick's voice sprung up in my ear, 'Standing by for report.'

This was where I needed the spy equipment. Printing was restricted inside the server room and the servers didn't allow any writable drive for copying any data.

I clicked a small button on top of my glasses to take a picture of the screen. As a back-up, I started reading the account information to Nick who waited in the coffee shop. When I was done relaying information I pressed the ENTER key again to let my ghost code really become a ghost and disappear.

It was done. I had no idea whose information I had just stolen, but I had done the unthinkable. All that for my family.

I hastily walked out of the data centre and blended into the running crowd of employees down the stairs.

work life—Week 5

One week later, I was stressing out rocking back and forth in my chair in my office. It had been a week since I hacked my own company but I have not heard anything about money. I was fidgeting with my phone, waiting anxiously for any news from Vincent. Every night, I had nightmares about the breaching. I was sure that there was no evidence left which could link the breach to me. Only two people knew about this, and I trusted both of them more than anyone.

My phone buzzed in my hand, startling me. Vincent's text scrolled up. It said: 'I've what was promised.' It meant the buyers verified the accounts I gave them and they had paid Vincent seventy-five thousand dollars.

I took a sigh of relief, a huge weight was lifted off my shoulders but it was not over yet. We were still short of a lot of money, specifically 175,000 dollars.

The quickest seventy-five grand I ever made, not the easiest or cleanest, but quickest.

Vincent had already lined up a second assignment.

I needed to focus on that with careful planning. Suddenly two of my employees, Raaj and Jacob, barged into my office.

Jacob Farmer, a young African-American, winked and gave me an impish smile. He whispered, 'Hey, Chief! Did you check on that new Indian chick in Billy's team? What's the lowdown on her?'

'Why don't you ask Raaj? He took her out for lunch. Didn't he tell you?' I quipped. Jacob stared at Raaj.

'Raaj, you dawg, you never told me that.'

Raaj said sheepishly, 'It was a very boring lunch. You wouldn't have enjoyed her company. She doesn't speak good English.' It was evident he was lying openly.

'What's her name though?' Jacob asked.

'Even her name is boring—Anjali! I mean what kinda old-ass name is that?' Raaj tried to hide his excitement.

I couldn't take it any more. 'That's enough guys, you two go back to your desks and stare at the computer pretending to work, and for the last time both of you watch your language in the office. I won't save you from HR if they come down again. This is not a locker room.'

'No-no problem, boss man,' they both said in unison and scurried away. In the next instant, Raaj's head popped in my door again.

He said, 'Boss man, are you coming for Patrick's farewell tonight at the Laguna Beach Club? You should come today. There will be tons of girls from all departments. *Muchacha Bonitas.*' Both Raaj and Jacob were embodiments of horny dudes.

'No. Probably not! You better leave now!' I replied, annoyed.

He walked backwards still facing me, and he pounded his fist on his chest making the peace sign with his fingers.

'Telling you, Bro... It will be cool shit.'

Apparently Patrick's happy hour was on everyone's mind. I looked at my inbox and saw at least seven emails asking me if I was going. I had no desire to go. I had left my party shoes behind me in my past. As I watched Raaj walking away thorough the hall, I started thinking about the name 'Anjali' he just mentioned. That name stood out to me. My brain raced through the new, richer and vivid memories to its old dusty cabinets, and then it all came naturally to me, just like an old black and white flashback movie unreeling in front of my eyes.

Naina Sharma—my second heartbreak.

Naina—the second love

It's hard to believe, but after Maya, I gave up on life. I was hurt deeply. Very stupid move but I was a kid—a heartbroken kid. I didn't handle the abrupt ending of my first love well. I withdrew into myself and it affected my grades. Once, I was considered a notable IIT aspirant, but now I could barely pass any of the entrance exams. Somehow I got lucky and got through to a Delhi college.

In 2002, I settled for a less-reputed but overly hyped— Technical Institute of Engineering in Delhi. I hated it because it was in Delhi, and I wanted to run away as far as I could from the city. I also hated that it was not IIT.

Going to an engineering college was like studying in an all boys' school. Male presence totally dominated the long intra buildings corridors, sprawling landscapes, libraries and canteens. Girls made up only 10 to 15 per cent of the total student population.

For me it was a blessing—no girl, no tension.

Naina Sharma joined computer engineering halfway into the second semester. She wasn't like other girls in the class, keeping to herself most of the time. I always saw her lost in her thoughts. Her gloomy eyes had a hidden spark. She was a bright student and was always on top of her assignments.

I was intrigued by her behaviour.

I felt that she lacked confidence. She never spoke in class, always wary of her surroundings as if something would terrify her.

She walked from hostel to college and college to hostel with a group of girls. She never smiled more than required and always held back. I didn't understand what she was afraid of and why in the world a beautiful girl like her had such low self-esteem.

I started to think about her more than I should have had. What could possibly have happened to her that made her so aloof?

Many a time, I saw her in the library lost in her books and listening to music on her iPod. Music was her escapism, it was her trip to a vacation away from ugliness of the world, where she wasn't scared by every sound around her. She would jam with the music by shaking her head and shoulders in rhythm. Although, she would immediately stop as soon as she realized where she was.

We crossed each other many times in the halls and in class but never spoke to each other. Our first year of engineering passed just like that. Life for me was coming back to normal. I slowly started taking interest in college life and did what normal students did—smoked a cigarette, tried a bit of weed, ate a lot of Maggi noodles—engineer's soul food, borrowed money from friends, lost money by loaning to friends, participated in debates and got myself a place in the cricket team and in dancing competitions.

In the midst of finding myself again, I also found that Naina fascinated me.

In our third semester, one humid summer day, our substitute assistant professor of applied mechanics, Mr Sahni, decided to take a long nap after a heavy lunch of rice and beans instead of showing up in the class. We all waited for Mr Sahni to show up but after a few minutes most students trickled away for a smoke and tea.

All the girls decided to stay back in the spacious lecture room. They soon broke into gossip while some started studying.

Naina, as usual, was sitting at the far end, on a bench and looking out of the window that overlooked the Mechanical Engineering building.

Suddenly, I felt my heart pounding fast. Heat emerged from my body in a flash partly due to the humid and stale air in the auditorium and mostly because of my decision to talk to her.

'Hi... Hi... Naina!' I walked up to her and mumbled.

My voice echoed through the quiet room. The boys who had stayed back pinned their eyes on me so hard that I felt their gaze on my back.

Naina spun her head towards me. It was the day of many firsts.

A first for Naina to hear her name in the class. A first for others to hear her name in the class.

First for me to talk to her—also first for me to talk to any girl in years.

First for other girls and boys to see my ass kicked publicly. They were going to witness my roast, my death and my cremation all together.

It was like the first day first show for all of us, and nobody even had to buy any tickets for it.

I extended out my hand nervously.

'Naina... Right! My name is Aditya. You must have heard my name,' I said and immediately regretted my cheesy filmy words.

She gave me a confused look and said bluntly, 'No, sorry, I have not heard that name ever before.' I wasn't expecting to be roasted, so I told myself to initiate a recovery mode. I blurted out some words again.

'Yeah...you are right, how could you? We have never met before.' My hand automatically withdrew itself.

'I mean we have met of course in hallways and in lecture rooms but never met, like this… I mean spoken to each other.'

The girls giggled and gushed when Naina got up from her seat and shook my hand.

She didn't leave me hanging. Thank God.

'Yes it's Naina Sharma and you are Aditya Malhotra… I know we have been in same class for a semester! By the way your zip is open!' she smiled and spoke fearlessly. That was a big first for everyone. Everybody was astonished. I thought she was a completely different person in that moment.

I immediately looked at my zip. It wasn't open and she laughed at my silliness. I literally cried with embarrassment and mimicked her laugh because I couldn't come back with a good line.

Her confidence threw me off, and I forgot what I was going to ask her next. A thousand-watt spotlight was affixed on me. Everyone in the room was enjoying my misery.

'Sorry, that was just a joke, but seriously, are you here to show me that you tattooed my name on your body or are you here to score points with another girl by talking to the quiet girl by making her jealous?' Her voice grew louder as her eyes pierced through my soul.

'What? No! Is that what you think I am here for?' I quickly replied, trying to salvage pieces of my dignity.

'Then what do you need? I'm sick and tired of this. I'll tell my boyfriend to teach you a lesson like he did with the others— you guys don't understand unless a couple of ribs are broken.'

'You… You… have a boyfriend!' I tried to find my male ego but my soft heart gave in.

She got in my face and put two fingers on my forehead, 'He's from Bihar and you must have heard how they roll in Bihar with guns.'

I pursed my lips and shook my head, confused.

She laughed hard again. 'Aditya—you are so gullible!'

She fooled me three times in less than a minute—she was either really smart or very mean. She served me fresh sizzling pieces of my attitude and ego on a tray. My mouth fell open to say something but words didn't show up; I brushed my fingers through my long hair and put my sweaty palm on top of the nearest bench for support in case my legs gave up on me. I scoffed, trying to show her I wasn't backing off easily and I was better than other boys.

'I'll tell you why I'm here if I can gather my thoughts for a second... Just give me a sec to tell you the business of my walk up to you.'

She literally gave me time to think and stared at me. I never felt anyone be so cold before. I drew a blank and cursed the moment in which I decided to talk to her. I found myself struggling for breath.

Say something... Anything... Ask her about the notes on applied mechanics... Any subject! C'mon you can have a decent conversation! One second... four seconds.... Where's she from? What she likes? What day is today?

Ten seconds passed.

Why don't you just kill yourself?

Moron! At least you didn't say I love you!

In that whirlwind exciting encounter she said something so mundane yet deep, which I didn't catch at that time. I am gullible because I'm an idiot.

happy hour

'A re you coming? Patrick's farewell drinks... Let's go!' A familiar voice from my office door rang in my ears and I shot back to reality at my office. It was my boss Balvinder Tyagi who goes by Bill in the US.

A short and stocky man in his late fifties, Tyagi reminded me of a corporate office character from Dilbert cartoons. He wore a necktie with a half-sleeve shirt and came to office every single day of the year. His goal was to blend in as an American so he chose to dress like Dilbert, but of course his skin tone didn't help him. He had tripped the company's security alarm twice in two years accidentally and had burned a pizza in the toaster oven. During my hacking heist plan, I took advantage of that known fact and instructed Vincent to put a slice of bread on fire to start the fire alarm on the heist day. It was a simple and yet very effective plan which eventually worked in my favour. When the burned food was determined as the root cause of the fire, everyone's first intuition pointed to Tyagi but due to lack of evidence and Tyagi's strong denial, the investigation was closed.

'Tyagi... I got to go home.' I looked at my watch and saw it was 5 p.m. already, time to pick up Karan from baseball practice.

I lied. 'Koyal and I have some plans tonight and I didn't RSVP either.'

'Come on, boy! No one calls me Tyagi, What is Tyagi—call me Bill like Bill Clinton and who RSVPs for a company party?

There's free beer so don't have any more second thoughts.'

He patted me on my shoulder and then shook my chair. My cell phone buzzed, I picked it up.

'Koyal... I was just about to leave in a few minutes.'

Obnoxious Tyagi shouted in my ear, almost spitting on me 'Let him go, Koyal, for tonight. Unleash him. We got to go to an office party.'

I spun quickly on my feet and walked away from Tyagi.

Koyal asked, 'You have an office party tonight?'

I reluctantly replied, 'Kind of... Somebody is leaving... it's a farewell.'

She got upset. 'Why didn't you tell me earlier? How were you planning to be at two places?'

I stood silently. She must be having a bad day at the store. I summoned up the courage to ask her, 'What happened—is everything okay at the store? Maggie? Himesh?'

She quickly shook off her gloomy voice. 'Nothing—sorry just usual stuff—I'll manage. 'As soon as I hung up, Tyagi danced like a pervert.

'Tyagi, who's driving us home? If I get drunk I'm not driving and I don't want Raaj or Jacob to drive me,' I said while entering the elevator.

'Stop making excuses. I'll get you an Uber or drive myself. I drink only one beer because my body is my temple and I worship my body. *Om Namah Shivaya*.'

He folded his hands and closed his eyes. I looked at his gut and tightly strapped belt on the lower waist holding his pants.

As we entered the club which overflowed with young people, I felt like an old man in the suit. The DJ had already begun his magic and was blasting the latest hip hop tunes on a massive sound system.

Raaj pulled me to the bar where Jacob and three double

shots of tequila waited for us.

I was ready to do it, no questions asked. Raaj counted to three and at three we poured the crystal clear liquid down our throats.

We slammed down the glasses on the bar table. Jacob shouted like a madman, 'REPEAT MISTER BARTENDER!'

A cunning smile appeared on the bartender's face. He tilted the tequila bottle upside down and filled all three glasses, which we emptied in a heartbeat.

They sucked the wedge of lemon and licked salt to kill the burn. I didn't. I liked the burn in the throat.

DJ changed the tune again and I felt my mind and body losing control. My feet started tapping, and I clapped with the music. I spun my neck and shook my head with the beats. I didn't know when my feet took control and when I reached the dance floor and let myself go completely with the music in a trance.

The last tequila shot gave me an instant kick, and I was riding high.

I danced and danced without any inhibitions for the first time in years. When the alcohol started to wear off, I stopped and got off the floor. I heard applause.

I hoped the applause was for the good show and not for giving the dance floor back to the annoyed dancers.

I traced my steps back to the couch and fell onto it, panting. I hadn't danced like that in years. My legs were burning. I leaned back, staring at the ceiling to catch my breath.

ice break—Naina and Aditya

Fourteen years ago, I felt the same burn in my legs after practising for the upcoming dance competition in the second year of my engineering college. It was a prestige issue for our batch. Second year students had not won any competition in years and I had decided to reverse that curse. I was alone in the abandoned canteen of our college. The structure had large windows and big ceiling fans.

I was sitting on the foldable chair catching my breath under the fan when I heard some footsteps.

I saw a silhouette of a girl against the backdrop of the lamp post and the moonlight.

'Who's there?' I said.

The silhouette stepped ahead in my direction.

'It's Naina.'

'Naina... Here at this time? Is everything okay?' I stood up instantly.

She stopped a couple of feet away from me, standing in the centre of the huge open hall of that neglected structure.

She looked amazing in dark blue tight jeans and a polka dot top. Her eyes sparkled and her skin glowed under the moonlight.

She reached forward and pressed a button on the stereo. 'It's the Time to Disco' started. She held my hand and raised it to her shoulder height. My other hand automatically caught her other hand. She moved her hips and waist in a serpentine-like move with straight legs and an arched back, stepped back quickly and threw her head back. She paused, looked at me, smiled and started moving to the music. I realized she was doing the salsa with me. I was impressed, more than impressed.

She continued dancing while I supported her brilliant moves with lifts and twists. Her dance moves were breathtaking. Rejuvenated, I joined the dance with full energy.

She swirled on her toes in my arms brushing my hands and caressing her hair on my face gently. We split up and then danced our way back to each other. My moves were mostly contemporary and heavily inspired from Bollywood and Michael Jackson. I wondered where she had learnt those exotic moves.

I stepped aside and watched her letting herself go in the moment; she looked happy without any shackles of inhibition and in pure bliss. Everything about her was magnificent, and I had no choice but to simply admire her for her talent, beauty and above all, mystical personality. She caught me ogling at her.

She stopped when she couldn't breathe any more. I handed her a water bottle. She finished half of it in one gulp and took deep breaths. She was happy with a big smile on her face. I loved her smile.

'So what! You dance at night because during the day real dancers own this place?' She took a crack at me and my pride.

'Very funny. Day or night, no one can compete with me,' I said.

'Maybe you should choose worthy opponents.'

I liked our banter and flirted a bit. 'You are right. Never came across someone like you, Sexy Salsa. Where did you learn that by the way?'

She winked, 'It's a talent, Bro; I was born with it.'

'Here we go, ladies and gentleman! We have a big bragger here in the house who loves to belittle and make fun of people,' I said loudly. My voice echoed.

'It's not bragging if you are good at something... If you got it, you flaunt it!'

'Not to burst your big ego bubble here, but I can learn it in a couple of hours and even show you some new moves you may not know.'

'Don't kid yourself, Aditya... You are good at this cheap Bollywood dance; I give you that, but please don't expect anything more than that from me.'

Sweat rolled down her face, onto her neck and vanished in the centre of her cleavage. She caught me staring at her breasts and nodded her head dismissively, smiling.

My lips started to form a smile but stopped midway, confused in that awkward moment. I took the water from her and took a big sip.

'Are you checking out my boobs?' she said.

Her blunt accusation caused me to spit water from my mouth and nose. I turned my head away at the last second, and I sprayed the water on the floor. I decided to fight back, enough of taking shots from her.

'What? Everybody likes boobs,' I said, shrugging my shoulders and wiping my mouth and nose with my arm.

She looked impressed with my comeback.

'So, you like to stare at every girl's boobs?' she said with a cunning smile.

'No! I'm not a pervert. I was, however, trying to read you.'

'Read me? What are you, a psychic now?'

'That under this charade of sometimes melancholic and sometimes spunky, there's a woman of strong character who could be inspirational to others.'

'Whoa! Let me stop you right there—I'm no superwoman, I bleed when I get hurt, I cry when I'm sad but thank you for your flattery. I'll take your compliment, but you don't have to work so hard to sleep with me—you are not getting any of this strong character and inspiring woman.' She indicated her body.

'That's okay, We don't have to do anything today, but at some point I'd like this friendship to turn into a physical relationship you know—hot and sexy,' I touched my chest and bit my lip and even grunted in the end to add extra effects of the nineties' Bollywood villains.

Her jaw dropped. She didn't think I would go that far to win the war of the words with her. It made her burst into laughter. I watched her come alive first time in almost a year.

She was something—a mixed bag of nice and naughty with a touch of mystery.

'So I hear you hail from Mumbai, the big city.'

'Don't believe everything you hear,' she whispered while wiping happy tears from her eyes.

She gave me the biggest hint in our first meeting which I failed to grab. I couldn't foresee the enormous life-altering effect of that in my life. We came out of the hall and sat down on the steps. She didn't leave me right away—I must be doing something right.

She faced the sky and leaned back on her hands while stretching her legs. She gave me a mischievous smile.

'Aditya—you are a very nice guy.'

'I know—that's my biggest problem. I can't not be nice. But more about you—those moves—man, that was amazing. Would you like to participate with us in the competition?'

'Why? I thought you had no competition and didn't need anyone!' she quipped again.

'I know I'm good and our dance is really good, but we don't have a X factor in our group. If you compete with us, nobody can stop us.'

'Okay, but I'll have to ask my Spanish boyfriend,' she laughed again.

I wasn't falling for that again so I fake-yawned. She was impressed and patted my back. She had the world's most beautiful smile. I had already fallen for her and her hypnotic smile

'If you don't mind me asking, why are you so hushed in the class? You are not arrogant, and now we all know that you are not shy at all,' I said.

'Again. That's me, a mysterious girl! And did you think you would know everything about me in one dance? Mister Aditya, this girl is no easy walk in the park.'

She was clearly teasing me and I was bewitched by her.

I sat upright and turned to her and said, 'Okay, we wasted a lot of time last year, let's get to know each other quickly.'

'What's your favourite movie? Mine is *Zakhmi Aurat* (Wounded Woman).'

'Eeeu! What is that...? Never heard of it! Are you making stuff up?'

'You should watch it...mind-boggling...too good! The girl goes on a rampage and takes revenge by cutting the penises of the bastards who raped her... WOMAN POWER!'

'Ha ha... You know you are crazy... *Titanic* was my fav. movie! Best ever romance.'

Enjoying this ride I said, 'What about first love? This hunky dude did fall in love and got dumped after a chemistry exam without any words... Clearly our chemistry was not right!' This was the first time I joked about Maya.

She taunted, 'Ouch! With those Bollywood dance steps, who would stick around with you.' A moment later she got serious.

'Well, I'm in the same boat... My first love was very difficult... very painful, but it's over now.'

Sensing that I might have touched a painful point, I switched the topic.

'How about your bad habits? And don't give me chewing nails or not brushing. Let's both say it aloud. So here we go. One, two, three…'

'PORN!' We both yelled at the same time, amazed and embarrassed, laughing until both couldn't breathe. Later she told me that she was from Mumbai and came from a big family. She talked and talked for hours until we realized how late it was.

We started to walk back to her hostel, our hands touching on the way. Love was in the air for me. I left her at her hostel gate.

The hostel pretty much resembled an old fort with a big perimeter wall around it. When the world's oldest doorman opened the little entry door in the big gate, I caught a glimpse of the beautiful and well-cut green rows of shrubs along with well-lit corridors. The boys' hostel barely even had working light bulbs, forget about any kind of landscaping. There were many girls sitting outside with big books in their laps. They clearly wanted to keep an eye on who was staying out late, which conveniently translated into who's dating who. They stood up in awe when they saw Naina at the gate. It was apparent she never stayed out, and as the door was closing I saw the girls were falling on top of each other to see which moron had taken her out.

The next day was the hardest for my classmates to digest. After the third lecture, when we had a fifteen-minute break, I walked up to Naina and brushed my fingers through my long hair, my signature move. She looked at me and smiled, waiting for me to speak. I gave her my hand which this time she shook with a soft smile.

The boys gasped in utter shock. The girls knew about this from last night, so it was already old news for them since they had beaten it to death all night gossiping about it in the hostel. Naina and Aditya became a thing in the college and that news spread like a fire in the dry bushes.

'Naina—will you join our dance team and help us create history?'

'Hmm. What if I say no?'

She snatched her hand back and folded her arms. Annoyed, I frowned. She was literally playing with me again. The boys were ready to declare me a loser for the rest of my life.

'Well, if you say no then I have no choice but to try and win your approval by only two methods I know,' I was not backing down.

'What two methods?' She was curious.

'One, I can try the old-fashioned and trusted method of electric shocks to correct the wiring in your brains, or I will sing for you. Yes, I will sing for you until you say yes!' I exclaimed.

She looked confused, clearly not amused with any of the two options and asked, 'How about a third option, like taking me out to dinner or buying me flowers?'

'Dinner and flowers are for idiots, not for you,' I said.

She rolled her eyes and said, 'How many electric shocks are we talking about? I think that may be safer than your singing.'

The whole class exploded with laughter, and I had to admit even I couldn't stop myself from cracking up.

She laughed and ruffled my groomed hair violently with both hands. She leaned forward and whispered in my ear that she was going to buy the DVD of *Zakhmi Aurat*. I looked at her, bewildered, and we both laughed again. She was so cool!

A few weeks later we watched her favourite movie *Titanic*

together and kissed for the first time. My respect for Leonardo DiCaprio increased ten-fold, but I also hated the fact that he had raised the bar so high. I wondered if Naina expected me to sacrifice my life for her if push came to shove.

She wasn't thinking about sacrifice at all. A couple of weeks later, we went on a date to India Gate and that's where she revealed what she learned from the eternal love story of Kate and Leo in *Titanic*. She was thinking about getting her sketch done like Kate had in the movie—nude.

'Hey, Adi... Listen! Will you do something for me?'

'Anything for you, my darling,' I responded in a cheesy tone.

'I want you to draw me...like in *Titanic.*'

'Draw you... You mean like in the movie... Naked!' My mouth fell open. I couldn't believe it. 'No way. It's not happening.' I shook my head as if that was a final decision.

'Why? What are you scared of? I'm doing all the work!' she complained.

'For starters, let's just say I'm not comfortable with that, and I'm not sure if I'm a good sketch artist... It's ridiculous. What if I end up drawing an ugly sketch?'

'I think it's very cute! Come to my hostel one day and we will do it in my room. I trust you, you are good at everything except singing.'

'In your room? What about your roomie?' I tried to resist.

'Don't worry, I'll be very professional and will not take advantage of your vulnerability.' She rolled her tongue then blew a kiss in the air, teasing me.

I blushed. 'Nahi (No)! What if we get caught or my thing shows some activity?'

'It better show some activity. If it doesn't, then I would like to know about that in advance before we plan our future together,' she laughed hysterically at my misery.

'I'm not doing it, Naina Sharma. Go ahead and laugh your ass off.'

For the next few weeks whenever we met, that was the topic of discussion. After a month, I relented.

We spent a week scouting for a proper place with the right ambience. I wanted to do it perfectly. She tried to reason with me, saying that it was not a movie, there was no James Cameron to stage such exquisite sets for us, but none of her wisdom changed my mind. We tried at her hostel room, but ever since she had ditched her quiet façade, she had become hot stuff for the college. Every girl in that building wanted her opinion to find solutions to the world's biggest problems like how to win guys, what outfit to wear for dates, or how to get rid of stalkers. I had to hide many times under her bed on the cold floor for hours, until I passed out, cold and hungry.

One Sunday when the hostel was empty because many girls had gone back home, we tried again. She brought nice pillows and sheets and slowly undressed herself and slipped under the sheet on her bed. She adjusted herself with the pillows, leaving her upper body and one leg exposed, just like Kate. I stood there with a sharpened pencil, holding my breath. I asked her a stupid question.

'Naina! It's very cold here. Won't you be cold?'

'Shut up, Adi! Concentrate. I expect your best work!'

I shuddered with excitement and then slapped myself a couple of times to snap out of it. *How did Leo do this?*

For the next two hours, I worked on my masterpiece with undivided focus and was able to revive my childhood hobby of sketching. Meanwhile, her cheeks showed different shades of pink when she blushed. I could feel she was trying to curb her emotions.

'Adi—this is harder than I thought... In the movie they showed it so elegantly, with such ease.'

'Don't talk...let me focus and, yes, I know this is real hard.'

I chuckled, without looking at her. She smiled again and her eyes widened at the thought of what I had just said. Just like my guru Leonardo, I finished my work professionally and handed her a decent sketch which she loved. I waited for her to get dressed outside the room.

Nothing happened—I had a different plan for a special day. Bangalore was the next stop for my love story.

Soleil—the other 175k

I zoomed back into the club from 2003 to 2018. Laser lights were flickering in sync with the beats. My pupils were getting photosensitive because I was getting high due to all the alcohol.

The DJ continued to count 'eight', 'nine' and at the count of nine sparks crackled on a maze of thin hanging pipes on the ceiling and didn't stop for good 20-30 seconds. The popping sound of fireworks was crisp and thrilling.

I realized Tyagi wasn't sitting next to me any more. I scanned and found Tyagi with an attractive woman who looked like she was open to spicy experiments that night. I was happy for him.

He was typing on his cell phone. Suddenly I felt my cell phone buzz. I fished it out and checked it.

Tyagi had texted, 'That was fucking HOT, DUDE! You are an awesome dancer, you are a true son of India—Ekdum Mithun Da (Totally like Mithun)!' I smiled and put my phone back in my pocket. My eyes popped when I looked up at a stunning girl wearing a shimmering, low-cut, shiny satin off-shoulder dress which reached just near her knees. She complemented her dress with an expensive designer leather jacket which was belted around her slim waist. Her presence oozed luxury. I had not seen such a stylish blonde in my life. Her full lips sizzled in red hot lipstick. Her shoulder-length blonde hair complemented the dress.

'By the way, that was fucking cold, man!' she said seriously.

I looked behind to ensure she wasn't talking to someone else—her exotic French accent was mind-blowing. I tried to snap out of my drunken state of mind by blinking.

'Hi! I'm Soleil, Soleil Paulette.' She extended her beautiful arm out.

A loud explosion of fireworks marked the end of the show on the floor. Her perfect face, big eyes and high cheekbones looked spectacular in the rapidly changing lights.

I got up and said, 'French?'

'Man, you are cold for an Indian, saying it like being French is a sin.' She grinned, shaking her head. I felt like a jackass instantly.

Her accent was electrifying. I felt I needed to clean up the mess. I held her hand and shook it nervously, 'Oh no. I didn't mean that at all...'

My phone buzzed again. I wanted to escape from that dreadful moment.

Another text message from Tyagi.

'That FRENCH chick is SO HOTTT.'

Before I put it back, it buzzed again. This time the text was from Raaj.

'My sources tell me she doesn't like to be called French.'

That information was useless to me now.

She was staring at me smiling. I cleared my throat to say something.

Suddenly out of nowhere, a Jason Statham-type bald guy appeared and wrapped his hand around the French girl's slender waist.

I prayed that he was her boyfriend so he would take her away from me, saving me from any further embarrassment.

The guy had a chiselled, sculpted body under his club shirt. He gave me a condescending look and said in a meek voice, 'Don't you think you are a bit too old to be in here? FATHER!'

I didn't appreciate the disrespect. 'Hey c'mon, man! There's no need to put me down. I'm rooting for you, dude. If you can take her away with you—if you are man enough!'

He didn't stop and went on mocking me in a miserable imitation of an Indian accent. 'Don't you have to go back to your "arranged" wife and fix peoples' computers?'

His theatrics made me laugh.

'That's enough, asshole!' Soleil jerked her body away from him.

'Man! Get the fuck outta here, I don't like guys who are full of shit and you are a big pile of shit.' She said all of that in her fumbling French accent which sounded so sexy but was hardly threatening. She signalled for him to walk away with her index finger. She looked wasted.

Soleil and I watched him walking away. She said, 'So, you were saying?'

'My apologies! I didn't mean to come off blunt. I said French because of the way you exuded beauty in this club. I mean look around—you are killing it—everybody's looking at you. You are pulling off what's known for French women—the chic style with a touch of sophistication and you are direct as you should be and you put that grown man back on his tracks.'

I offered her a seat on the couch. I sat uncomfortably next to her to keep a distance between us.

'Bravo!' Her face lit up. 'You know a lot about French women? How many have you dated so far, Mister?' she asked me in my ear, getting really up close—she smelled great.

'My name is Bond, James Bond,' I laughed. 'No I'm kidding. The name is Aditya and I've not dated any French women.' My heart was pounding. She rehearsed my name and then pronounced it perfectly. 'Aditya. What a nice name—what does it mean?'

I said, 'It means the sun,' and pointed upwards.

Her face lit up again. 'No shit! That's what my name means

too—Soleil the sun. That's so cool.'

She raised her hand to high-five me and automatically I responded.

'So, what else do you like about France?' she put her hand on my knee and slid it softly on my leg, flirting was full on.

I cleared my throat and moved in my seat a little. 'Ahh... What's not to like—there's just so much. It is by far the most romantic place with its exotic language, accent, food, museums and architecture.'

She crossed her sexy legs and took a long drag on the hookah before passing the pipe back to me.

'You sound like fucking Wikipedia, you know that?' she said, unimpressed. She was a tough girl, I needed to up my game.

'I need another drink,' she said, looking around.

'Grey Goose on the ice with a touch of Red Bull!' I said with a sparkle in my eyes. She was surprised and impressed, 'You are very observant! Observant and talented. I like talented men.'

Almost magically a waitress appeared through the fog, and walked up to us with four shiny shot glasses in a tray.

She poured the crystal clear vodka in the shot glasses, handed the glasses to us and said, 'This is from that gentleman for you, and he's sorry for being an asshole.'

She pointed to the Statham guy who was rubbing his body behind a skimpily dressed girl. He looked back at us and dipped his head and folded his hands in a namaste. We picked up a shot glass and looked at each other—her eyes were already giving me an inviting look.

I felt a chill run down my spine and couldn't take my eyes off her. She bumped her shot glass to mine and said, 'To our better halves who made this fun night possible for us by not being here.'

I need to get out of here. I reminded myself. *The whole office is here.*

We gulped our drinks down, and for a second, my senses went numb again. The music came back exploding in the ears as soon as I put my shot glass down. By the time I was done, she finished the remaining three shots. *Shit, she's something!*

'By the way, why did you say "that was fucking cold" when you walked up to me?' I yelled in her ear.

She rolled her eyes and said in her sultry voice, 'You left me on the dance floor.'

'I did? When?' I yelled.

'What the fuck? You don't remember rubbing our bodies against each other on the dance floor for two songs?'

So much for being subtle, Aditya! The whole office has already witnessed your loose character.

'You and I! On the floor... That was you I was dancing with?... I'm sorry. Really!'

'Don't be! You won me over with your moves. I want more of that!' she said, biting my earlobe. I thanked the fog in the room for hiding us from the rest of the folks. I was trying to restrain myself, but I was so tipsy that I didn't realize that my arm had already reached around her back. I pulled her closer and whispered in her ear, 'Your name...Soleil Paulette reminded me of someone.'

'Really... Who? Your one of the many girlfriends?'

'Someone for whom I had strong feelings... A guy,' I winked at her.

She looked at me surprised.

My head dipped giving all signs of how drunk I was, 'Sunil Paul. An obnoxious hairy dude. He was so hairy even his teeth had hair!'

'Soooneeel Paul, hey it's just like my name!' she exploded with laugher, 'You are too funny, Aditya.'

I thought it was time to go.

I texted Raaj and Tyagi to take me home.

They buzzed back instantly. Tyagi said he was busy with an Australian girl, but Raaj replied right away:

'I've got your back, Bro—Raaj.'

I saw Raaj, drunk, stumbling towards me. I signalled to him with my hand to go back right away. I turned to the drunken angel on my arm—she took a deep hit on the hookah and quizzed me. 'I think I'm going to go home now. Do you want to share the cab? I live on the East Side.'

'So do I... Fifteen minutes from here,' I said.

'Cool, drop me first and then go on to your wife.'

Suspense in my heart was building up, I looked at her and asked her in a serious voice, 'You know what will make this night more fun? Just a bit of ex to hit the peak?'

'You mean the drug Ecstasy?'

I half-smiled. 'What do you say we get to a quieter place, just us?'

She chuckled, rummaged through her purse quickly and took out two pills. Without wasting any time, she popped one in her mouth and then gulped it down with her leftover drink. She put the other pill in my hand and I immediately knew this night was going in every inappropriate direction for a married man.

She put her head back and closed her eyes.

We came out of the club into the dark cold night. She held my hand to walk properly. Her face glowed under colourful neon signs. The city's streets were coming alive with every minute as more and more club-goers poured in.

She held my hand and extended her other arm to signal for a cab.

I stood with my Ecstasy pill clutched in my fist.

Ecstasy brought back bad memories.

Ecstasy and I had a long dreadful relationship.

love in Bangalore

'Do you know what this is?' Naina sat in front of me, on top of the wooden desk in the big lecture auditorium. She had two brown pills in her open palm.

'No, ibuprofen? Why… Are you sick?' I said.

Naina was looking sexy in her shimmering glitzy low-cut light pink top and her tight black jeans. She had coloured her hair burgundy about a week ago. This was a recent transformation, during which she also upgraded her clothes and changed her looks. I was surprised with all the extravagance, but she looked hotter. She was from a rich family and had easy access to money, but in the last few weeks she was on an unlimited shopping spree.

When I enquired, she promised to tell me everything in Bangalore. She admitted that I was the best thing that happened to her and that I had made her come out of her shell. I knew something was up with her. She was not herself.

We had been in relationship for over a year and she had never hidden anything from me before. I gave her space to deliberate on whatever she had on her mind with the hope that she would share what was bothering her with me one day.

We were in Bangalore for a week for an Annual Young Engineers Consortium. I stood like an enthusiastic nerd in front of her, outfitted in my best jeans and a black Reebok cricket T-shirt.

I had also changed my hairstyle. I had bid farewell to my long locks and had embraced the short crew cut look.

'Naina, what's going on? We are getting late for the party, let's go.'

I felt that I was way underdressed for the party, but then I thought I was with the hottest girl who was going to blow everyone's mind the moment she entered the room.

She didn't say anything, but she didn't ignore me either.

She gulped down one pill with water.

I got worried and touched her neck and forehead with the back of my hand. She was cold.

'Now you are freaking me out, Naina... What is going on?' I said.

She hugged me and asked, 'Why'd you bring me to Bangalore, Adi?'

'Because I love you, and I was getting tired of seeing you lost in your thoughts... I brought you here so we could spend some quality time together, and you can share what's going on in your head. I have so many questions. Like why have you coloured your hair.... I miss the old look... The old you... Now I look at you and see so much distance between us.' I palmed her face in my hands and looked straight in her eyes.

She gave me the pill. 'It's the fun pill... Take it and I will tell you everything.'

Naina had never been so mysterious, and I needed to find out what was up with her. I took the pill and shoved it into my mouth. I guessed what that pill was. I hung out with notorious Vincent—the drug peddler of our college. I just hoped that it wasn't fake or bought from the street.

The pill I took was Ecstasy, a highly strong stimulant in the same category as cocaine or heroin.

Almost in a psychic connection she read my mind, 'Don't worry it's safe, I got it from Vincent.'

Vincent was the resource to arrange underground

recreational drugs in the college. He worked only on a contact basis and would arrange anything and everything for parties at hostels.

'Adi, why haven't you made love to me yet?' Naina asked me.

No way. That shit can't be working on her so quick. I looked at her, perplexed. Her eyes were beginning to dilate, and she smiled—the first time in almost two weeks.

'Hey, I thought I was going to get answers to my questions. Why am I on the stand?' I laughed.

'No, don't play... I already know you wanted to make love to me since the first night we met at the canteen. I don't blame you for that, in fact I will let you in on a secret...shhh.' She winked at me, pulled me closer and said, 'All this time, I wanted the same I just couldn't... The circumstances.'

'Right, the circumstances! Easy on the shirt please... I don't have another for the party,' I gently held her hands.

'Adi... My life has been rough. We talk about feeling bad because of petty things like having a bad exam or missing the train. I-I've been at the bottom end of my life and no words can describe the pain, the panic, the anxiety and the suffocation I've felt at this young age. No kid at eighteen should go through what I've been through.'

She went on, 'I can't live a lie any more, and I will tell you everything starting with my real name... It's Anjali... Anjali Mishra.'

I had no idea what to make of that information, but the name echoed in my brain and I felt my heart stopping.

She took my hands in hers, 'Yes Adi... I'm sorry. My name is Anjali, not Naina, and I'm from Bihar, the most violent place in India. I know it because I have been a victim of that violence.'

Suddenly the door of the classroom burst open loudly,

surprising us. A few guys and girls stormed into the room, laughing.

She jumped off the bench and dragged me behind her while skipping down the stairs towards the door.

'Where are we going, Naina?' I asked while running.

'Dance… Let's dance. I want to dance all night,' she screamed.

'I need to know… What was all that about, Anjali? What's going on?'

'You will… Tonight you will know everything.'

I stopped running and pulled her arms, bringing her closer. I felt the moment was right and put my lips on hers. I felt a knot in my stomach as soon as our lips touched. Our stiff bodies suddenly relaxed and started to get a bit cosier with each other. Her breath was warm and minty. I sucked on her upper lip slowly and passionately then our tongues met and we both shuddered, kissing until we felt our lips swelling. At that moment, we heard footsteps down the hall.

We broke apart and collected ourselves. We ran towards the sounds of beats.

I shouted on the top of my lungs, 'Naina, I can't live without you. You are so beautiful, smart, funny and witty… You complete me.'

She skipped steps ahead of me and looked back at me and yelled, 'And you are an Oxford dictionary.'

Naina's revelation

We swooped onto the floor making our way through the explosive and energetic college crowd. People were dancing like there was no tomorrow and I guessed Naina also wanted us to have that night like it was the last night. We danced for more than an hour until my legs gave up. I screamed in her ear so she could hear me in the midst of the deafening music.

'I'm going to sit out for a bit and check out the food. I'm getting hungry.'

'Yeah me too… I'm hungry for you!' she screamed back and gave me a sensuous bite on my lips.

Naina came running and hugged me from behind, 'I love you, Adi… I love you so much.'

'I love you too, Naina,' I said without hesitation.

'Not Naina…Anjali, and I'm not afraid any more. And I will love you forever,' she made a plop sound with her tongue and crossed her heart with her finger.

I watched her disappearing in the pack of dancers. That was the happiest I had seen her in the last two weeks. Many questions were floating up in the air around my head, and I needed the answers. I traced my steps to the makeshift cabana bar made out of bamboos and banana leaves.

I made eye contact with the bartender, pulled my wallet out and dropped two hundred rupees on the table. The bartender put out a small wooden bowl of spicy peanuts and a glass of cold water in front of me. I started drinking water when I felt a tap on my shoulder. I looked back and saw a stranger with a picture in his hand.

'Hey buddy! This dropped from your wallet,' he said.

Shaken. That was the right word to sum up my feelings at that moment. Mystified, I took the picture and looked at it. The guy patted me and walked off leaving me perplexed. *His job to shake my inner core was done. Well done random stranger!*

The poor quality headshot picture of the girl in the picture was taken out of the school records and had the standard half-notarized government stamp across it.

The girl's hair was pulled back tightly into two tight ponytails, and she was wearing a blue blazer on a grey sweater and white shirt. Facial hair on her brown complexion indicated her young age, I didn't know who she was, and my intoxicated mind wasn't helping either. I turned the picture over. The caption read, ANJALI MISHRA XII Section B.'

I felt the ground beneath my feet shrink, and my head spin. I had to put one foot down on the floor to balance myself. I was looking at the picture as if I had seen a dead man walking. My hand holding the picture started shaking nervously. I looked at my hand as if it didn't belong to me. *Is that Ecstasy or the picture's effect?*

The girl in the picture was indeed Naina, and Naina was Anjali.

I needed answers fast. I ran back to her.

The crowd was thicker now and the music was louder. Flirty couples were grinding and caressing their partners.

I glued my eyes on the crowd until I found her. There she was in the middle of the floor, moving her body to the beats. I made my way through the crowd and pulled her out.

Holding hands, we ran through the quiet empty halls, up the stairs and then stopped to catch our breath. We looked at each other and immediately kissed each other while panting. We laughed and then ran out of the main building to a waiting car out in the front. I had a surprise planned for Naina that evening—Vincent helped. We got into the back seat of the luxury car, and a well-groomed driver took off as instructed earlier. Naina's face said it all. She was impressed and we couldn't keep our hands off each other. Our hearts were racing and our breathing was laboured.

The excitement was intoxicating. It was not the right moment to ask about the picture.

After a short drive, the car stopped in a residential area in front of a duplex house. The driver quickly exited and opened the door for Naina. I came out from the other side and ushered Naina into a flat Vincent had arranged for. I unlocked and pushed open the heavy wooden door and immediately shut it behind us. The flat was beautiful—everything in it was impeccably decorated. I asked her to wait, and I stepped forward to flick on the light switch. Suddenly the flat was illuminated with colourful lights. It was covered with heart-shaped balloons. I let her absorb the arrangement.

She pursed her lips, indicating she was very impressed. She half cried, half smiled and pulled me closer, placing her lips on mine. I melted away again, nothing else mattered in that moment. I wanted to live that moment eternally.

She was the one. She made me laugh and laughed with me and sometimes laughed at me too.

My body started feeling numb with the anticipation of what was coming next. I slowly cupped her warm cheeks with both my hands and I slid my tongue into her mouth. Her fingers brushed my hair and her hands caressed my back. My hands automatically found their way to her butt and squeezed slowly. I picked her up in my arms—she wrapped her legs around me while we kissed. I carried her to the bed in the adjacent room. I lay her down on the soft bed, moved away a lock of her hair from her face and told her that she looked exquisitely beautiful and that I was crazy about her while my hands slowly went up to her soft breasts. She mirrored my hand movements and rubbed my chest.

She wiped her tears and bit my earlobe gently. She told me to stop talking and to make love to her.

I stroked her breasts and then put my face on her right nipple and kissed it gently—she clutched my hair hard, the catalyst in that fire. I lifted her top above her head and took it off, picking her up in my arms and hugging her tight.

She whispered, 'I love you, Adi... More than anything in the world, tell me you love me.'

I responded, exhaling, 'I love you, Naina! So much... So, so much.'

I was in love with this girl, I wanted her and she desired me and that's all mattered. I undid her bra and removed it from her soft shoulders. Her skin was warm and soft. She was aroused and so was I. I removed my shirt swiftly.

She looked at my stretched out naked chest next to her. I traced her neckline with my lips and then kissed her shoulders and moved slowly to her breasts. I made soft circles around her nipples until she moaned and grabbed my head and put my face in her breasts vigorously. She smelled amazing.

She pushed my hips gently, and I aligned my body on hers and brushed my crotch against hers. We both moaned with pleasure. I kissed her neck again and watched her shudder. She slid her hands inside my pants and stroked my butt, and then we both unbuttoned each other's jeans and took them off. We lay there naked on each other. I kissed her body from top to bottom. She held my fully stretched out penis and stroked it up and down slowly while I kissed her. I sat on the bed with my back resting against the wall, while she straddled me. I would see the face of my beautiful girl while I made love to her.

She flung her hair back, tilted her neck and bent down to mouth my penis. I stopped her immediately, and she looked at me with aroused eyes. I didn't know what to say.

She spoke in a sultry voice, 'Adi? I've fantasized about this for a long time... Let it happen... I want to live fully in this moment... Don't deprive me of my fantasy.'

My hands retracted, and I let her continue. She brought her mouth in line with my penis and worked on it, at first slowly and tenderly and then with urgency until I started feeling the build up.

I pulled her face way before it was too late and took a deep breath to make the sensations subside while she caressed me affectionately. She pulled herself up and then sat on me and looked at me with her angelic eyes.

She gently slid my hard penis inside her. She was wet with anticipation. We both moaned while she pushed her hips onto mine. I lost track of time, She kept going hard on me until we both gasped with the ultimate explosive orgasmic pleasure of life.

We gazed at each other the whole time. I felt an unbelievable rush being with her that night.

Picture. Anjali. Secrets. Nothing mattered. In that moment.

I let go of all the complications of life and felt pure intimacy and joy.

If only life was that simple.

A few minutes later, we were in a dreamlike state, lying naked next to each other with our eyes closed. We had transcended into a whole another world. It was amazing. I drifted in and out—aware of everything but focusing on nothing. Vivid memories of boyhood, school, the school trips, laughing friends, Maya's fading face flitted in and out. Suddenly, I drifted back to reality, to the earth, to that room, that bed and with renewed energy and devotion to the girl next to me—I pressed my body against hers with a need for something we both badly wanted.

I love you, my love.

I pulled my face down and kissed her soft nipples—she smiled softly with eyes closed.

She also visited the whole another dreamy world just now; I hoped she would let go of her past in the depths of the forgotten memories. I promised Naina that I won't get hung up on her past. I found her in my present and that's all mattered to me.

I nibbled on her nipples until they became hard; she pressed my head into her breasts and wrapped her legs around my back.

How long could it go on?

I timed my breathing against the beat of my heart and pushed inside her. Our hips started working in tandem. Desire and urgency slowly started building inside her, and I felt her nails digging into my back. I felt her shuddering, signalling her peak. I controlled myself to enjoy more of our intimacy until multiorgasmic electrifying zaps struck our bodies.

I didn't keep the count of how many times we made love that night before our tired bodies gave up and we fell asleep in each other's arms.

Our passion kept coming back even though our bodies couldn't keep up. I dreamt of her and made love to her in my dreams also.

Sunlight glinted through the holes and crevices of the window. I woke up to the birds chirping outside. It was an splendid morning, but my head was hurting from Ecstasy and a night of relentless lovemaking.

The smile on my face vanished when I didn't find Naina

in bed. Instead, I found a scribbled Archie's light blue paper note next to the bed.

My heart jumped as soon as I saw the letter. Ominous dark feelings started to build up inside me. I had seen such scenes in countless movies—where the heroine or hero would leave the other one in bed, for good.

I scrambled open the note and read it in a jiffy.

And read it again. And again. I felt that I might throw up. The note said:

Adi, I'm so sorry for doing this to you.

I wish I could change the past, but I can't. I have to leave you so we both can live.

Adi, you and I are not so different. We are very much alike and that's why we were destined to meet each other in Delhi and eventually fall in love. Our fate was playing hide and seek with us for a long time, longer than you and I know. It dawned upon me only later when we started to know each other.

I had my eyes on you the minute I saw your pained and burdened heart in the college. I was running away from my traumatic past, but my past has followed me here, and I can't run any more, and I can't see you getting hurt.

Your life will be in danger if I'm in it. I have lost too much in my life, but losing you would be unbearable for me.

I loved you since the day we met. I loved you more and more every passing minute and I'm crazy about you after last night. I want to stay but I can't. I wish I had told you the truth. I know that you will hate me for doing this to you, but believe me this is for the best.

Don't try to follow me—I'm the wind and don't know where I'm going, but I'm gone.

Love you forever!

Anjali

That was it! Naina was gone like the wind—leaving behind me, and my broken heart, sleepless nights and the mystery of her identity.

to the dark side

I dropped the Ecstasy pill in the sewer secretly while getting into a taxi on the street.

'My boyfriend is out of town. Do you want to come in for another drink before you go to your wife?' Soleil said in a sultry voice. She popped another pill and settled herself in the middle of the back seat.

I looked at my watch.

She noticed me checking the time.

'Our partners, they don't need to know, my boyfriend isn't even in town.'

She scooted close to me, put her leg on mine and ran her hand up and down my inner thigh. I knew she was alone that night and the shit was driving me crazy with the riveting drama, and I was struggling to keep up with sexed-up horny Soleil. I simply took her smooth manicured hand and kissed it.

I said, 'That's good to know, I didn't want to get my ass or derrière kicked as soon as I walk into your house.' I spoke to her in a raspy voice, trying to sound suave.

With a big smile on her face on hearing my French, she said, 'Your French is quite exquisite, Monsieur. What are you, *vous bête* sexy?'

'You just said it—"A sexy beast"!'

She took out a cigarette from her purse and lit it up. The driver yelled in a thick Turkish accent and signalled to the NO SMOKING sign in the car.

She plucked open her purse, took out a twenty and slid it through the small circle in the plexiglas.

He looked at it and swallowed his pride instantly.

'No smoking rule, my ass!' she laughed hysterically and leaned back on her side.

In two minutes, the cab stopped at a beautiful duplex in the expensive part of the town.

Her townhouse was the first in that deserted street and had big tall trees in front of the property. I kept my head down in an effort to hide my identity in case a neighbour walked by.

We got out and I handed the cabbie a twenty when the meter read only nine dollars. He thanked me and took off.

She took me by her hand and walked to the beautiful French door where she punched in the code and put her palm on the electronic key pad. She glanced at me to ensure I was not looking at her code. The door had no knob to twist and push.

While I was wondering how the door might open, the screen turned green when the code and her palm was accepted, and the thick wooden door slid open with a whoosh sound. Heavy security as expected.

When we got inside, she pushed a button and also disarmed the security alarm. The door shut itself behind us and lights lit up the whole bottom floor.

I suddenly thought about Koyal and Karan. Karan must be playing games on his computer and Koyal and Maggie must be chatting away.

I felt low. I wish I could turn back and call it a day, but my feet were stuck heavy on the ground.

I had no choice but to go down to come up in life.

She fumbled while taking her heels off.

The interior of the house looked like it had been copied from the modern home magazines. A two-storey foyer held a sparkling crystal chandelier, and gleaming wooden floors sprawled as far as I could see.

She wasted no time. She dropped her purse on the nearby table and came in front of me.

'I want you. I wanted you since you danced with me on the floor. I want you to fuck me real hard.'

Millions of thoughts swirled in my mind again—words from different people echoed and my heart started to sink. Vincent's words flashed, 'Use your charm.' Nikki's words, 'You are naïve, you are playing with fire.'

I wished there was another way, but there was none.

That was the first time I looked at her properly, while she gazed at me lustfully.

Finally I was about to have a physical relationship with a woman other than Koyal after years of marriage. I felt nervous and guilty.

Soleil took a step towards me. She was an absolute diva with her flowing blonde hair and lightly tanned skin. I held her hands when she started to unbutton my shirt.

'I don't feel safe here in front of all these cameras you have in the house,' I whispered.

'Relax! I turned them off remotely before we got here. Let's go upstairs, if that eases you.' Her speech was slurred, and she was having difficulty standing up straight. I removed my jacket and loosened my shirt. She ran her fingers on my chest, untied her jacket belt and dropped the jacket on the floor, opened her arms and signalled for me to take her upstairs. I carried her light body in my arms and walked up the stairs to the first bedroom on the right.

I put her on the bed and adjusted the pillow behind her head. She moaned with pleasure. She took my hands and directed them to her breasts.

'Come, get in the bed,' she spoke to me slowly, with her eyes closed. 'I miss my Franky. He's a good boyfriend, but he's away all the fucking time.'

She started rambling, half-unconscious. 'It was all sexy and exciting in the beginning. We were happy, but now it's too dangerous. He's worried all the time. I miss my Franky. I wish he was here.'

I knew she was ready to doze off with all the alcohol and drugs in her system. I had no desire to take advantage of a woman in an inebriated state.

I sat by her side, shook her softly and asked, 'Where's Franky now?'

She moaned again, 'Noooo, I told you don't worry about him. He's gone to Juarez, Mexico, doing something for his boss, Mendes. Now come to Mama!'

She tried to raise her arms, but she was so hammered that she just turned sideways and started snoring almost instantly.

Her beautiful face glistened in the dim light. I, with trueness in my heart, had wished for a miracle at that instant and uncanny as it sounds that miracle happened and under the influence of drugs and alcohol she fell fast asleep. I covered her with the sheets and tucked her in perfectly. I exhaled in relief. I had saved myself from another guilt trip.

My phone buzzed and broke my thoughts. I immediately remembered the main reason I was there. I got up on my feet and scanned the place. That's right—I wasn't there because of my charm only. This time, I had done my research. Meeting with Soleil was not a coincidence. I was there for a purpose.

Her boyfriend—François aka Franky, was my next assignment. To get to him I had to go through Soleil.

I was on the tail end of the fifth week and I didn't have all the money to buy our lives back from Terrence. I listened to

Nikki's advice and this time I did my homework. I had watched Soleil for more than a week, followed her every day, saw her leaving the club with a different man every day. I knew she always ordered Grey Goose on ice with Red Bull. All I needed to do was dance and flirt with her to get inside her house, which apparently was like a fortress with all those security measures.

My real work was about to begin, and my heart bumped against my chest loudly.

I took the stairs down to the lower level. I answered my phone. A calm, husky and serious voice resonated on the other side. 'Are you ready?'

'Yeah,' I replied confidently while loosening my tie and tucking my shirt into my pants with the other hand.

'This scum Franky is no good. I don't know much, but he's done very bad things because of which a lot of people ended up dead, so don't feel guilty. I know you. You are doing the world a favour,' Vincent tried consoling me.

'Vincent! There's no choice right now... It's too late to think... Time to finish the job.'

'You already slept with her?' he asked.

I didn't know how to answer that question. Poor Vincent had so much confidence in me. I blew his confidence with Nikki by getting blackmailed by her and Soleil was sleeping peacefully solo without any action.

I decided not to say anything.

I had not shared with him Nikki's desire to make me her brother and send me rakhis annually, poor guy would die of a heartbreak.

'Fine!' He continued, 'You have a plenty of time. Nobody is scheduled to be home and that bastard Franky is out of town, which you know already.' He took a deep sigh, 'Remember, we want to know where he's going exactly, who's he meeting or sleeping with.'

'Franky is in Mexico.'

'Mexico! Do you know who is he meeting?'

'Yeah, she mentioned his boss.' I had forgotten the boss's name already.

'Okay, that's good so far. Now get to work and call me when you are done. I will come to pick you up, James Bond! Having sex with beautiful girls and stealing information from bad guys—you are the man! Live it up.'

I grunted and hung up the phone. *Big difference—Bond is not fucking married!*

I patted my pockets to ensure I had my wallet, company access card and car keys—I had everything intact except my dignity.

I was leaving behind that one.

I felt charged with adrenaline kicking in. I picked up my suit jacket from the floor and put it on. I quickly put on the rubber gloves I had carried with me. I wanted to start from the basement. I had seen the map of their home on the Cook County public real estate website.

On the main level, there was a big china cabinet and opposite it a bookcase filled with books. I had no time to go through books. I quickly scanned the room, looking for a computer, printer, but there was nothing. I hurried and found the door to the basement behind the kitchen.

I opened the door, peeked in the dark and listened for any movement.

There was none.

I treaded down the stairs carefully and saw a string hanging down next to a bulb. I pulled it and the whole basement flooded with lights. It was a vast open area decked up with cool stuff which would blow anyone's mind.

A poker table was set up in the corner next to big speakers connected to a vintage vinyl player. Next to the player was a large glass cabinet with vinyl records. A lavish pool table and a full bar was set up in the opposite corner, along with a wine rack.

I kept walking and came across a long dark room. There was a large dark mahogany wood office desk in the centre. A laptop and a bunch of stationery was on it. I opened the laptop and quickly got to work.

I took out a USB stick from my pocket and stuck it into the computer. The software I brought with me was designed to bypass the administrator account by creating another account in the background and then copy over all the files from its cache and hard drive.

The software did its magic and started displaying its activity.

'Bypassing Admin Security...'

'Creating temporary account...'

I had more work to do. I had also brought an iPad in my other inner jacket. I pulled the chair back, went under the table and found the Wi-Fi router and a mess of cables behind the footstool. I moved the footstool aside and pulled out an available network cable behind the router and connected its end to the adapter on the iPad.

I wanted to see if there was any other network device like a hard drive or another computer in the house. I jumped through the screens while sweat started to build up around my forehead.

Suddenly my phone buzzed, jolting me. I almost dropped the iPad, hit my head on the table and knocked over the footstool. I came out from under the table and quickly took out the phone.

Koyal was calling. I pressed my lips and clenched my teeth. *Not now, Koyal.*

I let it go to voicemail. I needed to hurry. I focused on the iPad screens to find what I needed. The phone rang again with Koyal's name on the screen. I let it go to voicemail.

I dropped the iPad and decided to do something else. I ran back to the laptop—copying was in progress.

Thirty per cent done...

I ran to the vinyl cabinet and started rummaging through, looking for clues.

The phone buzzed again. It was a text message, 'Come quickly! Help! Himesh is here!' My blood boiled instantly on reading Himesh's name. I had to hurry. I started panicking. I was trying to find a needle in a haystack. I ran towards the walls and started slowly tapping them. *Shit* it's a basement, all the walls sounded hollow in Chicago and I had no time to dig through the walls.

The phone rang again. This time it was a voicemail from Koyal. I cursed in frustration, swiped to listen to it, and heard screams of Koyal and Karan.

I felt like my legs would fold under me. I texted Vincent to come pick me up as I couldn't stay there any longer.

I decided to leave and ran back to the computer room. I dived under the table and unplugged my iPad from the router. In the process my head bumped the bottom of the heavy desk. Suddenly, a hidden drawer dropped open at an angle that enabled me to see the contents in it. There were many pistols, clips, some cash, drug packets and a pocket diary. Trembling, I picked up the diary and carefully flipped through it. The old yellow wrinkled pages of the diary contained the coded information of accounts and names of people and GPS coordinates of some locations. I thought immediately that this could help absolve me, if Franky was as bad as Vincent said.

I retraced my steps to the laptop and found that the copying was done. I unplugged my USB drive, closed the laptop and ran upstairs.

Twenty minutes later I was riding with Vincent in his car. My heart was still drumming. I sat with a raging storm inside my head. I was terrified for my family—I was doing all these crimes to save them from outsiders while the imminent danger loomed from the inside—Himesh.

I was blatantly pissed at everything at that moment; I fisted the power knob of the radio system.

Surprised, Vincent looked at me and his broken radio knob. The car swerved off the lane and escaped a near collision with a truck on the right lane. Vincent cursed in Hindi and brought the car back in the lane. I wobbled in my seat and yelled at him, 'Can you at least drive straight, asshole?'

I adjusted myself in the car while connecting the USB drive to the laptop in the car and started going through the data it had copied. I was looking for temporary data which resides in the caches of browsers.

'Adi, forget about this Franky shit, it's not important right now.'

'How is it not important, Vincent? I fucking risked everything to get this. Let me finish this because I don't know what I'm going to do to Himesh when I see his ugly face. We need money, and I can't do this if I'm in jail after bashing his face.'

He nodded and left me to it.

My fingers moved quickly and started reviewing the cached files. I drilled deeper and after a few minutes, I was able to find a list of coordinates.

When I thought I had found a lead, I spoke up, 'Okay, there are four pairs of coordinates I found in his recent history. I'm plugging these in the map, hopefully one of these will be close to Juarez. That's where Franky is going to be.' I started working with the coordinates.

'Okay, so here's the list. First one came as Centro Municipal De Las Artes. The second one, Plaza De Armas. Third one, Aguilas Café. The fourth and last is a building that is under construction.' I closed the laptop and threw it on the back seat.

'My man!' Vincent clasped my hand, 'Terrence will be off our backs. I'll pass this information back to the buyers. This is great, only you could do this.'

I looked at Vincent. It was almost midnight, but he still looked dapper in his fitted three-piece blue and grey chequered suit and tie.

I had another battle to fight now. I missed the old restrained, routine life with Koyal and Karan.

Vincent flicked the indicator and careened the car off the highway towards Edgewater—my house.

I sat at the edge of my seat and prayed for the safety of my family.

I'll kill that bastard.

an intruder

The scene at the house was eerie. All lights were off. I realized that Koyal and Karan were at Maggie's which was two houses down.

I shouted pointing to a house, 'There!'

He put his big foot on the pedal to accelerate. As we reached near the house, I started to have a gut-wrenching feeling.

Vincent yelled at me, 'I will hang back and call the police. I can't be seen with you when the police arrives. Sorry, Bhai!'

I jumped out of the car and continued running.

I stopped at the entry door.

I patted my pockets to find my keys, singled out the one which worked with Maggie's door lock. I shoved the key and twisted it hard, pushing open the door with force.

I lunged forward and heard Koyal's shriek.

I slowly made my way to the kitchen where Koyal came running to me. I hugged her tightly for a second and then pulled apart to see if she was okay. She had blood on her hands and cheeks. My blood boiled.

I scanned the kitchen for Karan and saw a hand on the floor behind the kitchen island. I looked closely and realized that it was unconscious Maggie.

I looked at Koyal, 'Where's Karan?'

Koyal, scared to the core, couldn't speak and exploded into tears. I lost my mind. Himesh was standing behind the counter.

I screamed at the top of my lungs, 'Himesh! You son of a bitch!'

I ran forward, grabbed the chandelier's ring and swung it in full force towards Himesh. It hit him on his forehead and he lost his balance and fell hard on the floor. I walked around the island, while Himesh struggled to get back on his feet. Karan was in the kitchen's corner. He leaped towards me. He was shaken. Crying. Himesh caught Karan by his arm and drew a gun with the other hand. He spit blood on the floor and said, 'I will not let you steal my family! I own her.'

'Cops are on their way, Himesh. Don't be stupid!'

He yelled, 'Shut the fuck up!' and lunged forward and kicked me in my chest. Himesh was of average height, but he was heavily built. His kick was powerful enough to knock the wind out of me and make me fly in the air for a few metres. I shook my head, took a deep breath and tried again because he was still holding Karan's arm.

'Ok, you want me—great! You got me! Let the kid go! He idolizes you. Don't hurt him,' I pleaded.

But I was a fool. I didn't read his eyes clearly. He wasn't there to bargain. He was there to finish off everyone in the family, starting with me. He slid and cocked his gun, letting go of Karan's arm for a fraction of a second. It was my moment to do something.

He fired the gun. I dodged the bullet and scooped up plates from the island and threw them at him. One of the plates hit his throat and choked him. He was immobilized for a few moments. He coughed and swore at me and then gasping for air, fired one more shot.

I stepped forward briskly, pulled his gun arm with one hand and punched his throat. I slammed his powerless body against the fridge and continued to choke him. He punched me with his free hand. I lost my grip on his arm and fell backwards—he immediately fired another shot. The bullet grazed my back, and I screamed in pain.

Himesh took a big step towards me. 'Why don't you just die?' he yelled again. 'I-I tried to let it go, let it all go, but I can't. I can't walk away knowing that you are screwing my wife. I can't.' He stood up, pointed his gun at me and said, 'That's why we have to go. We all have to go.'

I closed my eyes. I couldn't get away from this. I realized this is how I was going to die!

Everything went quiet for a second. I waited for his move.

Suddenly a baseball bat came from nowhere and hit his face. It was Koyal. I heard his jaw cracking. His body fell on the dining table shattering the glass. I limped up to him and jumped onto his chest, pinned his arm holding the gun under my knees and punched him hard in his face.

One punch, two punch, three punch. I reached towards his hand to grab the gun away, but he kicked me in my chest again. I fell back, hitting my head on the island which knocked me out for a second. I shook my head. I couldn't die. I told myself to get up. He tried to get up with the support of the dining table frame. I kicked his face, he lost his grip and he fell back, hitting his head on the pedestal. I scrambled to get up, grabbed his gun and stood, pointing the gun at him.

I wanted to finish him off, to end the agony once and for all. But Koyal's scream stopped me. He laughed weakly at me and then threw his head on the floor. He stopped moving. I pushed him with my toe. He didn't budge.

I threw the gun on the island and quickly turned to Koyal. She lowered her bat and threw it away which made a loud thud. She screamed, 'Maggie!'

We both hurried towards Maggie. I picked her up from

the floor with Koyal's help and put her on the couch. She was breathing. I was relieved.

I said, 'She's not hurt, but she has passed out due to trauma. She and her baby will be fine.'

Maggie was the sweetest girl in the block. The sisters cared for each other a lot.

Koyal learned about life the hard way, and Maggie learned everything from her brave sister. She left her parents' house to live with Koyal after college. Nick fell in love with her and pursued her for a long time. Maggie didn't believe in love after seeing Koyal's disastrous love life, but Nick managed to win her over. They got married a year ago and were expecting a baby in a few months.

Since the day they married, Koyal wished only one thing every day—don't let Nick become like Himesh.

That was the reason I decided to help Nick. Fear and desperation can break any gentleman.

Koyal rushed to Karan, but, fortunately, he was unharmed.

Koyal's right cheek was swollen and her eye was bruised.

The floor was in an utter mess with shards of broken glass and plates everywhere. Suddenly the flashing lights of cop cars appeared in front of the house.

Behind us the door of the house burst open and the police swarmed in armed and ready. The ugly night was finally coming to an end.

Maya returns

Night slowly shaped into Friday morning and the clock on the wall read 4 a.m. when we reached the courthouse. We were worn out both emotionally and physically. Nick, after returning from his shift at the O'Hare airport, stayed back with Maggie and Karan at our house.

Himesh was taken to the downtown precinct where he was going to be booked, locked and possibly wait for his appearance in front of the judge before going to prison.

I drifted into sleep on the wooden chair in the cramped office, while Koyal sat next to me, holding my hands. This was the longest night in my life, considering so much had happened starting with the clubbing, Soleil and then Himesh.

The medic team had cleaned up our faces after forensics took pictures of our bruises. We both had to endure some stitches.

I woke up, perplexed, in the chair, and looked at my watch on my wrist. It was 7 a.m. The empty office started to show some activity. The early staffers had arrived.

'I'm sorry guys… The attorney should be here any minute now. Your assigned domestic violence attorney on the case is out of town and the on-call officer-in-charge is now on her way here,' an elderly African-American woman spoke politely to us.

I got up—everything in my body cried in pain. I took off my jacket and tie. I touched Koyal's shoulder and said, 'I'll get us some coffee and something to eat.' She nodded briefly.

'There's a café down the hall—follow the signs—it's hard

to miss,' said the clerk lady softly.

I returned with coffee after ten minutes. In the hallway, I saw Himesh's parents exiting from the room.

'You won't do anything of that sort. You can't let this man go unpunished again, Koyal!'

My feet stopped at the door of the office when I heard a demanding female voice. I stepped aside to listen in.

'Koyal! Please listen to me—on my way here I read the entire case history, including the restraining order on the assailant, Himesh, and both physical and verbal abuses on the victim, YOU. Mrs Koyal if you don't put this man behind bars today—I guarantee you that he will come back again and the next time he may very well succeed in killing somebody in your family.'

I stepped inside the office and found the attorney, arguing with her back towards me. Koyal was still at the same place I had left her in. Her face was swollen. She was a mess.

The woman spoke again, 'I know they are his parents and am sure they will ask you to forgive him. But you are done! He's not your responsibility. He deserves to go to jail for a long time for this.'

She knelt down in front of Koyal and held her hands, 'Believe me, you will be doing the world a favour. He's socially unfit and is a danger to the world. You have to let him go.'

The attorney heard me scraping my feet. She turned and saw me and I saw her. Our eyes met and, just like a dramatic film sequence, we stood there looking at each other without blinking.

No thunder—no lightning bolt—just silence.

I took five seconds to realize who was standing in front of me.

Our attorney was Maya, my first crush in Delhi who had left me abruptly.

She had grown into a fine woman and was looking absolutely stunning in a professional crisp black pant suit with a light, lemon-green shirt. Her hair was pulled back tightly into a ponytail. No make-up. She was looking beautiful.

Meeting your long lost teenage love in the midst of a family feud, after seventeen years in another country, on the other side of the world? That was the stuff straight out of movies.

I froze. She spoke first, 'Adi, is that you? Aditya Malhotra?'

I felt a lump in my throat and shook my head. My eyes welled up. Surprisingly, I was happy to see her and to find that she was all right, alive and well.

She came to me and hugged me tight, her eyes gleaming with delight. I hugged her back. We broke apart, realizing that Koyal was in the room too. Koyal stood up.

Maya turned to Koyal and said crying, 'You are very lucky, Koyal. Adi is the best man I have known in my life.'

Maya turned back to me, wiped her tears, 'I hurt you bad, really bad and not a day passes when I don't think about apologizing for what I did.'

She looked up, shook her head and chuckled. 'You know I had a speech for you. I thought that if I ever ran into you, I would say it. And now, I can't remember any of it, and I am a lawyer for God's sake. I'm supposed to be good with words.'

I spoke. 'It's fine, Maya. I've moved on. I'm just happy to see you here.'

It was weird how all the anger I had built up for years just subsided. I had devoted a huge part of my life blaming her for every bad thing that had happened to me after she left me. I should have been strong enough to accept that and should have worked harder on myself to fulfil the ambitions I had. If I had channelled the energy and time I had spent hating her into something productive, it would have made a big difference in my life.

I was thinking clearly now, and that's why I wasn't mad at her any more. I felt like I found the closure I needed all my life.

Maya wiped her tears. She transformed into a lawyer and addressed Koyal. 'One of two things will happen if you don't put your ex-husband in jail. After a few days, he will come back— better prepared and more dangerous. Either he will succeed in killing everyone he desires, or you will kill him trying to defend your family.'

'None of those options are good for your son! Think about him. I'm a living example.'

She looked back at me, 'I'll tell you why I left you seventeen years ago without saying anything. Why I am a lawyer not a fashion model like I always wanted to be.'

'What your son is going through right now, I've seen it, I lived through it. Truth is that we vanished from Delhi overnight because of my cruel father. He...he was abusive... Very abusive and would beat up my mom every day and night. We escaped his fists and punches and came to my uncle's house in the US. My life seemed so glamorous to everybody in school, but inside it was so vile. I was ashamed and scared of sharing that with anyone...even you.'

'On that night after our final exam, I reached home to find my father in another abusive fit. My mom was sobbing in pain. She was tying a towel with her mouth on a fresh wound on her arm but blood was gushing from it. Glass pieces were scattered everywhere, the belt on the floor was coloured with her blood. My heartless father stood in front of her. He saw me and told me to go to my room. He shouted at her about some major loss in his business because her brother didn't help him financially. Mom had had enough of him, and she shouted back with a new-found energy, talking back for the first time. His ego couldn't swallow that, and he slapped her. But on the second attack, Mom pushed him back. I stopped midway on the stairs and decided to help her. I ran down, picked up the belt and wrapped it around my palm. When he charged back at her, I knew I had to do something. Suddenly years of watching my mom suffer and living a double life fuelled my will and my arm swung in action. The belt flew like a snake and wrapped around his neck. I jerked the belt and started flogging him; I kept screaming and whipping the belt on his body for a long time. It felt like we were finally liberated. I remember Mom pulling me away from his unconscious body. In the next two hours we were sitting in a train to Mumbai where we stayed for a few days in a hotel and then flew to many countries before we were able to get asylum visas to America with the help of my uncle. The violent past still haunts Mom.'

I had goosebumps listening to her harrowing experience.

'My dreams were shaken. I turned my life around. I studied to go to a law school, and I chose to make a difference in the lives of women who had gone through what we had. I chose to help scared and helpless women. I fight every case as if I am fighting my father, and I do not stop until justice is met. Women are the strongest species, but they need to be reminded that they can fight any injustice and I'm doing just that.'

Maya looked at Koyal with hope that her story reminded Koyal of her own strengths.

She had narrated her incredible horrific story effortlessly. I felt so small listening to her. I was speechless and looked at her in disbelief. She was a real-life hero.

Koyal held Maya to comfort her.

I said apologetically, 'I'm so sorry... This is terrible. I had no idea, Maya. You were going through such a traumatic life.'

'And that's why I didn't tell you anything. You loved a pretty, sophisticated and ambitious girl. What could I possibly tell you at that moment? We were just kids, dragging you into that would have not helped any of us.'

conspiracy

The taxi driver dropped me at the Navy Pier taxi pick-up spot on Grand Avenue at almost midnight. I paid him exactly what was shown on the meter. I followed the signs in the freezing cold to the east parking lot—my hands were clutching Sullivan's cold gun.

I ran hysterically towards Vincent's BMW in the almost empty parking lot. Very few cars were parked in random spots only.

I pushed myself in the car and touched the cold muzzle of the gun against his skull. 'Vincent! It was YOU! You set me up! I'm gonna kill you!' I screamed.

Vincent pursed his lips and looked defeated.

He said, 'Calm down, Bhai. I'll tell you everything, but please move this gun away from me.'

My eyes widened when Vincent gave up so easily.

I looked at him in horror. I was shaken to my core. I growled in anger.

'You did... You messed up my life? You were my friend... my brother... you told the DEA... sent them in my house, they took away the money, all of it. They knew everything about Soleil, and Franky.'

I slid the gun to his ribs. In the distance, I heard the blaring sirens of cop cars, but they soon sped away.

'What did you tell them? Only you knew about Franky. He's dead, and they think I've something to do with it.' Angry as hell, I pushed the gun deep into his ribs.

Vincent sighed, turned up the heat in the car and set the fan to blow hot air on my side. He said, 'Look, Aditya! You are not going to shoot me—your gun is still on safety. Listen, I'm on your side, so let's pause a moment and talk.'

His head lurched forward and he gazed at me as he spoke sincerely. He was right, the gun was still on safety. I was annoyed that he was right. I placed the gun away from him.

He shifted in his seat and faced me. 'It goes back to our college days. You remember that I was pulling small drugs jobs back in our college. Where do you think the drugs came from? My father ruled the drugs business in Goa. He was a ruthless, conniving businessman but a family man. He wanted me to have a good life—a safe, clean, normal life, that's why he sent me thousands of miles away from Goa to Delhi. He didn't realize that I had his wayward blood in my veins. I wasn't going to be an engineer or an MBA. What the fuck! That shit wasn't meant for me. I automatically got into the drugs world and did well on my own.

'I was young, but I wanted to show my dad that I could take his empire to other countries like Columbia, the Czech Republic, Mexico...the whole world. I established myself and made some associations with some bad...very bad guys in the business. You remember that night in Goa, that was the foundation between me and my father and you helped me back then. After that night, I chose to drop out of college to live life king-size. I earned a good name in the drug cartel world in Goa, after wiping out the competition. My father accepted me as his heir, and he was proud. You are wondering how all of this is relevant.'

He paused, looked at me and continued, 'The drugs world is full of money and power, and I was riding high. I had no idea where you were in your life until six months ago! That's when the DEA busted me in their massive raid in El Paso. They had all the evidence against me. Heck I was busted with twenty-six kilograms of narcotics in the back of the car.'

'Your DEA friend, Richard ran that bust. They froze all my money, houses and brought me down to rockbottom in twenty-four hours. Richard offered me a deal to go undercover and help them with information about drug smuggling, money laundering plans, the contacts—everything possible—you know. Or else I was looking at straight seventy-five years in prison.' He looked in my eyes trying to find sympathy.

I said, 'And you took the deal.' *Son of a bitch.* I gaped at him in disbelief.

I couldn't control myself. I swung a solid left-handed fist at his mouth.

My other hand poked the barrel of gun just below the kneecap harder. He cried in pain. I held the gun from the barrel and hit the base with force on his knee. He coughed and spit on the steering wheel.

I watched him coughing hard. His eyes were turning red, he panted and he wiped tears from his eyes. Just when he thought the worst was over, I hit his knee again with the gun.

He thumped his fist loudly on the wheel which made the car honk. I glanced at the other cars in the parking lot to see if there was any movement. There was no one to hear us.

'Bhai...I'm really on your side. Would you let me finish?' he cried in pain. I had the urge to beat him up more, but I needed him. He was tightly coupled with my fate.

I stared at him and said, 'You do realize that you deserve every bit of that. Go ahead, I'm listening.'

He took a deep breath and started narrating, 'Of course, I shook hands with Richard. What choice did I have? I'm a bad guy, but I'm not built for prison. You tell me what you would have done, in fact, I don't have to ask you that. To save your family you have done so much. You showed you have more balls than me. You fucking escaped from the DEA! How crazy is that! Really crazy but dope, super dope! Anyway, I started helping the DEA by supplying them with information, and they were able to catch more drug dealers along with hundreds and hundreds of pounds of drugs.'

When Vincent realized he had me hooked deeply, he took the liberty to look for a cigarette. He lit one up, which I removed from his lips instantaneously. He understood that I was in no mood for his dramatic pauses.

He asked me, 'Ever heard of Carlos? Carlos Lopez? His name has been published in the *TIME* magazine and once they did a cover story on him.'

I shrugged my shoulders.

'Of course you don't... I know you. You don't do anything except sobbing over your sad life. Sorry! I digress.'

'Richard's lifelong mission is to catch the Mexican drug lord Don Carlos Lopez. He has a personal vendetta with him because Richard's daughter died in exchange firing with Carlos's gang. "No Carlos, no deal"—that's what Richard told me,' he said, shrugging his shoulders.

'I had no information about Carlos. So we started digging. That's when I found Naina.'

I stared at him astonished.

'Bhai, Naina is alive! Imagine my state when I found that out—it was unbelievable. I wanted to share that with you and started searching for you on Facebook, Twitter, Instagram and shit. But you were nowhere to be found. You are a ghost. I paid 5k dollars to a private investigator just to find you.

When I found you, I thought you were the saddest person,

pretending to have a happy married life.'

Suddenly, he got all serious and almost choked up. 'Finding you was the best thing I had done. We were great friends back in college and I felt a bond with you. I decided not to tell you about my deal with Richard. I didn't want to stir up your otherwise calm life, but then this Terrence thing happened. I wanted to help, but I had nothing to give you. I couldn't let you die. Not while I was around.'

He paused again. This time I allowed him to light up a cigarette. His words seemed honest.

'So the next part is what I'm not proud of, but I did it only to help you and also actually myself. I didn't want to hurt you or anything. I thought you still had the playboy charisma and we could use it to arrange the money for Terrence. By that time I had found that Franky was working for Carlos—he was the only solid human link we had. I needed to know if you could seduce Soleil and as a test I asked you to get the accounts information from the sexy black girl—Nikki. Nobody needed that information honestly—that was a pure test in which you failed to seduce the girl, but hey, you came through in the end—that's all it mattered.'

My turn to be surprised again. 'But why! That's just stupid, Vincent. You realized how risky it was if we were caught.'

'It's not stupid if it works—besides we didn't get caught, thanks to your out-of-the-box thinking,' he responded. 'The DEA has no idea that we did something like this. Did they ask you about Nikki or about hacking information from your company?' He looked at me.

I nodded my head in a no.

'So after Nikki, I was confident that you would get Franky's whereabouts one way or the other. You did really good, you prepared well and got in her bedroom and slept with her. I apologize for that part. I didn't mean to push you, but I was very happy for you—you were living your life again.' He slapped my shoulder in a friendly manner.

'I'm happy to have you back. My friend.'

I decided not to tell him about what happened between me and Soleil and that Koyal and I were trying to make things work between us. I had different priorities right now.

'I passed on the locations you gave me to Richard. Richard used that information and they set up "Operation Spyglass" along with Mexican Federales to catch Franky and Carlos in Juarez, Mexico. But…'

'But shit happened! Carlos was too smart for them. He already knew about the DEA's plan. They ambushed the security forces and killed two of Richard's men and five Mexican agents.'

'So that's it! You are on my side, Vincent! You know everything, that I have nothing to do with Solei's murder and Franky's disappearance. I don't know any of these men and have nothing to do with their world. Call Richard and tell him everything you just told me. You hear me! I don't fit in this drug world story!'

'He is on his way… I texted him before you got inside my car.' He pursed his lips 'Look on your side.'

A deep gruff voice echoed from my side, 'I will tell you the rest of the story and how you fit in.'

Startled, I looked to my left and found Richard Nelson standing next to me, outside the car. I almost jumped in my seat. He was still in the same suit as before. There were some scruff marks on his arm due to the skirmishes on the rooftop.

He opened the rear passenger door and slid himself into the backseat. He offered his open palm in front of me, signalling for me to hand him the gun.

'C'mon, son, give it to me. Is it still on the safety lock?'

'It still is, and he doesn't know how to remove it... Richard, tell him that we are on his side,' Vincent jumped in.

'I suppose I will. But I suppose that Mr Aditya here is facing another dilemma about the gun. Am I right?'

I slapped the gun in Richard's palm. He grabbed it, and quickly released the magazine from the gun base to check if it was fully loaded. He put the slithering magazine back in the gun slot and then pocketed the gun. 'You are quite a runner. I almost had you, but luck was on your side. Hopefully, luck continues to stay on your side if you want to get back to your life.'

I had nothing to say.

'Okay, Mr Aditya. I will make it quick. We want Carlos, and we want your help to get him. I will tell you why you will help us in a minute. Vincent is working with us, and has helped us make high profile arrests in the cartel world. We busted many money-laundering systems because of Vincent's help, which is all good. But it's not complete if Carlos is not behind the bars. I look at you and my heart tells me to believe a different story, but being in this tough profession, I don't give a fuck about what my heart says. Not any more!'

He spoke calmly, but his words pierced my soul.

'Soleil is dead, Franky's dead too, most probably. Your DNA is all over Soleil's house. Now we know that Vincent used the DEA's informant money to get the information with your help. The money we found in your house belongs to the DEA and that complicates things very much. Your friend may have been trying to do right thing for you, but it makes the DEA look bad that an Indian nobody like you took the DEA's money and got their only substantial link to Don Carlos killed. We have every reason to believe that you sold Franky's information to someone else, and that's how they expected us to walk in an ambush and killed our many good soldiers.'

He interrupted me as soon as I opened my mouth. 'Vincent has a plan. I wasn't onboard at first, but when he told me how you manipulated Soleil to get Franky's information, I got interested.

'To tell you the truth it's too James Bondish with tons of risk.'

'Again, I'm no James Bond—he's not married—I am! And I didn't know anything about what Franky did,' I said.

'But you escaped our DEA facility in front of five agents, that shows a lot of courage and heart. You jumped off the roof, you proved that you are no ordinary man. Mr Aditya, there's a lot at stake here. A French national is dead. Now, it's possible Carlos's men killed her when they realized she knew too much, but where's the proof? The only solid theory which exists today, puts YOU in the middle of everything. Can you fight that in court? Will your lawyer friend be able to convince an American jury?'

He took no time in showing me the reality. *I was fucked.*

He shifted in the seat to face me. I stared at his face, holding my breath.

'Listen to what we have to say carefully. We have established a credible link to Carlos. Her name is Selena a.k.a Naina a.k.a Anjali. I understand you had a relationship with her when she met you as Naina.'

He let me absorb this information.

Vincent spoke after a long time, concerned. 'I know this is very difficult for you, Bhai, but Naina is in Mexico…and she is Carlos's wife. In Mexico, she goes by the name Selena.'

The car creaked when Vincent's shifted his big body in the seat. He arched his back and lifted the right flap of his jacket. He took out a yellow manila envelope and handed it to me.

Yellow manila envelopes never bring me good news.

Reluctantly, I opened it. I pulled out photos of Naina. She was alive, she was well and she looked fabulous. The numerous shots were taken in secret, while she was getting in and out of the cars.

We all sat in silence, while I sifted through the pictures.

'Richard, you said in this profession the heart has no place, so why are you playing with my heart? Why would I trust any of you? It could be another lie. Another set-up. Vincent has watched too many movies and this plan seems like it has been lifted straight out of the movies. Those are fake pictures, right?'

They exchanged looks. They probably hadn't expected the kind of response I gave them.

Richard spoke, 'If you must know, this kind of deal isn't uncommon in the DEA, FBI, CIA or any other national security agency. We always need assets and informants, and I'm a firm believer in giving people a second chance to redeem themselves.'

'What do you guys want from me? I've not been in contact with her. How can I be of any help? I shot back.

I gave them the response they were looking for. Vincent put a sympathetic hand on my shoulder.

'Don't worry Adi, she is not in danger, at least not yet. We have some intel that soon something big will happen, which could potentially be risky for her life. If anything happens to her, that will sabotage our attempts to get to Carlos,' Vincent said. 'Look! She obviously meant a lot to you. When I was gathering information about Carlos, I stumbled on the fact that Naina was with Carlos and we think that she was a major driving force in Carlos's business expansion. You and I both know that Naina was not an ordinary girl. She was a fighter.'

I fired back, 'She left me without a word—how was she a fighter? And why should I care about her well-being?'

'Oh man, you don't know anything do you?' Vincent said.

I looked at him, perplexed. 'What else I don't know?'

Vincent started talking. With each word he said, I understood how wrong I had been about Naina.

'Do you recall the night, fourteen years ago, when you told me that she left you and you were heartbroken. There was no Google or Yahoo back then, but I did manage to find out a lot about her. She had a troubled past—her family burned her school and her boyfriend alive because he was a Christian. She got her dad and brothers arrested in the murder case and ran away to Delhi. She was being hunted in India by her family and when they learned that you were her lover, you also became a target. That's why she ran away again and left India and somehow ended up in Mexico with Carlos.'

Finally the truth about Naina came out after fourteen years.

I shoved my face in my hands. I felt suffocated in that closed car.

I had misunderstood her so much.

I pushed open the car door and immediately felt the icy cold breeze on my face. I screamed aloud in the parking lot, thinking about what Naina had had to endure.

I should have saved her. I was the love of her life.

Goa

Fourteen years ago, we were young and Vincent was skinny. The beautiful sun was setting in the background, hypnotic Goa trance music was playing in the car stereo. I was looking outside the rapid changing visuals from beaches to the white lighthouse careening through the winding roads with palm trees on either side.

Vincent drove the car with ease. He was looking like a coastal boy, dressed in white denims, a green polo shirt, yellow tennis shoes.

This was my first time in Goa. It was beautiful, but I was mourning the loss of Naina. He took me to a party on Anjuna Beach. The scene was straight out of a movie. Lots of girls and boys, skimpily dressed hot girls in bikinis, chiselled guys with six-pack abs were flying high.

Vincent found the shack he was looking for. It was one of the largest shacks on the beach. As soon we entered, the owner came running to greet Vincent.

'Tell the boys we have to leave in fifteen minutes—tell them to come prepared,' Vincent ordered. I knew he was famous in Goa, but he acted like he owned the place.

We took seats in the corner where a private lounge was made for VIPs. It was cordoned off from the public.

'Adi, tell me what happened. I hope the flat in Bangalore was okay?' he asked.

'No Vincent, the flat was fine, rather it was better than

expected.' Before I could finish even my line, we were brought tequila, ice and two glasses.

Vincent shook, 'Bring two chilled beers.'

I started talking, 'I've been going over what happened and trying to connect the dots. Wondering if I did anything wrong. But nothing makes sense.'

'You said something about the picture—Anjali something?'

'About a month ago, Naina and I went to see a movie in Vasant Vihar. We were holding hands and mingled with the crowd when the movie ended. Suddenly, two guys came running up to us and one of them pushed me. By the time I got up, the guys had disappeared and so had Naina.'

The beers arrived. I took one from the man's hands and took a big swig.

'I looked around but didn't find her anywhere. Same guys came back and followed me into the cinema's lobby. They were asking around by showing a picture to people. One of them rushed to me and without any warning, punched me in my face. He shouted and cursed at me in a thick Bihari accent. He started questioning, "Where is she? Tell me or I'll kill you!" I was pissed off. People stopped and watched me getting beaten. He hit me again in my stomach and tried to hit me again when I swung out of his way and slapped him really hard. It was so hard that I felt his jaw break. By that time the second guy showed up. He was twice my size. I didn't want to mess with him, so I asked them what were they looking for. He gave me the picture, and it was the same picture we are talking about. I didn't recognize the girl, so I shook my head in all honesty to them. They realized they had got the wrong guy. Someone shouted that the police had arrived, so they left in a hurry, leaving the picture with me.

I got worried about Naina, so I started looking for her. I

found her in front of a cigar shop. I showed her the picture and told her the whole story about my scuffle with the guys. She simply stared at the picture.

On the way back to the college she didn't say anything. After that day, she changed. She bought new clothes, changed her hairstyle, everything.

I was done with my story and my beer. I looked at Vincent, hoping to find an answer. He had none.

He said, finishing his tequila, 'I don't know what to make of this, Adi! It looks like she had a troubled past. I will try to find out what I can. I'm just surprised. She was so excited to go to Bangalore with you—she even took some Ecstasy from me. Did she tell you that?'

I nodded. He bent down, and with a rolled hundred-dollar bill, snorted a long thick line of drug powder, that the owner had brought him. He shook his head like a madman.

'Forget that bitch who left my bro! We will figure it out. For now, you have to enjoy! You are in Goa—the party capital of India. I'm taking you to a Russian club!'

Half an hour later, Vincent's Toyota Landcruiser SUV rolled into a long winding driveway of a night club. In the background, lively music was playing. Expensive cars were lined up outside.

Vincent exited first, he lit up a cigarette and puffed big smoke clouds. He looked like a dapper gangster. He had put on a blue leather jacket in the car. I exited from the other door, wearing black cargo pants and an army shirt.

Vincent reached into the car and took out a large Mexican hat and wore it. I noticed a sudden shift in people's moods. They looked tense.

I asked, 'Vincent, they all looked pissed at you! What's going on?'

He replied, 'They are pissed at my skin, Bro! Russians don't like us Portuguese or Mexicans.'

We started walking to the club. Vincent's bodyguard followed him with a packet in his hands.

'What do you mean Mexican?' I said while walking.

'You know that my dad has a Portuguese lineage. His father, grandfather and great-grandfather have Indian origins. My dad, however, married a Mexican woman, so naturally I'm mixed,' he chuckled.

We entered the club. Its large dance floor was filled with smoke and people. Waitresses walked around with loaded trays. Rich Goan and Russian people smoked cigars, made business deals and ogled at half-naked dancers.

'I'm here to meet Boris. Why don't you have some fun with the Russian girls there?' he screamed in my ear and pointed to a large round stage in the centre filled with showgirls in sleek clingy dresses. Their sensual bodies were moving along to the music.

He walked away to the upper level followed by his bodyguard.

I looked back at the girls and decided not to go there. I had no desire to be part of the group of horny middle-aged guys who were ogling the girls. I went straight to the bar.

My head was still trying to solve Naina's riddle. I ordered a beer and sat down on a bar chair. I noticed one of those dancer girls was settling down on the chair next to me.

'I like it when boys wander into places like these and they have no clue what to do!' She chuckled while lighting a cigarette.

She was breathtaking and smelled of an expensive fragrance. Her low-cut red shimmering gown was barely hiding her assets. The gown had a side slit which ran all the way up her waistline indicating she wasn't wearing anything underneath.

'I thought you needed to be rescued,' she said.

'Rescued from whom?' I asked with a faint smile.

'From yourself. You are lost. Everyone here is searching for something or someone,' she whispered into my ear, trying to seduce me. I couldn't believe this was happening to me.

'Yeah and they go home with an empty wallet after they find someone like you!' I smiled. She laughed.

I was glad I made someone laugh. I missed Naina.

'Since you asked, I'm looking for Boris! Do you know where he is?'

Her eyes widened and she looked at me up and down. 'Wow! Big business for such a young boy. Everyone who comes here first goes to the centrestage to see us for free, but you are the only one who didn't go there.'

'No, I just followed my heart and it lead me to the bar,' I shrugged my shoulders in all honesty.

'Good, all those other motherfuckers follow their dicks!' she shot back.

That made me chuckle, I didn't expect that coming from her. She then asked me, 'How do you know Boris?'

'I'm a long-lost friend—we spent a night in a jail in Moscow,' I lied so effortlessly that even I was surprised.

'Oh shit. You missed him—he's in Puducherry for a few days.' She lit up another cigarette.

Suddenly, the scene in the club changed. I heard a few gun shots. People stopped what they were doing. I saw a few men hauling Vincent with a bloodied face down the stairs, through the hallway into the back door.

Suddenly the hallway was filled with Russian bouncers. I thought I was going to die. I exited the club from the front gate and walked quickly through the winding driveway, keeping my head down to avoid any attention. I located the SUV and quickly jumped in it.

'Go around the back of the club and follow the cars. They have taken your boss!' I yelled at the driver who pulled the SUV out abruptly from the parking

We followed a black van for twenty minutes though the city, traffic lights and out of the city until it reached the ruins of an old fort. It was a moonless night. We stayed behind the exterior wall of the fort, inside the car.

Inside the fort, in the open field, three Russians stood in front of Vincent. The headlights of their van shone on Vincent's blood-smeared face. Three of Vincent's bodyguards who were also in the SUV with me, drew their rifles and exited the car quietly.

Scared shitless, I exited behind them and crouched behind the wall.

Suddenly, a revving jeep filled the eerie calm fort with noise. It emerged from the left of the van, and before the Russians could do anything, it ran over the two of them. I cringed as bones crushed under the tyres of the jeep and bodies flew in the air.

A lone surviving Russian started shooting. The jeep came to a jerky halt as its tyre got stuck in the dirt.

The Russian emptied his gun, shattering the jeep's windows, head and tail lights.

In the pitch dark, the gunshots looked like fireflies. The men who came with me sprang into action and took out the remaining Russian in seconds. He was no match for Vincent's cavalry.

Gunfire stopped, there was silence for a few moments and then another Russian emerged from the van, surrendering himself by falling on his knees. He faced Vincent who was still on his knees.

It was an eerie scene. Three dead bodies were scattered. The battered jeep was stopped, fresh blood dripped from the jeep's grills. The door of the jeep opened and a broad-built man of average height came out. He wore loose cotton pants and exquisite cowboy boots. He had a thick moustache, a wrinkled face and a cigar clubbed between his lips. He looked like a villain straight from the movies.

He walked briskly, angry as hell, and stopped in front of Vincent. Right at that moment, the remaining Russian started gagging, coughing and spitting froth from his mouth. The man kicked the Russian who fell on his back and started choking on his own spit. His shaking body came to a halt after he died.

The man turned to Vincent and spoke to him.

'*Por qué? Vincent. ¿Por qué no puedes mantenerte alejado de todo esto? Te envié para tener una vida decente* (Son, why can't you stay out of this life? I sent you away to have a decent life. Why do you keep coming back here in this shit?).'

The man was Vincent's father, Carlito Fernandes. I had heard quite a lot about him I got closer to them.

'You are my son, I can't see you dead.'

'Papa, I belong here. I was going to take Boris out tonight, making Goa once again, only ours. That *puta* didn't show up. I had the whole plan.'

'How?' Carlito asked. Vincent gestured towards the dead Russian.

Carlito's eyes widened with anger. '*Mierda*! You were going to poison the bastard with tequila.' He kicked the dirt and said, '*Estúpida película drama* (Stupid drama)! Bloody immature! Now we have no Boris. And wherever he is—he knows what you have done.'

I understood the drama and tension between the father and son. Vincent wanted to follow in his father's footsteps even though his father didn't want him to. I agreed with his father, but Vincent was my friend. I took out my phone and sent him a text.

His phone beeped. He read my text and eyed me. It was his time to shine and rise. He touched his father's shoulder and said, 'Papa! Boris is in Puducherry. I'll lead a team to finish him off. Let me go, let me do this, Papa. I am good at this.'

Carlito edged closer to Vincent and stared at him. He smiled. It seemed the complex relationship between them had made some progress. That night I saw another side to Vincent. He was an emotional fool like me. He was trying to win his dad's attention.

Carlito yelled at his men to bring the Land Cruiser in there. He looked at me and said, '*Gracias a tu amigo* (Thank your friend), son. He's a good friend. He led us here and saved your life.'

Vincent walked to me with open arms. He hugged me, lifting me off the ground. 'Bro, you saved my life and helped me rise in my Papa's eyes. I will never forget this. How did you know Boris is in Puducherry? That's what I wanted to find out, but those motherfuckers shot my bodyguard in the storage room and they brought me out here.'

'That's what happens when you poison people and expect them to answer you. I just asked the dancing girl very nicely,' I winked and bragged a little bit.

Vincent laughed like a wannabe gangster. 'Shit! In five minutes you got information from that girl. Man, you have a gift—this is the talent. Some day that can change your life.'

'For me engineering ends here. I'm not meant to be in school, *amigo* (friend)! You saw what happened here—this was the first time my Papa ever liked what I did. You carry on, do big things, build some rocket and super computer shit, but believe me you have a gift. Some day that can change your life.'

the homecoming

'Some day that can change your life', that phrase echoed in my mind. Vincent was right, it did change my life for the worse.

I felt a hand on my shoulder. I returned from my flashback into the present. I was back at home after spending a long cold, tiring and strange night in the streets of Chicago, standing at the front door. Koyal hugged me. Karan came behind her and clung on to my leg. Her eyes were red. I felt guilty for having them go through this trauma. She held me from my shoulders and helped me inside the house.

'How are you, Adi? What happened? What did the police want from you? Where did they take you?' She asked several questions before realizing that she was pushing too hard. I dragged myself inside and sat down on the sofa. The house was a mess after the party.

Koyal pulled a chair and sat facing me.

My heart was in my throat. I lost control and started crying. I fell on her feet.

'Please Adi... Tell me what's going on? Why won't you tell me what's hurting you?' Koyal exploded and threw her body onto mine, hugging me really tightly. We cried our hearts out. I was so blessed to have that little family who cared so much about me. We were each other's worlds, and I had started to realize that.

After a few minutes, I undressed in the bathroom and

looked at my bruised body in the mirror. A blizzard of blurry images flickered in my raging mind. The DEA dragging me in the crowd, sitting in a locked facility, escaping into frigid cold, running down the cold stairs, loud car horns and police sirens echoed in my mind and then Naina's pictures and Richard's words came to me.

Half of the DEA agency believes that you are responsible for the DEA's failure.

We need Carlos. You know Naina, use her.

Get back in her life, that's the only way.

Only way.

If you don't comply then forget about your wife and son.

You will rot in a prison for a long time. You have twenty-four hours. Think about it hard.

If you do what I say then all of this goes away, Terrence goes away, his threats will not matter any more and you will be able to play ball with your son.

I stepped in the shower and closed the glass door. Soon the room was filled with steam. My body ached wherever the hot water touched it. I felt unbearable needle pinches all over my body before the steam and hotness took over. Slowly, my muscles started to relax.

I turned the knob to cold water, soaped and shampooed. I checked myself again in the mirror after coming out, and I still felt the same way. My body was clean, but my soul was still dirty.

the choice

'They don't have a case! You are part of a big conspiracy. They indirectly misled you to do all that,' said Maya in a decisive tone.

I nodded in disagreement. Maya paced in the kitchen furiously. Koyal sat opposite of me. I had come clean with Koyal and Maya and told them everything. I told them about Nick's debt to Terrence, Terrence's death threats to the family, Vincent's elaborate plan of stealing information from Soleil and how I was trapped in the midst as suspect number one of America. I decided to hide my intimate encounters with Nikki and Soleil. I couldn't tell that.

I told them about the DEA's proposal. Koyal listened to each and every word and had not reacted. I wanted her to react, scream at me even, but she sat there listening to me and Maya.

Maya, on the other hand, was not pleased with what I had told them.

Birds chirped outside the kitchen window. It was a beautiful Sunday—a perfect day for skiing. That kind of a sunny day was rare for Chicago.

I showed my palms defensively. 'Soleil and her boyfriend are dead, allegedly. They are pinning their deaths on me.'

'Yeah, but you didn't kill her, right! They don't have a case,' Maya said.

'I don't know, but they have my DNA and fingerprints in her house. I may have left my hair or something behind. They are also saying that I somehow sabotaged their operation to capture some Don Carlos in Mexico, and they also lost Franky and some of their agents. They are ready to declare me a traitor!'

'Carlos—the don? He was in the *TIME* magazine,' Maya said quickly.

Apparently everyone except me knew about Mexico's drug warlord.

'Is the DEA saying you gave Franky's location to Carlos's men and they thought he was working with the DEA, so Carlos ambushed the DEA team and also killed Franky?' Maya connected the rest of the dots herself, which was commendable.

She turned to me and looked straight into my eyes. 'So did you do all of those things they are saying, Aditya?'

'No! Absolutely no!'

'Great. Then have them dig through your phone, email and internet records. If you never connected with these people, then they won't be able to prove anything. They are just phishing— these are the DEA's standard textbook threat and intimidation tactics.'

I thought for a second about that, but immediately rejected the idea. I couldn't risk the DEA digging through my life because that would lead them to my hacking theft. *Shit! I was fucked from all sides.*

'I don't know if it's worth it. They have piles and piles of fake evidence against me,' I said dejectedly.

'So what, Adi? You are just going to give up and put your life at risk again for this suicide mission? Who do you think you are? Shahrukh Khan?' Maya questioned my motives.

I stayed quiet and looked at Koyal for some help. I needed her support to make my decision.

'Should I even dare ask you about your decision?' Maya asked another question.

I looked at Koyal again, shaking my leg nervously.

Koyal spoke, 'Adi, if I was in your place and was given a chance to find out what happened to the love of my life, I'd take that chance. I'd take that chance to find the closure I need, so I could move on.'

She turned to Maya and said, 'He has no choice. If he doesn't do it, he will not forgive himself.'

I stood up and Koyal held my shoulders. She said, 'You did so much for this family, and I had no clue! You saved Maggie's life by saving Nick, and it's my turn now to support you.'

I was so lucky that I was surrounded with strong women like Maya, Koyal and Naina. All of them wished nothing but the best for me. And for them I knew I must go to Mexico to fix what I had broken. Koyal was right. If I didn't do this now, I would never forgive myself. It was time to close the Naina chapter and heal the wounds.

I had to go to Mexico, I had to meet Naina.

no half measures

My fingers clutched the arms of my airplane seat, and my back was sweating. My anxiousness was getting the best of me. I was going to Mexico to meet Naina, risking my life to do so. I looked out at Chicago's expansive concrete jungle sprawled beneath me. Who could believe that half of this city was reduced to ashes in the 1870s during the Great Chicago Fire. The city is considered the birthplace of skyscrapers. The criss-cross network of streets, ramps and highways is an amazing example of engineering marvel and looks like a complex labyrinth.

On my side, Vincent was dozing off. He wasn't kidding about flying high when he gulped down six shots of tequila right before we boarded. I still didn't know what I felt for him after he had pulled me into this mess. I studied his face and thought how much he had changed from our college days. Back then he was a skinny dude with a flamboyant style and was instantly popular among guys with his Goan swag. He sported shoulder-length hair, cool sunglasses and flannel or polo shirts with accessories like bracelets and chains.

Now he had put on weight though still handsome.

His taste in clothing was still impeccable. He had ditched the three-piece suit today and instead wore a maroon leather jacket over a black turtleneck sweater.

I stretched my legs which ached from the rigorous crash course I had gone through during the past two weeks. Not just my legs, the muscles all over my body and even my jaw ached due to the excessive clenching during gun practice at the range.

In the past two weeks, I underwent a rigorous crash course with experienced trainers hired by Richard. I was pushed, pulled and dragged on the dirt and was made to run through narrow lanes over and under the obstacles. I took two weeks off from work and did only three things: train, eat and sleep.

A two-week boot camp was supposed to help me fight a dangerous drug cartel who lived and breathed death their entire lives. Even Richard had started showing concern over this suicide mission. But Vincent was optimistic.

'He will come through, Richard! Don't worry about Aditya. He's a fighter. He may not look like a fighter, but he's tough as nails.'

I also trained in handling guns—lots of guns—handguns, fully automatic, semi-automatic rifles. *Yeah, I also learned to take the safety off.* It was all for the contingency plan because I was not expected to engage directly in any hostile activities. Richard had arranged an empty warehouse, a closed textile plant, to run the training. Two weeks ago, we stood in a large old stock room which still contained unused threads and yarns. The room was lit with natural sunlight. We stood around a worn-out table.

I hesitantly asked Richard, 'How can I help you with this?'

'Bhai! Of course we are not going to drop you in a snake pit and expect you to get us the precious stone. Like we said, we have been working on this plan for a long time and we have thought through every possible angle,' Vincent said, trying to reassure me.

Richard carried the conversation forward.

'They are very dangerous people and will show no mercy in cutting you into small pieces if they smell anything fishy. Carlos's downfall is very important to us, but I also want you to come back out of this alive, believe it or not—I do have some heart for my own people.' He looked at me and then signalled Vincent to carry on.

'When you are in the world of drugs and extortion, you automatically make enemies. Call it turf war, competition, conflict of interest or sometimes families turning on each other. Carlos is no different. He has made many enemies, and his main enemy is Mendes who's been killing Carlos's men and his business. When we agreed that you are the right man for the job, we concocted a fake drug lord from Dubai—his name is Charlie and you will pretend to be him. Charlie, which is you, has expressed a desire to meet with Carlos and work on a new strategy to exploit access to Afghanistan's drug market. Using homeland security, we have created fake internet chatter about drug deals worth millions in Charlie's name. Carlos has agreed to meet you in Mexico City. Your name "Charlie" precedes you, Mr Aditya.'

Smile.

'You are very famous in Mexico and you didn't even know.'

'With Charlie's partnership, Carlos expects his net worth will multiply in a few months, leaving Mendes behind like a street cockroach,' Vincent stopped talking to gauge my reaction to the plan. They both looked at me.

I was impressed, very impressed with their stupidity. I pursed my lips and said with sarcasm, 'Too good! Great plan! Straight out of a Bond movie.'

Richard didn't like my smartass comment. 'I suggest you keep listening carefully if you want to come out of this alive. For the record, let me tell you for last time—this is what we do every day. That's why we are called DETECTIVES!'

Vincent picked up again. 'You will be meeting with his number two at a place which is not decided yet.'

'Wait a minute! I'm meeting his number two? Not him or Naina? You don't need me, anyone else can meet this number two.

'His number two is Naina.'

I froze.

Richard spoke, 'We cannot send anyone else to meet her. Only you! You will somehow plant a satellite tracker on her which will help us track her and Carlos. And then at the right time we will raid his house and capture him alive. We have no intention to kill him, men like him are worth more living than dead.'

I started pacing, thinking about the plan. My heart started racing.

'How many people know about this plan?'

'Nobody else. Just the three of us,' Richard explained.

'Great! What if you die, Richard? Why would anyone listen to Vincent—he's an ex-crook? I will be fucked!' I resented their plan, which I had seen in the famous Bollywood movie *Don*.

I was stupid to be even part of this, but the mere mention of Naina threw all logic aside.

'Nobody will die, Mr Malhotra, we do this all the time and don't forget, Vincent is accompanying you to help you all along.' That didn't comfort me because I no longer trusted Vincent the way I used to.

Richard continued, 'You have my word, you will come back home.'

I shook my head. 'Your plan is very complicated. Many things can go wrong. I can't act as a drug lord. I don't know the business even if you teach me. Shouldn't we try to bring Naina in directly, so I can convince her to give away Carlos?'

Vincent shook his head in disagreement. 'Lover boy! That's impossible. Nobody meets Carlos until Carlos wishes to meet.

This is our only opportunity.'

'Can you not track them with their cell phones? Why do you need to mark them with a tracker?'

'We don't know what numbers they use, they change phones like models change clothes.'

'Before you ask anything else, we don't have any clue where Carlos and Naina live. They own countless houses in Mexico City.'

I was quiet for a few seconds. 'What about drones? Can you use drones to track them?'

'This is not Afghanistan or Iraq. You want to start an actual war between the US and Mexico?'

I exhaled, rubbed my forehead and tried to make sense of all this. It all sounded too Hollywoodish to me with very little probability of success. I was not a trained spy. I was a lover boy. That was my only talent plus a bit of computer hacking.

'This is a half measure plan, I know me. I know what I can do. I cannot get past those loyal killers and you know that too, and I can't die... I simply can't afford to die and we can't afford half measures. Let me meet her—find out a safe place she visits—place me near her, and I will take care of the rest. The pictures you guys showed me of Naina. Where were they taken?'

'That was a school where her son goes.'

'That's it, that's perfect—put me there. Mother and son— that's my zone.'

Vincent's neck danced again in disagreement and scepticism. He wondered how a rookie like me could reject their well thought-out plan and propose a new one at the last minute.

'Bhai, that's impossible. We can't get in touch with her directly. She is a fucking walking-talking fortress with an army of specially trained bodyguards. It's gonna put a lot of civilian lives, mostly kids in danger if we try anything stupid on a whim,' Vincent stared at Richard for support, but Richard was thinking of something else.

'Will you be able to execute the mission as planned if we place you around the school?' Richard asked me.

'In all honesty, I say your whole plan relies on this engineer's shoulders,' I smiled. Richard did not.

Suddenly my stomach dropped and I zoomed back to the present. The plane was cutting through a pack of clouds and was facing serious turbulence.

I looked at Vincent in fear and no surprise there—he was still out.

The flight went smoothly. I should have taken the turbulence as a sign of caution sent directly from heaven. It was clearly warning me about the bumpy ride I was going to have in Mexico.

Soon we were descending into Mexico City. I gazed out of the window and thought about Naina. I tried to imagine how I would react when I see her.

What am I going to say to her?

How will she react? Will she even recognize me?

I recognized her from a picture in a heartbeat.

I threw my head back and asked myself why I was there really!

Am I still in love with her? Am I mad at her for leaving me behind?

I always wondered why I couldn't let her go from my life.

Now I know because that story was not finished; the story shifted locations and introduced new characters, but it was far from over.

I looked out of the window. Beautiful stars in the big clear sky. The glitzy city was sprawled out below.

At a distance I saw the Angel of Independence—the most

distinguishing symbol of Mexico City. The stone monument glimmered in flood lights and stood majestically in the middle of a busy square. I had heard about it at work from Alejandro. He had talked about how when Mexico won a prestigious football championship, fans gathered around the square and celebrated.

'That's the stock exchange—Mexico's financial hub,' Vincent reached over my side, heaving his heavy body and pointed to a pair of gleaming tall skyscrapers.

'Your alcohol breath stinks—get off me.'

'Bhai, you still mad? You should be thankful to me—I turned your life around.' He giggled. I scoffed at him and wondered what he was made of.

accidental spy

Three days before the flight to Mexico, I met Richard in his office. I felt weird coming back to the same building I had escaped from, a few days ago. His office had an amazing view of the John Hancock tower and other skyscrapers. The wall behind his desk was full of bravery placards. He had pictures with the president, secretary of state and other dignified personalities of the free world.

He was a man of simple tastes. His office furniture was mostly black. Tough Richard looked like an ordinary man with something heavy on his mind that day.

'Aditya, this war on drugs is not just a job for me. It's as personal to me as it is to you. I lost my beautiful sixteen-year-old daughter Carrie to cocaine. She had a life ahead of her, and I lost her on the way to the hospital when Carlos's men ambushed me in the US, can you believe it? I hate that bastard—he's always two steps ahead of us.'

I studied his sombre visage and was surprised to learn that this stone-faced man did have a heart.

He paused, fighting back his emotions, and walked to the end of the desk. He scooped out a small glass capsule from the drawer and a special gun with another hand. He signalled for me to come closer and emptied the contents of the glass capsule in his palm. He showed me the glass and steel tracker which were as big as a rice grain. He put that in the special gun and signalled for me to turn around and remove my shirt.

'This is a micro tracker. This is your second back-up. Only my tech team and I know about this, not even Vincent.'

He rubbed my skin with a swab patch and injected the tracker in.

'Wherever you go we will be monitoring your activity on large screens in the tech facility somewhere. Don't worry, it will not hurt at all.'

I put my shirt back on and rubbed the back of my shoulder. I didn't feel a thing. He pointed to a shoebox next to me on the floor. 'Wear these boots in Mexico. They have another transmitter, a bigger one. I got you the most comfortable shoes,' he smiled.

'I told you I want you back alive and I'm not taking any chances, this is also your lifeline. Make sure you don't lose it.'

I shook hands with Richard and handed him the pocket diary I had stolen from Franky's house.

'This is now full measure, Sir!' I said confidently. That diary was my ticket out of jail.

welcome to 'Mehico'

In forty-five minutes, we were out of the airport and found ourselves standing in a line, waiting for a cab.

I demanded an explanation, 'What? The government can't afford to rent us a car? And here I am putting my life on line to disrupt the multibillion dollars drug market.'

Vincent heard it but ignored it and unzipped the front of his jacket.

As people boarded the taxis, the cars moved and finally the ground transport guard marshalled us to the next cab in line.

I complained, 'What kind of a cheap ass mission is this— can't even afford a car with a driver.'

'It's a stealth mission, you get that. It's not a vacation.'

The weather was much warmer than in Chicago, the sun had descended and the golden street lights burnished the streets and the tired faces of locals.

Vincent opened an email on his phone and instructed the cabbie where to go in fluent Spanish. The driver smiled with excitement to see an Indian speaking Spanish. Like a chameleon, Vincent could easily pass for an Indian and Mexican based on the demand of the situation. The traffic reminded me of Delhi.

Vincent spoke first. 'It's a stealth op, that's why this charade of cab and hotel. To tell you the truth, I'm sorry for pulling you into this. I thought I was doing the right thing, but on the other hand, I am excited—it feels like a road trip—two old friends separated in Goa and now we are in Mexico....going to see another old friend. Well, your ex-girlfriend.' He punched my shoulder in a friendly way.

I didn't share his excitement. We wouldn't be there if it wasn't for him. My blood boiled.

He winked and this provoked me further. I grabbed his neck and shook his big head. I yelled, 'I'll kill you. I'll kill you.'

He mimicked my scream and started laughing.

Now I was even more pissed, I punched him on his knee, and he yelled in pain. I hit him again. 'Enjoy your road trip with weak legs, asshole!'

The cab veered abruptly and came to a screeching halt on the side of a road full of street shops. I didn't realize that we had passed the posh urban area so quickly and now were in the middle of an area which reminded me of Delhi's Chandni Chowk. The cabbie got out and yelled at us in Spanish and threw our bags on the curb. He had kicked us out.

We were standing right in front of an impressive monument. I didn't know what it was, and I didn't care much at that time. I looked closely and realized that it was some sort of monument for fallen soldiers.

Will I be considered a fallen soldier if I die helping the DEA in this matter of national security?

Honestly, I was a bit relieved that the cabbie only kicked us out. I had heard horror stories of tourist-cabbie Mexican experiences which generally do not end in the tourist's favour. After a few minutes, I decided to walk and Vincent followed. We walked as the shopkeepers stared at us; some ran after us to sell handmade small wooden guitars, wicker Mexican hats and Mayan souvenirs. The streets were bustling with traffic and vehicles lined up one after another. I looked up at the grey sky which was filled with smog. It had looked so pristine from the airplane. The upward billowing smoke formed a blanket layer to cover the city.

Vincent stopped a boy and asked him something in Spanish. The boy responded quickly by pointing in a direction.

Vincent trotted towards me and spoke between heavy panting. We had barely walked, and the guy was losing a lung.

'It's not too far, let's cut through the back roads—this street is clogged. We can cut ahead and catch another cab in front,' he said.

I was not too enthusiastic about taking back roads in a city notoriously famous for abductions and mugging incidents. As much Mexico is famous for its tequila, food and culture equally it's shamed for the absence of law and order, street killings, abductions and drug wars. We walked for about fifteen minutes and didn't get anywhere.

'Check the walking directions on Google to the hotel,' I said.

'I'm trying, but the service is going in and out...damn network!' he said.

'You fat bastard! You don't even have a working phone in a foreign country?' I yelled.

'Bhai... calm down... I'm being nothing but nice to you. I'll figure it out.'

Our dispute was cut short when we heard footsteps in the dark alley. Out emerged the faces of five boys. They laughed in unison and one of them stepped forward. Getting down to the business, he quickly waved his knife in front of Vincent.

'Fat bastard? Americano or Indian?'

His sidekicks laughed at his joke because he was their boss.

The leader turned to me and asked, '*Habla Ingles* (Do you speak any English)?'

I stared back at him, unmoved.

Vincent shouted from his spot *'Como estas amigos* (How are you guys)? Yes. We are Americans and we know English.'

The leader strode to Vincent in an authoritative manner. 'Shut up, fat man!' he said.

His men laughed again. Vincent raised his hands defensively and stepped back. The leader poked Vincent's neck with the tip of his sharp knife and snatched the phone from his raised hand.

'Welcome to Mehico!'

Their school uniform gave away that they were students and part-time thugs. The gang fanned out and encircled us. Two wore their neckties on their heads like bandanas and another had wrapped his tie around his right wrist. The last guy looked out of place as if he was forced to come on a field trip so he could fit in with his classmates. *Peer pressure.* He was scared to his core.

The leader signalled to the frightened nerdy kid to step forward. He had his school shirt nicely tucked in. Even his shoes were spotless shiny. In nervousness, he fumbled and dropped the knife from his hand. The eight-inch sharp, jagged blade glistened under the moonlight and made a splat sound when it hit the rocks.

It was a heavy knife. He quickly collected it and strode towards me awkwardly. I waited for him to say anything but he forgot what he was supposed to do.

I helped him and asked, 'I don't have a nice phone. Do you still need it?'

My guy looked surprised. He stumbled and dropped the knife again. The other guys started shouting at him in Spanish.

I really wished he wouldn't take my phone. It was one of my lifelines. It was a secure and encrypted phone with a direct line to Richard.

The leader sneered at the poor fellow. He took the knife

and placed it on my throat. '*Turistico* (Tourist), huh? Remember this night... Remember Mehico forever. Give me cash, watch all of it... Keep your shitty phone; even my dog has a better one.' He chuckled when he saw my red flip-open Motorola phone.

I was stacked against the wall. The leader's teeth shone under the lamp post light. I saw his face clearly. He was calm and seemed very good at robbing people.

He threatened me, 'If you want to stay alive, learn Mehico! Speak Mehico. Your English no good in Mehico. Stay in hotel... Stay safe! *Turistico!*'

I stayed calm thinking I was there for a greater purpose.

'Take the money, guys!' Vincent shouted from where he was held by the other three guys. The leader growled at him, reminding Vincent what he just recommended to us travellers. Vincent quickly translated that in Spanish '*Toma el dinero amigos* (Take the money, friends)! *Nadie tiene que lastimar* (Nobody has to get hurt).'

He winked, impressed with Vincent's eloquence in Spanish.

Vincent and I emptied cash from our pockets into their black bag.

The leader signalled to his dudes to leave the area. They obeyed and disappeared in the darkness of the alley.

The leader took off the knife from my throat and stepped back, 'Don't hate Mehico for this... We are not all that bad... My name André! Like André Agassi only no play tennis.'

He fished out a fifty Mexican dollar bill from the bag, and gave it to me with a wicked smile.

'Catch the taxi at next right...*vamos* Jamie!'

The nerdy kid's name was Jamie, he followed him into the dark alley.

Vincent spat in disgust, grabbing his bag from the street. 'Fucking dumbasses! They didn't take our bags.'

'I can call them to come and get these. They have your phone.'

Vincent looked at me angrily but then started laughing.

I chuckled and said, 'Fucking great start to your road trip!'

a point of no return

We reached the hotel without another incident. Vincent checked us in. According to the plan, he was supposed to go and meet a local undercover DEA agent and get the guns and money for the mission.

I went straight up to my room which was luxurious and had a spectacular view of the dreadful city. I ordered some food from room service, and decided to take shower while I waited. I wanted to call Koyal and tell her that I was safe, but I was not allowed to make any calls other than to Richard.

The food arrived after thirty minutes. I ate the empanadas, a snack much like a samosa while looking out into oblivion. After I ate, I drank beer and lay down on the chaise in the balcony facing the city. It was a little over 10 p.m. and the traffic on the sprawled arteries was getting thicker. I stared at the shimmering lights and started thinking about Naina.

Tomorrow was a very big day of my life and probably of hers too. She had no idea that her life was going to change forever. I wondered how she would react when she saw me.

I let my mind go back and thought about the time I had spent with her. Images flashed in front of my eyes—the strolls we took in the green gardens of India Gate, the dates we had in the ancient ruins of the Qutub Minar complex, the sketch I had made of her in the hostel. I fell asleep dreaming about the night in Bangalore.

I was running ferociously in the dark towards the sound of music.

With each stride, the fear in my heart grew. I heard screams—Naina's screams in the distance, and then, all of a sudden, her smiling face appeared. We were in the canteen in New Delhi—she was dancing like fire. Her moves were breathtaking. But suddenly she fell.

She was dragged by a pair of hands, she screamed my name. I ran blindly after her. I was back in the disco in Bangalore. I was running through the intoxicated dancers, laser and disco lights blinding me. Someone pushed me and I went airborne for a quick few seconds before landing on the soft carpet of a cinema in Delhi.

I rolled over on my stomach to push myself up when I heard the growling and howling. I wanted to scream but nothing came out of my mouth. I heard footsteps around me. Those goons found me and had returned to finish their job. I felt like I was going to die. My body started to give up, but my heart fought back. I wanted to see her beautiful face again. I swung my arm punching the faceless person overlooking me.

'Ow Aditya!' the voice echoed.

My eyes opened. It took me a couple of seconds to adapt to my surroundings, then I heard my name.

Vincent was crying in pain while cupping his jaw with his right hand. He thumped the floor with his foot.

'Not cool, Bhai. What's wrong with you? Don't hit Naina like this when you meet her.'

I got up and looked at the clock on the bedside. It was 12.30 p.m. I was having a nightmare.

'Tell me you are serious about this shit. Our freedom is depending on this.' He marched in with a backpack and threw it on the bed.

He unzipped the bag and looked back at me. 'Go get ready. You have fifteen minutes. We are doing what you wanted. Instead of following the plan which I meticulously made over three months, we are going to rendezvous with her at her son's school.'

He stopped what he was doing and almost proudly said, 'Meticulous! Rendezvous! Those are nice-sounding words. That's the DEA impact, man!'

'Tell me you can do this, man. You need to bring your A-Game. A lot is riding on this.'

He was exactly what a desperate man should be. He unzipped some more pockets in the bag and muttered something nervously. I was already tired of him speaking non-stop, I headed for the bathroom. Vincent yelled at my back, reminding me, 'Ten minutes okay! Hurry the fuck up! School dismisses at 2 p.m.'

I came out in thirty minutes with an effusive smile. Vincent's face was red like a ripened tomato.

'Today is a big day, Vincent, look alive.'

'Do you know what we need to do? Do you want to go over the plan once again?'

He followed me to the closet where I had kept my bag.

'Okay go ahead, tell me the plan once again.'

'It's simple and effective. We will be driven to the school where her son goes.'

'Of course, why would we go to any other school?'

I chuckled, realizing how stressed out he was. He threw his hands up in the air and stomped off to the chair in the corner like a kid.

'All right! We are just staying here to listen to your jokes.' He was furious.

C'mon Vincent! You know I'm just messing with you... Let's go!"

I started dressing up and narrated the plan.

'Naina arrives daily with her convoy of two cars about ten minutes prior to the school's dismissal. She steps out of her car occasionally, and when she does, she is surrounded by at least four armed escorts. She picks up the kid and on the way back, she stops at a café. That's our best shot to get close to her. Richard has arranged for local law enforcement and there will be a few undercover agents in the area. I will approach her in the café and plant a tracker on her. I will also convince her to meet again.'

Vincent relaxed, comforted by the fact that I had a thorough understanding of the plan. 'All right, we are at a point of no return now. Stay vigilant all the time. Don't fuck up!' he warned me.

I finished dressing up. I had picked out khaki cargo pants with a loose white shirt; I put on a maroon thin leather jacket and slung a soft leather messenger bag around my shoulder and chest.

Vincent looked at me and rolled his eyes. 'You know, you are not going for a model show! But you do make anything look good. Get your sexy on, Bhai! You are going to need that. Also, I saved my new number in your phone in case you need words of wisdom when your mind stops working in front her.'

mean Mexican streets

Ten minutes later, we were cruising on the mean streets of Mexico City. We barely drove for about five minutes until we started seeing the real traffic. The driver tried his best to get us to the school as fast as possible through the clogged traffic.

Vincent poked my leg with something in the back seat. I jumped up when I saw a black bolt metal gun.

'What the fuck, Vincent.'

'Now that you know how to use it...keep it for your safety.'

'No way... I don't need it and tell our men not to fire a single shot. Keep in mind, I'm just here to talk to her... Also, there will be school kids.'

Vincent took the gun back and shoved it in his pocket. I wondered if I should have taken the gun.

Our car stopped moving. I checked the time. We were getting late. I unlocked the door and stepped out in gridlocked traffic as far as I could see.

'Vincent, I will just walk from here. Meet me at the café in an hour.'

'All right, Bhai! But take care. You sure you don't want the gun?'

'You want me to walk around in a foreign country with a hot loaded weapon down my pants?'

'Bhai, you already have a hot and loaded weapon in your pants, I've no doubt about that,' Vincent giggled.

'When you stop giggling like a girl, make sure you track

me on the phone and tell Richard to be ready. If we get lucky, we might be going back home tonight.'

The stale air was smoggy and humid. The school was on the right, on a one-way street after a three-blocks' walk.

We were in the business district of the city, I was on the left lane, and had to cross four lanes to get on to the busy sidewalk on the right. I walked past luxury vehicles and rattling two and three-wheelers on the same road. As I reached the middle of the third lane, the traffic started moving, and my surroundings immediately filled with buzzing noises and honking from excited drivers.

It stopped again after moving for ten seconds. I decided to get across quickly before I became roadkill in a busy Mexico street. Sweat broke out on my forehead. Vehicles were stacked next to each other with little or no space to walk through, I walked briskly through the labyrinth.

My attention shifted when I heard a male voice a few feet ahead of me. I looked in that direction and saw a lanky boy in a school uniform. He spoke to someone in Spanish in the beat up Toyota Corolla.

My head felt a lightning bolt when I heard him shouting, 'Selena' in the backdrop of buzzing car horns. He was the same guy who robbed us and had given us an unforgettable Mexican welcome. *André*.

I followed him. He turned around quickly and trotted through the vehicles in a zigzag way like he was on a mission.

My heart started racing with excitement and fear at the same time.

André made it to the busy walkways on the side of the street.

I was trying to keep it unnoticeable but in a strange nation all faces looked hostile to me. After two blocks, I saw the signs for the school. André stopped near a beggar sitting right below a big window of an expensive clothing store in the corner of the street. He dropped a few coins in the bowl in front of the old homeless person who wore a torn army shirt. From a distance, I, watched his every move.

The beggar handed him a gun wrapped in a newspaper. I flipped out my phone. It rang and crackled as Vincent answered it.

'What's up, Bhai?

'Vincent, something is wrong, something big is going down here. André from last night is here with a gun, and I heard somebody instructed him about "Selena". It's related to Naina.'

'Okay, I'm on it. Stay on the line.'

'I'm following André.'

'Okay, but don't make any move yet, we didn't plan for this.'

'Well, nothing goes as planned, Vincent! We are going to have to improvise,' I responded desperately.

Vincent came back on the line. 'I'm calling Richard... Give me a minute.'

I took a few steps to get a closer look. André lit up a cigarette and dragged a long pull on it while watching the street. He had already pocketed the gun in his school pants.

I treaded carefully through the crowd of people.

André's composure changed from casual to alert. I followed his eyes' direction and saw two black Lincoln cars coming slowly onto the school street. Suddenly, I had a revelation about his plan.

He dropped his cigarette on the pavement and crushed it under his shoe while both cars went past him.

My heart sank, thinking of Naina sitting behind those tinted windows.

I paced and I wished I was carrying a gun at that time. I glanced at my wrist watch and it was five minutes past the school dismissal time. The traffic had delayed Naina.

When I reached the corner, I saw kids coming out of the school, wearing the same uniform André was wearing. Luxury cars were lined up to pick up the kids.

The school street had three one-way lanes, lush green big trees on either side. One side of the street had the school's castle-like buildings and the other side hosted a plethora of designer shops.

I raced across the street, following André.

The phone buzzed in my hand and I quickly flipped open the phone. It was Vincent.

'Adi, hang on... No idea yet. What does it look like from there?'

'It looks like deep shit, Vincent. Naina is late, so no café break, and I'm smelling something fishy with André being around here... Tell your men to keep an eye on André.'

'Okay, tell me what is he wearing?'

'Shit, he is in school uniform like the others... Dammit! Just track my phone, a big storm is coming.'

I scanned the area hoping to catch a glimpse of our undercover officers, so I could draw their attention to André, but it was madness with so many people and school kids on the street at that time. I wished immediately for a traffic jam in the street, but despite the honking, the cars continued to move at an even pace.

I closed my phone and followed André. He walked past the Lincolns searching for someone in the cars through the dark glass windows. He noticed something and walked across while talking to someone on his phone. I watched him disappear behind the cars. I was a few feet away from Naina's car, which was approaching the school's pick-up point.

shootout in Mexico

Over 1,00,000. This is the estimated unofficial number of abductions which occur every year in Mexico. Of course, the official number which gets reported is less than 2,000. For years, the country has been immersed in unending drug wars which has left the people in despair and made its own people turn on themselves for ransom money. School kids are the most vulnerable.

For the kids' protection, the school deployed its own security measures and cordoned off every street except one during pick-up time. Two heavily armed school guards stood behind their posts on either side of the large iron gate. One by one the cars pulled up in front of the gate, a kid's name would be called out on the loudspeaker, then he/she would come out of the school and would get in his/her car.

I crossed over to the pavement on the side of the school. I came close to the second Lincoln car and walked alongside it. I glanced through the tinted glass windows from the corner of my eyes.

Call it a psychic connection, but I felt that Naina would be in the first car. I stepped up quickly. The passenger window was down. I picked up my pace again, and as we got closer to the school, I lost my sense of the surroundings. My heart pounded with the thought of seeing Naina. I gripped the strap of my bag and taking big strides, approached the first Lincoln car.

Cars stopped again, I heard the next kid's name was called

out in the background as my eyes were fixated on Naina in the car.

There she was—in front of me after so many years. She was as gorgeous and elegant as before. Her skin looked vibrant and tanned and her styled lush hair was coloured dark brown like models.

I was awestruck and kept looking at her while she was unaware of me staring at her, next to her window. She craned her neck to look out at the gate and saw me. She looked at me for a second. Our eyes met—my heart stopped, but her attention and eyes diverted to the gate the next moment.

She said something to her driver and he speeded up the car, leaving me behind on the pavement. I walked faster and came into her frame of vision again. She looked at me again and then dropped her sunglasses onto her face.

Dammit! That was not how I expected it to happen!

The cars stopped again and this time I took a step closer to the window. She scrambled to reach for the window button. I spoke in the midst of the cacophony of cars, horns and students. 'Naina! It's me, Adi.'

That caught her attention and she looked at me in amazement. We were about to have our moment when a loud honk from the second Lincoln shattered it. The driver from Naina's back-up car honked twice and then rolled his window down, waving his arm for me to step away.

I didn't move. The cars inched forward and Naina glanced back at me. I smiled and skipped two long steps to her. Then somebody shouted an unexpected name, 'Arjun'. Bewildered, I spun around and saw a young boy running to the car. He almost bumped into me.

He reminded me of Karan. Naina's face lit up with smile, and she quickly pushed open the door for him. He jumped in screaming something in Spanish, and Naina laughed with him. She looked back at me and then slammed the door on me.

I stood there stunned, like I had been stung by a poisonous snake. Her car moved up, leaving me behind.

The second Lincoln car had now moved next to me. A hand emerged and pushed me away, an angry face with big moustaches and eyebrows, flashed an AK-47 at me. The driver gave me a stern look and drove past me.

While I was debating my next move, both cars had pulled away from me and were making their way to the main intersection. I knew I would lose my chance once her car merged with the traffic. I picked up my pace and started chasing the cars.

My phone buzzed. It was Vincent. 'ADITYA! BACK AWAY! Listen to me, back away! Richard's team just picked up chatter that there's a positive intel on kidnapping Naina's son.'

'What? Why?'

'This is Mexico... just like our Bihar these fuckers know only this one way to get rich. The local police has been made aware of this, and they should be swarming all over the place, so you stay away from the scene for today. The last thing we want is you getting your ass stuck in the middle of this bloody cartel war.'

I hung up, kicked the ground in frustration. *Too late for that now, isn't it?*

I wasted no time and doubled up my speed. Up ahead at the intersection, I saw Jamie, André's nervous guy from last night. He was stomping his foot on the ground emphatically and shouting on a cell phone.

It was all going to happen now. The police were not going to make it in time. Naina was with her son and would die saving him. I couldn't let that happen.

My mind raced trying to figure out what the fuck was going

on. I was running parallel to the second car now. Heavyweight bodyguard guys in the back seat noticed me and their arms moved frantically. They took out their guns. One guy pointed a pistol at me, hoping he wouldn't shoot, but those guys were trained to kill and not take any chances. He shot a few bullets at me but missed me, as I ducked.

Suddenly, in the distance, I heard the loud noise of tyres screeching. I looked on my right side and saw a speeding black SUV was heading towards us.

It was an ambush.

Naina's car was waiting, its passengers unaware of what was about to happen at the red light. Suddenly Naina's car spun out of the lane. Its tyres rotated and screeched on the asphalt. My nose filled with the smell of burned rubber. Naina's car swirled out of the lane, hitting cars in the front and in the left lane and raced towards the busy intersection where the traffic lights were still red. Her car entered the square at the same time a big semi-truck entered from the left. The truck driver pressed the horn hard, drawing everyone's attention in the busy corner. My feet stopped and my heart skipped as I saw the truck heading for her car. Her driver took off hard and then applied the brakes, causing their car to swirl out of the way of the truck. Suddenly, the sound of gunshots rattled in the air and sent everyone in the square running.

In a frenzy Jamie was firing, he let his gun loose at Naina's car and almost emptied his magazine. The guys in the second car retaliated. In those quick seconds, the whole scenery of the busy commercial square changed. People scattered hysterically, many dived down on the ground. Scared kids crouched behind trees, poles and stone structures in the middle of the walkways. The windowpanes of stores shattered and magazines and newspapers fluttered in pieces from news and magazine stalls.

I ran towards Jamie. From the corner of his eyes he saw me leaping in the air and instantly turned the mouth of his gun on me. I flung my bag at his hand, knocking the gun from his hand. I rammed him with my head, shoving his body into the back of a concrete bus-stop bench. His head hit the bench hard and he became unconscious.

I quickly rose on my feet and ran to the intersection where the light had turned green but the traffic had come to a halt due to the gunfight. In confusion, many drivers had abandoned their cars. The sirens of police vehicles blared in the far distance. But they were not going to make it in this dead traffic. I sprinted to slide my body over a car's hood and fell on the other side. As I fell, a flurry of bullets zoomed past me and impaled the vehicles behind me.

One car's front tyre blew up. *Dammit! I'm with you assholes!*

Henchmen from the second Lincoln fired shots at me. I dropped my body on the hot asphalt. I tried pointing to the oncoming black SUV to tell the occupants about the impending kidnapping. The black SUV charged and veering wildly from the right, smashed into the second Lincoln.

Window glass shattered and flew in all directions and the Lincoln got tossed up in the air doing a perfect somersault. As the car landed back on the road, the body of the driver got thrown out of the vehicle.

I covered my head to avoid the shards of flying glass. Before I could register what happened, I heard another loud bang. I looked up to see that another vehicle had rammed into Naina's car.

I couldn't believe what was happening in broad daylight in a crowded city. A gunfight broke out between the guys who emerged from the SUV and the cops in the street. The cops were no match against the heavy artillery firepower. They scampered and called for back-up which was stuck blocks away.

I threw myself behind an abandoned car and saw André jumping behind the car that had rammed into Naina's Lincoln. He no longer looked like a school kid, but a stone cold assassin. He had changed into black clothes and was wearing a bulletproof jacket. He was carrying an automatic rifle and looked fearless. He walked with an automatic rifle like a trained shooter, reminding me of Winter Soldier from *Captain America*. He had no fear. Looking through the scope on the gun, he fired a few shots and took out the bodyguards in Naina's car. Two more guys came out of the SUV and crouch-walked to Naina's vehicle, pointing their guns at her car.

One of them shouted at the back door and fired a few shots to break open the door. Another stepped in front, opened the door and reached inside. My heart sank as I expected the worst for Naina.

Instead, I heard a flurry of shots being fired and then saw both of those henchmen's bodies slumped down onto the street.

Naina was not going down easy, she killed those bastards. *Naina was a badass.*

She fired a few more shots and another bad guy dropped.

I needed to do something. I snaked under a truck and picked up a semi-automatic AR-15 gun from the street. I crouched behind the busted Lincoln's broken engine and started firing at Andre's men. I got three of them right away. I kept firing until I ran out of ammo. By this time Andre's men had started firing at me. I needed to get out of there before they put countless holes in me. I ran behind another abandoned car and pushed myself into it. I turned on the ignition and rammed the pedal. I ducked down and raced towards André. Bullets went flying past me, hitting all parts of the car. Suddenly, I heard a loud noise and my back hit the dashboard brutally. My car had come to an abrupt halt. My ears rang continuously and I felt my eyes closing against my will.

I knew that Naina was still in danger, I told myself that I had to fight; I needed to help her.

I dragged myself out of the car and tried to stand up. But my legs folded, and I rolled over on the street.

I had run over two of André's guys, pinning them on to their own SUV.

I grabbed a pistol from one of the unconscious men and rolled on my back to get in position behind the car. Naina took advantage of the diversion I had created and ran towards me with her son. She dropped herself down next to me and made her son lie flat. She seemed disappointed upon seeing me. Maybe she was expecting a known face or maybe she was worried about her son's safety more than mine or hers.

I thought we were doomed. We needed help.

A rain of bullets kept hitting the other side of the car until somebody yelled, and firing stopped. *They needed her alive.*

I was wrong. We didn't need help. I had forgotten that Naina was not the same innocent sweet girl any more. She pulled herself up and snatched the shotgun from the other dead guy. She pulled herself up and through the broken back windows, started pumping the gun with one hand and shooting with another. I decided to help, so I pulled myself up and started shooting through the window. I ducked when I saw André's gun pointing at me and he fired. His bullets pierced the car in front of me. The car which was saving us was getting annihilated.

A tyre hub hit me on my head as the tyre of the car next to me blew out. Suddenly, things started to fade out and all I could see was the big blue sky with its smoggy clouds. Then the clouds separated and Naina's face appeared. She looked scared. She had run out of her ammunition.

I heard her screams followed by a child's screams. I extended my arm to her while I lay flat on the hot tar of the road.

Just when my eyes started to give up, I saw André. I growled with frustration, and, my body struggled to get up. He stared at me with an inquisitive look, and then his lips formed an evil smile when he recognized me.

'The FUCKING TOURIST!'

I bared my teeth to snarl and scream, but I tasted sand in my mouth when his heavy boot shut me up. Things went quiet, and I drifted into another world.

dead man

My eyes opened and I found myself in a dark place. I lay there without moving, wondering how I got there and where I might be. A wave of revelation fell on me that I was in a box, a wooden box. I sprung up in fear and bumped my head on a solid rough wooden wall barely three inches above me. My hands searched for each other, and I moved my legs—all my limbs were there.

My body went airborne all of a sudden and then fell on the floor of the box. I was in a vehicle which was being driven fast and wildly.

Thank God! At least I was not buried underground in that coffin.

That gave me immense hope. I was alive and not buried yet. However, I was being taken somewhere. I wondered if I was going to be part of the abduction statistical data in Mexico.

I patted myself, looking for my cell phone. I felt a bump in my pocket. My phone was still there. The last call I made was to Vincent, so pressing the dial key twice would initiate a call to him. I needed him to answer the phone.

The cell phone light lifted up the menacing darkness of the box and my heart felt hopeful again.

I tossed my body with difficulty in that tight space and managed to put the phone on my stomach. The vehicle ran through another speed bump and my body went airborne again. The phone landed at my right armpit. I heard Vincent yelling. I got my mouth closer to the phone and yelled at him. 'I'm in a box in a vehicle, speeding on a dirt road. Vincent, trace this call!' I had made a mistake. I should have been discreet. My voice caught the attention of the men in the vehicle.

I heard angry and excited voices, followed by drilling sounds. They were opening the box. Three tanned mean faces peered over me and patted me, searching for the phone. One of the men grabbed my phone and handed it to someone who wasn't in my frame of vision.

He screamed in frustration and then broke apart the phone before tossing it out of the moving vehicle. I struggled to get up, but the other two men pinned me down and boxed me in the darkness again.

I yelled and screamed in vain. The crunching noise of loose gravel under the treads of tyres was driving me crazy. I felt like somebody was banging on my eardrums non-stop.

Thirty minutes later the vehicle stopped.

The front doors opened, the vehicle jerked while men stepped out.

Voices yelled at each other. I identified André among them. The back door opened. My box moved, my body moved with it. It was being dragged in jerky movements as if someone wasn't gripping it well. I was being transported somewhere. In the distance, I heard wild animal growls. My heart jumped in my mouth. Perhaps they were leaving me boxed in a jungle. I panicked and tussled in the tight box vigorously, and continued doing that until the guys carrying the box lost their grip.

The box tilted to the right before it fell on its side edge and then rolled once before falling flat on the surface. Inside, my head bumped twice on the board during the fall.

The heart-wrenching growling sounded like it was much closer. The fall had loosened the hinges of the doors on the box and thin streaks of light shone through the crevices, giving me hope. It wasn't a jungle. Upon listening closely, I was able to make out that the growling and howling was coming from dogs, hungry dogs. I hoped André was not a fan of the ruthless Ramsey Bolton from *The Game of Thrones*, who threw his enemies in front of his hungry guard dogs to be ripped apart to death.

Someone removed the wooden board above my face. Two pairs of arm reached down and yanked me out. My legs folded due to numbness and when they tried to make me stand, I rolled in their arms almost dragging one of them with me.

do you remember me?

Moments later, I was being dragged by my shoulders into a luxurious mansion. The floor felt smooth and marbled. I was being taken into someone's safe haven or hideout, and for the first time I heard a zealous cheering noise. I was taken through a spotless clean corridor whose walls were decked with expensive and meaningless abstract art. The corridor branched into different rooms. My captors continued walking to the end of the passageway and stopped in front of a large wooden gate. One of the guys opened it.

We stood at the brink of the stairs, and suddenly they pushed me down the stairs. I instinctively covered my head. I was at the mercy of gravity and was destined to feel a lot of pain.

When I opened my eyes, I was lying in my pool of blood with my face touching the sandy and unfinished floor. I exhaled and dust particles near my nose blew in the air. The air smelled of urine. I rolled onto my back. An old, slow moving fan whirled above my face.

Great! I'm stuck in the middle of a fucking drug war? I have the worst luck!

I sat upright with difficulty and scanned the place. A few wooden barrels sat incongruously in the corner. They contained tequila bottles.

The wall behind me in front of the stairs had a rack of pipes running flat against it—all of them rusty and covered in mould. A dirty washbasin was installed next to the pipes and there was a door next to it.

Must be the toilet.

A yellow light bulb hung on a thin wire from the ceiling.

My heart jumped on hearing the sound of faint footsteps.

Naina was standing in the corner with her son wrapped in her arms.

I blurted, 'Oh, thank God!'

They were shaken. She looked at me, full of disgust. It appeared that she held me responsible for all of this. Her dusty and unruly hair gave me the idea about the rough experience she had gone through as well. Her eyes lacked the usual glint and exhibited the true magnitude of the problem we were in. Her clothes were ruined.

'Are you okay, Naina?' I said softly.

She didn't move. I pulled myself up slowly. A shooting pain from my left knee stung me sharply.

I wished Naina would step forward to help me. She didn't. I inhaled and wiped the beads of sweat on my forehead.

While staring at me, she moved wisps of her hair from her face and tucked them behind her ear.

I looked at the kid. 'Are you okay, son? You speak English? What's your name?' He didn't respond either. Like mother like son.

'Naina, what's going on? Talk to me? It's me. Aditya Malhotra from Delhi. Do you remember me?'

She stared at me blankly. '*GREAT! She doesn't even remember me!*

'I can't believe you don't even remember me. First you dumped me and walked out of my life, and now, I, like the biggest idiot on this earth, came all the way from Chicago to Mexico looking for you, thinking you were in danger. Why don't you remember me?' I almost pleaded.

She doesn't have a clue! Adi, you idiot, she doesn't have any clue who you are and you like a Romeo didn't let her go for all these years. She moved on and you are still stuck in Bangalore.

I strode towards them, and they stepped back in fear. I stopped and retraced my steps.

Easy lover boy! You are scaring the kid.

I managed a forced smile. 'Hey! *Amigo!* What is your name? I have a son your age. His name is Karan.'

He mumbled and slowly lifted Naina's hands. She let him go. He stepped forward and spoke in broken Hindi and English, '*Mera naam* Arjun. My mom Selena.'

It took me a few seconds to register what he said. He didn't look like me at all. And he looked like he was around nine years old. He wasn't my son. I was relieved.

'Arjun? Why Arjun?' I questioned.

He shrugged his shoulder innocently which reminded me that he was only nine, and I was asking stupid questions.

'That's a very nice name. Arjun was a great warrior, just like you! And it's my favourite name too. You speak good Hindi. Did your mom teach you?'

He shook his head with a big smile. His necktie was missing.

'Naahi (no)...My dad!' he replied.

I didn't believe what he said. *Carlos knows Hindi?*

He asked me, '*Aap mere Mom ko jaantay hain* (Do you know my Mom)?'

'Yes, I do. Do you guys have a cell phone?' He shook his head in a no.

'I need water,' he said.

'Are you thirsty? Is there any water in the basin?' I looked around to see if there was any camera watching us. I found nothing. I was surprised to see no surveillance and no water.

I quickly pried open a barrel with an iron rod. It had a

large stockpile of guns in it. I picked one rifle to check if it had any ammunition in it. None of the guns were loaded. I looked into another barrel and saw that it was filled white powder packets. Drugs!

DRUGS, GUNS, BROAD DAYLIGHT SHOOTOUT and KIDNAPPING—*these guys are serious about their business.*

I didn't realize Naina sneaking up behind me. Suddenly, like Uma Thurman of *Kill Bill* she swung her right arm from nowhere and hit me in the face.

I stumbled, gasping for air.

She turned to Arjun, and said something in fluent Spanish. I tilted my head to catch a glimpse of him and saw that the boy had gone to the corner covering his ears.

She stared at me with her big black eyes.

'Listen motherfucker! Tell me who the fuck you are and what do you fucking need from me?'

I was stunned and at loss for words. I stuttered, 'Who-who am I? You don't know me?'

'No, I don't and we are in this shit because of you. What do you need from us? Are you with that asshole Mendes?'

'But-but we were in love...Naina... Remember—we made love?'

'Made love! With you?' Her face turned red and her eyes narrowed. This time she let her left arm do the damage and gave me a solid jab in my stomach. I let out a scream.

'The name is Selena...Selena Lopez... Why do you fucking keep calling me Naina?'

'I don't know you at all. Oh my God, what is going on? Where are we stuck?' she almost cried.

'Are-are you serious? I mean...you don't know me at all?' I stammered.

I wanted to hear her story—what had made her disappear

into the clouds of anonymity, what had pushed her to the edge. I wanted her to know how fate brought me back into her life, but I didn't know how and where to begin.

I was hurt, deeply hurt. She didn't even remember me.

scarface

Some time passed in silence before the door to the basement opened. Multiple pairs of feet descended on the wooden stairs, which creaked with every step.

Human shadows of different sizes appeared.

A big lanky dog came out running from the dark stairs, looked at me with his shiny pupils and cautiously inched forward. My focus shifted from the dog to the other three visitors. André was one of them. He wore a white shirt with a waist jacket, a long assault gun hanging around his neck and shoulder. His black glistening shoes clicked while he walked. A thick gold chain buried under shirt shimmered around his neck. He looked like Al Pacino just walked out from a dress rehearsal of *Scarface*.

I had to give it to him. He had an uncanny resemblance to Al Pacino.

He didn't waste any time and came right to my face. He sniggered, 'Fucking tourist! You are *loco*. Crazy. Man! You know *gringo*?'

When I didn't panic, he felt an urge to clarify himself.

'*Gringo* meaning... Umm...dirty foreigner!' He swung on his feet. 'This is my gang. My homies.' He sounded unpredictable and dangerous.

He swung his body and looked at Naina. He marched towards her. The two other guys gripped my hands and shoulders. He returned quickly after saying something to Naina in a barely audible voice. Naina followed him with her son. André smiled again and winked at me and made a lewd gesture about Naina's curvy body.

'I bring sexy translator,' he announced.

He signalled for his men who quickly went into action. One went past me and brought a chair from the corner. André brushed past me and plunged into the chair. He pulled the dog on a short leash close to him. The dog reluctantly obeyed him.

He caressed the dog's face, jaws and head vigorously. The dog clearly was not friendly with him and kept turning his head away.

'My English not good... My gang don't know ABC. But she must say for you, what I say... You understand?'

He didn't wait for my response and started speaking in fluent Spanish. Naina reluctantly translated.

'I told you. You are a tourist. Go places. Visit forts, cathedrals, beaches, go to strip clubs—watch naked *girls*, stay in the city. Then why are you following me?' As soon as Naina stopped, he threw many bills of hundred dollars at my face and said something in Spanish which Naina translated for me.

'How much money did I take from you? A hundred dollars? Five hundred dollars? Now we are even. Okay! Let's talk business!'

He signalled for his men to let me go. One of his men handed us bottles of water. Naina said something to Arjun, and she quickly took big swigs to make sure the water was not poisoned. Once satisfied, she passed the bottle to her son, and he gulped down almost half of the bottle.

André spoke to me while I took a few sips of the water. He leaned forward in his chair. 'Drink break finished. You know this girl?'

All eyes were fixed on me, waiting for an answer. I couldn't tell them anything which involved the DEA. I had to make up answers on the fly.

I nodded with a grim face. He spoke in Spanish and gestured at Naina to translate. She reluctantly translated.

'She is Selena Lopez—Carlos's wife... You know?'

'Who? No... I don't know that,' I lied.

'What do you know?' she said.

'I know her from the past,' I said while looking straight into her eyes. 'We are both from India. I loved her and then I lost her. I came to Mexico to see her. We have not seen each other in fourteen years, and yesterday, I saw her for the first time. I was at the right place at the wrong time. I had no idea what was going to happen. All I wanted to do was meet her, talk to her and find out how she ended up in Mexico.'

The room fell into silence. Naina looked surprised at what I had just said.

André sniggered. He didn't need Naina to translate that for him. He understood my dilemma.

'*Un amante...* A lover...'

I quickly corrected myself, thinking about the implication of what I had said. 'She didn't love me... Only I... One-sided.'

'*Si....* I know all about fucking one-sided love stories. Girls act like Jennifer Lopez, makes guys crazy.'

Suddenly André's dog got up and walked up to me. He sniffed at my feet and wagged his tail. André yelled at him in Spanish. I rubbed his head instinctively and looked at the dog in that dim light. His name was written on his collar.

CUBBY.

a blast from the past

Post the Nikki debacle and before Soleil's chapter, I had seen Frederick Smith, the homeless war hero, at different intersections of Michigan Avenue in the downtown area while driving home or to work.

One morning, prior to the Soleil mission, I went running in Lake Shore Park to clear my head from the stressful situation with Terrence.

Light snow had covered the park which was decently filled with brave people in that cold. I was getting ready for my encounter with Soleil. Following Nikki's advice, I went to great lengths to prepare. I watched Soleil's movements. Vincent and I followed her wherever she went. We knew her entire routine—zumba in the morning, nails and hair at noon, shopping and lunch, quick grocery stops to the market. In the evening, she would dress up to kill men at the clubs. I was ready, but deep down I was still not at peace with what we were doing.

I stopped after one lap of the park. I took off my overcoat and spread it on the bench. I felt suffocated, and I wanted to run fast. My feet started moving, slowly at first, and then picking up pace. I ran like a maniac, blowing the cold air out of my nostrils.

After four laps, I came back, panting, to the bench to retrieve my overcoat. It was not there. I looked around and saw that a tall man was wearing it. He was playing with his dog. I shouted and waved at him to come over. As he got closer I recognized the man and the dog.

Frederick, the war hero, the smelly homeless person, was wearing my overcoat. The coat hung loosely on his tall and skinny frame. He yelled at his dog to follow him, and the dog obeyed his master. His dog sniffed me when I patted him. Frederick apologized for taking the coat and tried to return it to me. I declined and told him to keep it. He needed it more than I did. We chatted briefly. He shared his teachings about the worldly dimensions, karma and the well-being of the human mind. I listened to him expecting some divine spiritual advice to restore my normal life. Nothing of that sort happened. He looked at my grim visage and asked me to share what I had on my mind.

I told him a shorter version of my story. How I was going to deceive a woman to save my family from getting wiped out by gangsters.

He mulled over what I had said for a few long moments. Then he said, 'This is your war, soldier! If I was in your place, I'd have done the same. Protect your home.'

I was taking advice from a homeless person. It was unbelievable, but in extreme circumstances, sometimes logic doesn't make any sense.

'That would be five dollars, Sir! The advice is not free!' he chuckled.

I gave him twenty dollars for food and patted the dog. 'Why'd you name your dog Cubby?' I asked.

'It's after the Chicago Cubs victory in the 2016 World Series baseball championship! He's a winner,' he hugged his dog.

I walked away from the park with hope in my heart and a decision to go through with Mission Soleil.

After that day, I didn't see Frederick for a few weeks. After I returned from the DEA, I received a call from the Chicago Police Department. They called me to identify a dead homeless man. They said that they had found my business card in the coat pocket. Frederick was stabbed to death trying to save Cubby. When I asked about Cubby, the police said they had no idea where the dog was.

a friendly canine

Cubby, who was lost in Chicago, was staring at me in Mexico. He was a white Great Dane with black patches. He looked meek and sad. André yelled at him again. I stroked his head and body gently, and he seemed to like it, perhaps reminded of his old owner, Frederick. He had recognized me the moment he had walked into that basement. André got up and pulled Cubby away.

He yelled, 'This dog from America like you…! All Americans are dogs! Fucking *gringos*! I give him food, he don't eat; I want him fight, he don't fight.'

My mind was racing, and I was thinking about Vincent. Maybe he was tracking my phone call. If so, I needed to buy time. I started a conversation, 'Where did you get this dog? He looks hungry. Do you have any food? We all need food.'

André waved his hand to Rico, a man behind me. Rico took out two paper bags and gave one burger each to the three of us.

Cubby wagged his tail and looked at me in excitement. I broke half of my burger and gave it to Cubby. He started eating it eagerly. André and his friends were shocked. André smacked the behind of Rico's scalp in embarrassment. Naina did not take a bite from her burger, but she helped her son to eat.

I approached her and picked up her burger from the floor.

She flicked her hair from her face and cut me an angry look. Every time I saw her, I found her irresistible. I wished we had been in different circumstances. She took the burger from my hand, leaned forward and whispered, 'Is it true what you said? About you being in love with me?'

Surprised, I responded, 'Yes, you don't remember anything… how's that possible? Believe it or not, I came here for you, Naina. I know you are living this life as Selena, but you used to be Naina. Why'd you name your son Arjun?'

'Carlos liked it. Said it's named after a warrior. This one stayed in my mind.'

I looked at her baffled. *A name stayed in her mind? How come I didn't? She was an enigma fourteen years ago and she still is one now. Nothing changed about her.*

I walked back to André who was sinking his teeth into his burger.

I told Naina, 'Ask him why we are here? Who are they and what do they need from us?'

Naina translated that for me to André. He responded casually. Naina didn't like his response. She looked furious.

'They needed Arjun. We two are just collateral.'

André licked his finger and strolled to me. He clutched his gun, a finger on the trigger. He spoke while circling around me slowly. 'Carlos killed Mendes's guy, Franky. Carlos thought Mendes is gay. *Incompetente!* Mendes will not hit back! No. Mendes is no *gay*. He kidnaps Carlos's son. Hurt where hurts most!'

His words hit me deep when I heard Franky's and Mendes's names in the same sentence. I started to realize the plot of this kidnapping. The kidnapping was a retaliation. My head started spinning.

Shit! André works for Mendes. Just like the DEA, they will also hold me responsible for Franky's death and when they find that out, I'm definitely dying in this basement!

Naina screamed and jumped at André. She slapped him

hard leaving a scratch on his face. I pulled her back.

I released my grip when she felt awkward in my arms. She exchanged a brief look with me.

'I'm with you, Naina... Trust me!' I tried to assure her.

'Stop calling me Naina! I can't trust anyone here. Let us go!' she screamed.

André reciprocated, matching the crescendo in her voice. 'YOU ARE CARLOS'S WIFE! YOU ARE NOT GOING ANYWHERE.'

This wasn't getting anywhere. I hoped that Vincent and Richard were able to track our location from the trackers I had on my shoes and body before we were slaughtered in this shithole.

'André! Listen, this is not good for anyone! If anything happens to his son, Carlos will go mad and hunt every man who belongs to Mendes's gang down. It's your time to shine. Let the kid and mother go. It's the only way to avoid a war, and you know it. It's serious shit. You have got to fix this,' I yelled at André, hoping he would see reason.

André jammed the gun barrel under my jaw. 'Damn right. Mendes coming to deal with this shit.' He shoved me back with the other arm and stared at me. 'Y' know tourist... You are more than what I see in you. Who are you in middle of this shit?'

I stammered, 'I-I don't know what you mean?'

He struggled to think of the words in English but got irritated and then stormed off. He went to Naina and grabbed her neck from behind, shook it vigorously and told her to translate. She resisted his grip and pushed him away. André yelled at the third guy, 'Jose!'

Jose, as if premeditated, rushed to Arjun and placed the gun on the kid's head. Arjun screamed in fear and pain. Naina's eyes widened and she immediately fell to her knees and begged

André not to hurt him.

Facing me, André spoke continuously and Naina translated.

'Who did you call in the van? And what did you tell him?'

'Believe me. I dialled it in the dark in the box. I called a friend in America, and I couldn't tell him much; I didn't know where I was.'

'Tell me the truth! You called a friend when your life was in danger? Is he a policeman? DEA? Federales? Tell me the truth, or the boy will die.'

Naina's eyes narrowed as she asked, almost pleading me to tell the truth.

I struggled. I looked at Naina while I contemplated. I had realized that André had no decision-making power. He was a pawn of Mendes and only Mendes was going to decide Arjun's fate, not André.

I said sternly, 'No, he won't.'

A silence ensued in the room. That challenged André's ego. He kicked me in my right knee hard; so hard that my leg folded, and I fell in pain. Before I could breathe, I felt another blow. This time his knee smashed into my face. I felt I was floating for a brief second, before I fell flat on the dusty floor next to Cubby. Cubby licked my face.

André sat on my back and pulled my head up with my hair. He whispered in my ear, 'My house, my rules, tourist!' After shoving my head into the floor, he got up and stepped away from me. I was amazed at how my body was still taking all that beating without giving up. Naina fell on her knees in front of me and spoke to me, concerned. 'Tell him the truth. Who are you and why are you here?'

I chuckled and spit the blood from my mouth. 'I've already told you the truth. That's the only truth I know.'

I flinched in pain and turned over on my back. I pushed

myself up. André came to me and squatted in front of my face. Naina translated what he said.

'Who is coming to rescue you?'

Surprised, I looked at him. He laughed and pointed to my shoes. I hadn't realized that they had been replaced. They must have done it when I passed out.

The GPS tracker! Shit! They found it!

'Looking for this, Señor?' André said menacingly. He opened his palm and showed me the broken tracker.

I lost all hope of getting out of there alive.

Naina translated his words. 'What kind of a tourist comes with a GPS in his shoe? You are not some ordinary guy? Are you an undercover cop?'

Naina's eyes narrowed as she spoke for André.

André kicked my leg and signalled for his men to pick me up.

He said, 'The kid and wife belong to Mendes. He decides their fate, but your ass is mine!'

One last tracker remained. It was in my body, and I hoped they didn't scan me with a bug detector. In the next second, I realized that they could also zap me with a taser gun to short circuit the tracker inside my body which would kill the bug and nobody would ever know where I was. I prayed to God and wished and hoped that they didn't think of giving me electric shocks.

Last lifeline, that was our only hope for survival.

gladiator

In the two weeks of boot camp, I was trained to shoot different guns with live ammo while running through obstacles on land and in water. Richard personally watched me the entire time getting trained in specially designed military-style courses to test my strength and agility without breaking my body in that short amount of time. I was also eating a formulated diet that helped me recover quickly from extreme stress.

Some of that training had come to really good use earlier at the shootout in Mexico. I had handled myself well for a family man.

André had planned something special for me, now that he figured out that I was not just a lover at the right place at the wrong time. His men took us out of the basement and through the rundown warehouse. Jose was walking behind Naina and Arjun, a gun pointed at them.

We came to an open unmaintained area which had high brick walls surrounding it.

Dogs barked randomly up ahead. Cubby was evidently nervous.

We stopped at the edge of a deep empty pool in the middle of a courtyard. Everything about the place felt wrong.

Rusty taps hung in the middle of a tall, ruined cemented wall. Stadium-style benches were installed on both sides of the pool. André clapped and suddenly the place filled with bright lights. Bulbs turned on one by one just like in a football stadium before the next big game. Cubby started circling me nervously. He squealed.

The lights revealed how scary that place was. The abandoned pool's tiles were mostly black now, and at many places they were red with blood stains.

Dogfighting! That's the first thing that popped into my head. I connected the dots—the bloody swimming pool, the continuous howling of dogs and André's desire to make Cubby fight.

Dog fighting was made illegal in Mexico only in 2016, but that doesn't stop heartless men from doing it anyway. This lucrative activity brings in dogs from all over, the world. They are trained to fight using smaller bait dogs. They are groomed and then sold with price tags of thousands of dollars. This explained how Cubby made it across the border into Mexico. Rico had smuggled him in.

I didn't have to think why André had brought me here. I just couldn't believe what was happening with me. I suddenly felt André sneak up on me from behind, and before I could do anything, he pushed me into the pool.

I lost my balance and flew uncontrollably. I was surprised that I survived the ten-feet fall and luckily landed on my feet.

A whiff of stench hit my nose, which smelled like a very cheap detergent with bleach used to scrub floors.

I yelled, 'André! You asshole! What are you doing?'

'You correct! I can't hurt the kid... But you I kill!' he laughed. I saw more people started to show up around the pool. They started sneering and hooting at me.

This was my death pit. I came to convince a girl, and now I was fighting with dogs.

The heartless crowd yelled, spat and threw pieces of meat at me. I stared at the walls of the pool for a way out and saw a metal door in the corner.

My instincts told me that my future depended on whatever was behind that metal door.

The door shook vigorously and I heard a heart-piercing scratching and growling behind it. Out came a four-legged jet black figure from behind that chamber. A pitbull, with its mouth covered in a dirty sock, angry as hell, his eyes red and gleaming.

I was standing in the middle of a dogfight pit. The dog was still on the leash but was ready to attack. He was black as death. A very painful death.

'André you fool, you can't kill me and get all the answers. Naina and her son don't know anything about me. You got to let me get out of here.'

André danced and laughed like a maniac at the edge of the pool. He squatted down and yelled at me. 'This your chance homie... Fight! This dog is a winner. You kill him, you come out.' He stood up and snapped his fingers. The sock on the dog's mouth came off and he let out a soul-shaking growl. He jumped with all his strength only to get pulled back by the leash.

Those assholes, torturing poor animals.

The dog was getting more aggressive and scratched his paws on the floor. He bared his stabbing canine teeth and showed me his bloody red gums. I was out of ideas standing in fear in front of a hungry and probably a diseased dog in that ten-foot deep slippery pool. How would I fight a rabid angry fighter dog? Richard didn't design any course on animal fighting.

Suddenly, the dog was released, he charged and then jumped at me. Fortunately, my reflexes kicked in and I grabbed his neck with both hands. I was able to keep his mouth and razor-sharp teeth away from my face. However, he scraped my arms with his paws and long nails. Thanks to my leather jacket, his nails couldn't get to my skin. The dog was heavy and best in health, and had a strong muscular body with no fat to slow him down

I screamed loudly as soon as I got my voice back from that sudden attack, 'Cubby, help!'

Cubby was already showing his earnestness to me, his new boss and was pacing around the pool. Cubby heard those words and I don't know what but something triggered in his brain. He paused for a second, and then he leaped onto me and the other dog. Cubby landed on top of the other dog and sunk his teeth in his back. Cubby dragged him away from me and then let him go. The pitbull slipped on the slick floor and hit the side wall. But he was a champion and wasn't going to be defeated so easily.

The heartless crowd went silent and then suddenly burst in to cheer for the pitbull and started placing bets.

The dogs didn't go at each other as everybody expected. My heart rooted for Cubby for showing up at the most unexpected time to save my life He was my hero. I admired Cubby's lanky black and white spotty frame. He represented everything that the pitbull was not. He was literally an underdog in that arena besides me.

They stared at each other, growling slowly, letting the aggression brim in a melting pot. At a perfect moment, they backed up a few steps and sprung up at each other with bared long teeth, long nails on paws pulled out like wolverine.

They collided in the air and struggled for a grip on each other's neck. Cubby used his tall frame and kept his neck higher like a giraffe to scratch the pitbull's petrifying face with his strong paw. They landed together on the slick tiles and then repeated leaps at each other in a rising aggression in front of the moronic crowd roaring for the pitbull.

I spun on my feet and scanned around for a ladder to get out of the death pool. There was none. I saw André consumed in the dogfight, sitting at the edge of the pool. Wasting no time,

I jumped up and grabbed André leg and pulled him down. He fell really hard on his chest.

I showed him no mercy and kicked his stomach with those heavy boots they gave me. The tide had turned and it was his turn to receive kicks and punches. He recoiled in pain and groaned. I kicked his face and heard his jaw cracking. André yelled like a madman and hit his head on my knee, making me fall. He quickly got up, took off his jacket and threw it aside and prepared himself to fight me. I grabbed his semi-automatic rifle in a swift motion and swung hitting the right of his head. André's lifeless body fell sideways on the floor. He didn't move after that. I quickly turned to Cubby to help him, pointing the gun, only to see that Cubby had already got his opponent down on the floor. No one expected the anti-climactic home team loss.

Cubby slowly walked towards me. Miraculously, he wasn't hurt at all.

A man and a dog from Chicago stood tall in that ten-foot deep pool of death, emerging as unpredictable winners in a cruel inhumane sport.

The crowd roared suddenly in anger. Suddenly, their protest was cut short when the place reverberated with noise coming from a distance, followed by gunfire in the air.

This place was fucked up. One thing after another.

A burly man with curly orange hair had just walked in, surrounded by his bodyguards. He walked up to the brink of the pool and stared at me. He looked at André, who was dead. The man did not look happy. He was severely underdressed for the occasion in blue faded jeans and a white shirt. He had a thick moustache.

Jose, from behind the crowd, pulled Naina and Arjun into the front row. She looked terrified. I knew she was afraid for her son.

Arjun was her weakness and she was mine.
The guy looked at each of us in disgust.
He must be Mendes.

Mendes—the don

We were in a stretch limousine with plush leather seats and a minibar with stacked glasses and branded liquor bottles. Mendes sat back, relaxed with a faint smile. He raised his crystal Scotch glass and emptied it into his mouth with ease and finesse. He handed the empty glass to his wide-chested protein-pumped bodyguard who happened to have different sizes of guns wrapped around his waist and shoulders.

I was holding a similar crystal glass filled with Scotch. I didn't want to drink even a drop of it. It was fucking 5 a.m.

We all felt a big bump when the vehicle went over a pothole. I wondered if Mexico had any decent roads. The entirety of my travel had been nothing else but bumpy. Nobody had said anything for the last twenty minutes. The vehicle slowed down again. I peered outside. We had reached another estate with guarded gates. The limousine snaked inside the estate's winding driveway.

Mendes's face showed a restrained anger. Finally, he spoke. He had a thick voice. 'Do you know me? I'm Mendes!'

Surprised that he spoke fluent English, I nodded my head in a yes instantly.

'I have many tales, tales of being a drug mule and smuggling drugs, weapons, money-laundering, assassinations, killing police and having turf wars with other cartels but all that is irrelevant to you. You are different. You don't even know half of me. No point in trying to scare you with all that gory stuff... Great fight there in the arena! You ever saw a dogfight before?'

I stayed fixed to my stance and he took it as a no.

'And yet you defeated my best dog. That can't be a coincidence.'

He referred to André as dog. I didn't react and looked to my right where Jose sat next to Naina. Arjun had dozed off in Naina's lap.

'She is Carlos's wife, I didn't mean to bring her in. André, son of a bitch did something right for the first time. That *puta* went to get me Carlos's son, but he got me a double deal. Finally, André does something more than expected. But you killed him, so I'm now down one strong person.' He paused. 'Will you work for me?'

That was the surprise of the century, even bigger than Naina not recognizing me. I must have done something right to have the CEO of Mendes Corporation offer me a job with some portfolio to manage. I scoffed, perplexed as if I heard him wrong. 'Work for you?'

'*Si Señor* (Yes, Sir)!'

Jose and the bodyguard exchanged surprised looks when Mendes addressed me as 'Sir'. The car came to a slow stop. A large gate opened and we pulled into the massive hacienda-style property, with old castle-type architecture. We passed many sparkling cars parked on the long and winding drive. A large expensive swimming pool sparkled under the moonlight. A few men spoke to one another while smoking cigars in a cabana; it was early morning hours but their party was still going on. Girls sat on their laps. That's how they enjoyed their millions.

'In Chicago, I had a French man. He worked for me, took care of my business—a real genius. He was my main channel in the US and made many contacts there. He moved my products in California, Florida and New York and made me millions. He makes good money because I pay well. He even bought an air-conditioned house in the good part of Chicago. One day, he said he wants more money so I sent him to spy on Carlos for me. He tried for months and finally won the trust of the people closest to Carlos. I didn't hear from him in weeks and then we found he was dead—murdered—cut into pieces. I suspect he was snitched out. My man Franky, who I groomed, is gone! You know how hard it is to find loyalty. My name is hurt; my business is hurt. I must do something to avenge Franky so I kidnap Carlos's boy. Hit where it hurts most.' Mendes raised his glass and tapped it against his heart.

One thing was getting clearer in my mind that no matter who I talked to, everyone was tied to Franky.

I needed a drink and some clarity. The Scotch tasted bitter as I turned the glass upside down in my mouth.

Mendes grinned. He looked at his bodyguard, who as if programmed, opened a secret box in the wall of the car and took out a smooth-looking cigar. He inserted it in Mendes's lips and lit it.

'Mendes knows winners. You and your dog are winners. Both of you are not dead. Believe me, I don't kill useful and dangerous things—they all have use in my world.' He signalled to the bodyguard. 'Phillip will train the dog. I will make use of him. A prize dog.'

Phillip gave me a strong hard look.

'Let the mother and son go, Mendes! Your war is with Carlos, not with his family. So what if he found your informant. He got him killed. Most certainly you would have done the same had you found his informant. That's pure business—an occupational hazard, that's the job—I get it but don't bring in family. If you hurt his kid, Carlos will hit you back with all he has got, and that would be bad for you and your business,'

I tried convincing the drug lord.

I gave a heartfelt speech. Maybe after all this settles and I am alive I can be a motivational speaker.

'The boy is going to die, that's for sure. Revenge is revenge! It cannot be forgotten or negotiated. Carlos can fight back for revenge—let him. But no compromise, *amigo!*' he said.

I lost the battle of words.

Naina screamed and yelled in Spanish, holding back her tears. I didn't understand a word, but I knew it was a mother pleading for her son.

Jose grabbed her with all his strength. Phillip crouched, removed his bandana and tied it in front of Naina's mouth. All this while Mendes continued looking at me, studying my expression. He spoke again, slowly. 'You look very concerned for them, *amigo*. I'm told you are the ex-lover of this woman, huh? You love Carlos's woman! You know how great it is! This makes you my special person right now. I thought you were *maricon*—a gay, but you are dangerous, and I could use your skills. You can be my Franky. You can be my second-best guy.'

'Mendes! Sir! I am not a dangerous guy like you think, but I will do what you want if you let them go.'

'*Amigo,* the deal is for you only! They are dying, no matter if you agree or not. If you agree, you live. Otherwise you die too.'

I looked at Naina, She was holding onto Arjun. I felt I couldn't buy any more time. I was done playing games. I couldn't risk their lives any more. I decided to do the unthinkable—give up and confess that it was all my fault.

I squared my eyes, knowing what I had to do.

'Mendes! There's something you must know. Something which can save a war between you and Carlos.'

I got his attention, his big eyes narrowed. My heart started pounding. 'I'm responsible for Franky's death. In Chicago, I stole information about his meeting with Carlos. I didn't know what I was doing. Maybe you are right and I'm a very dangerous man—dangerously stupid to get in the middle of two drug cartels. I tried to help my family in a crisis, and I kept making one mistake after another before I dug myself too deep. I fucked up beyond retribution of any kind.' I pointed to Naina. 'This woman… Selena. She had nothing to do with it. I'm responsible for all this mess, and I'm truly sorry about your man, Franky.'

With that confession, I had given Mendes every reason to kill me. He started to realize that I had hurt him even more than Carlos.

I folded my hands, seeking forgiveness.

'That's even more dope than I imagined! Now do you believe me? You have this unique way of doing things. You proved to me again that you are a man. I like you even more now.' He patted my thigh and suddenly got serious.

I gave him a confused look. 'Did you not hear a word I just said?'

He ignored me and asked, 'Did you kill Soleil also?'

'No-no… I didn't kill her, I don't know how she died. I had a family issue, and I needed money. I didn't know what I was doing. My friend offered me money for getting information about Franky. I didn't know my friend worked for the DEA. He was an undercover agent; he used me, but paid me good money. I used that money to save my family.'

Mendes interrupted me. 'Who's that friend? A latino?'

'No. An old Indian friend from Goa. I have known him for many years.'

'I think he screwed you! Yes, he helped the US government, not you. Do you know Carlos is from Goa too?'

Suddenly, something hit me and I started to mumble; millions of thoughts suddenly spiralled in my brain and many events started to pop up from my memory bank...

Vincent asked me to get a list of customers from Nikki.

I gave Franky's information to him in the car.

Vincent took off after dropping me at home, the night when Himesh attacked Maggie and Koyal. Did he go back to Soleil's house? Did he set me up so my fingerprints would be all over her house? Did he kill Soleil that night?

Vincent was working with the DEA, so is it possible that he tipped Carlos about Franky and they murdered him or did he murder Franky himself?

Carlos is from Goa? Do they know each other? Are they related?

In all of these incidents two persons were common—one was me and other was Vincent. He targeted Nick to get to me. Did Vincent create this complex web of lies and deception?

Why?

Suddenly, all the doors of the limousine opened. Stunned, Mendes exchanged looks with Phillip and shifted in his seat. A small army of gunmen had made a formation around the limousine.

Suddenly my night grew longer.

showtime

Our attention diverted to a big bulky figure entering the vehicle and we all felt the sudden shift in the car's suspension, as it skewed to one side with the weight of that one person.

The large figure, clad in a black three-piece suit, sat down next to Phillip. Phillip's nostrils flared with anger, but Mendes gestured for him to calm down.

Mendes moved back in the seat calmly, sipped on his Scotch and then asked the smiling man, 'Now... Who the fuck are you, *pendejo* (stupid)?'

'That man is Vincent, my friend,' I replied with a hint of confusion in my voice. I wasn't sure what to think of that moment. Was Vincent there to save me? Was he still my friend or had he used me as a pawn in this elaborate plan of his for the past six months?

The smirk on Vincent's face answered it all. *Yup, it was all this motherfucker's plan.*

My hands twitched to reach for his neck. My blood was boiling, but I wanted to know why he did all this. Why did he frame me?

He folded his hands and begged me nervously. 'Aditya, Bhai! Sorry I got stuck in traffic, my man. Mexico traffic sucks! I hope you didn't have much difficulty and hope Mendes took good care of you. You did good, Adi, more than I expected from you. Don't worry now. I'm here to help you. I couldn't have

left you here after all you have done so much for me and I ...
STOP STOP... you are killing me my friend.'

He started laughing hysterically and continued laughing for
a good fifteen seconds, turning my curiosity into anger. I shook
his leg, and he grabbed my hand and twisted my arm. I coiled
with pain and let out a scream.

He screamed, 'I bet that's what you wanted to hear from
me, Aditya! That I came back for you. Right? Wrong! I'm here
because of my genius plan. You all are my pawns, and I played
you all so beautifully. You, Soleil, Franky, Richard, Mendes and
Carlos. All of you! Although, nice work, Mendes—for executing
a secret successful plan of kidnapping Arjun.'

Naina shouted at Vincent, 'You are hurting him; let him go.'

'I knew you would warm up to him eventually. After all,
he is your lost love, and nothing can replace an old flame. By
the way, did you two get a chance to know each other in an
intimate manner?' Vincent winked at her, she turned her face
away from him in disgust.

'Don't make a stupid mistake now. I'm going to let your
arm go for old times' sake,' he warned me.

He released my arm, and I felt a sharp stab at my shoulder
joint.

Vincent leaned forward and rested his elbows on the tip
of his knees. His body language exuded an air of confidence
which I had never seen him display before.

'Ever seen an onion? You peel one layer and another layer
comes up. I'm like that. I have a multilayered personality and
have many secrets and lies hidden in every layer. I really am
an undercover agent working with Richard for the DEA. The
250k dollars you got was the DEA's money. I got that from
them and gave it to you—that's why they were pissed off. But
Richard only knew what I wanted him to know. He never saw

my darkest side—no one saw that. I gave him information to keep him close to me, to win his trust. Now that we have established the foundation, let me answer all of your questions.'

He continued, 'I'm sorry, Aditya... Nick was never in bad company. He was just stupid and wanted to get rich fast for his wife. I made it happen so that he owed money to Terrence. Terrence is my guy. On my order he threatened to kill everyone in your family. Two, I swayed you to have an affair with Nikki and Soleil. The accounts information you got me from your company—remember that I said it was a test only—well, guess what? It wasn't a test! Three, I got Franky killed in Juarez. You gave me the information about Franky's meeting with Carlos which was for the DEA only, but I also tipped off Carlos's guys. I killed Soleil on the same night and left your fingerprints there. She had to go. She wasn't needed and would have created problems for all of us. My working with the DEA was all crap. I wasn't going to let them get anything. Richard needed results to show progress in his operations on the drug war, and I gave him bones with a little meat on it.'

He smiled.

'Naina! I knew that you would not think twice about saving Naina. When I found out that Naina was his wife, I made this plan. Through Naina, you took me to Carlos. Wuhoo! WHAT a plan! It gives me chills, Bro. You have no idea how hard I worked for all of this to come together. I also wasn't this fat a year ago. I gained weight purposely so I would look pathetic to you and win your trust. Looks are deceptive, my friend.'

Vincent stopped talking. There was silence in the car.

Mendes finished his Scotch, handed the glass back to Phillip, cleared his throat and stretched his legs. 'That's brilliant—you did all that, took so much trouble. On top of that, you came to my house, took my men and took over my villa. I like it!

You have courage and a big heart.'

Vincent chuckled with pride and he spoke with enthusiasm.

'No shit right! I thought it was a dope idea, At first my people didn't think it was a great idea to ambush your fortress and have your men act as if everything was normal and let you inside in this trap, but I think I pulled it off brilliantly. Not once did you think that the girls in the pools and the guys in the cabanas were your men in distress. It all appeared normal to you, right?'

Mendes tapped at Vincent's shoulder and said, 'You are a wizard. What say we go out and talk business in fresh air?'

Vincent's demeanour changed to dead serious. He shook his head in disagreement.

'*Amigo*, it's me, Mendes! I control one-third of all drug trafficking in this part of the world. Name your price and let's shake hands. You won't be disappointed!'

'You don't get it, do you, Mendes! With you gone, everything that was yours is now mine! I already took out most of your men, and the remaining will have no choice. They will die if they don't work for me.'

Vincent held a revolver to Mendes's face and said, 'In short, I can kill you right now because I don't need you. But this is not between you and me. This is between me and Carlos. I'll let you go.'

Mendes was stunned.

Vincent thumped the roof of the car with his hand. The doors opened again, and he signalled for Mendes to get out of the car.

I was speechless at Vincent's new avatar. He was bold, confident, aggressive and a gangster. He was in control.

Mendes looked at Phillip for help, but Phillip had switched his loyalties upon hearing Vincent's speech. He didn't move and looked away from his former boss. Mendes spat on the floor and walked out, disgusted.

Vincent yelled at Mendes's back, 'Don't try to buy these men, I handpicked these guys. They have scores to settle with you.'

As the doors slammed shut, Vincent turned his attention back to the remaining people in the car. Without wasting time, Phillip took Vincent's hand, kissed it and put it on his forehead in respect.

'Ok, I like that you respect me, but don't ever kiss my hand again. Now go out and give me some privacy with my old friends,' Vincent ordered. 'Also, I am a great boss. You will get a job matching your skills, unless of course, you like refilling my drinks.' He exploded into laughter and looked at us for approval. None of us encouraged him. He looked at Jose and said politely, 'You, Sir! Need an invitation to leave us alone? Go-Go... Shoo...'

I looked at Jose. He looked pale and was sweating. My instinct was telling me that Jose had a bigger role to play. Jose nodded in fear and exited the car.

My rage started to build up the more I thought about how Vincent had pulled off such an intricate plan under everyone's nose.

'This is good! Just the three of us like old times. Three friends from college! Did you ever imagine we would land up in Mexico? I sure didn't!' He was ecstatic. His plan worked from all angles, and I was fucked from all angles.

I wished Richard would come to my rescue. He was my last hope.

'Vincent, why? Why did you involve me? You could have done all of this on your own, why me?'

He patted his pockets and when didn't find his cigarette,

he tapped on the glass and Jose peeked inside.

'Jose! Paco?'

Jose quickly took out his cigarette pack and handed it to Vincent, Vincent took one and laughed in disgust. 'Every fucking asshole here is named either Jose or Paco… Anyhow, why you, right?'

He let out a big puff of smoke. Naina coughed and it hurt my nostrils. I was dead tired and sleep deprived and couldn't stand the stench of the smoke. I snatched the cigarette from his lips and crushed it under my shoe.

'You know, Aditya… Bro! With this new power, I can have your head removed. But I'll give you a friendly pass.'

'Every story has a hero, a villain, a heroine and a scapegoat and a few other characters who either help to propel the story or just clutter up the storyboard. I can call myself either a hero or a villain by wearing multiple hats when duty calls, but I'm not the hero type—what I really needed was a hero with a conflict to take the fall.'

He pointed his finger at me. 'Honestly I couldn't have done this without you, Aditya. Carlos and I go back a long time. Long like Goa, like the same family, the same father.' He paused, giving us a minute to handle the info-bomb he had just dropped.

'Carlos and I are from the same father—he is my stepbrother. He is of course is a few years older and was my father's favourite. He was everything our father wanted his sons to be. My father saw us as two separate individuals with two different directions cut out for each. He was ruthless in business, but soft with the family. Carlos got everything easily, he was born to run the business—success came to him easy. His persona exhibited early signs that he would change the drug world, and he did. I was kept away from the family business and sent to boarding schools. Carlos was nice to me at every step, but the seed of jealousy in my mind had grown uncontrollably, and I despised him. My father knew what I was going through. He tried to fix things. I didn't care. It was too late. Things got more and more complicated. Father realized that after all, I had his stubborn and relentless blood in my veins. He took me under his wings after that Goa night, remember! Even that night, luck didn't favour me until you helped me. I found Boris in Puducherry and wiped the Russians off Goa's map. I started small things—sold stuff on the street, worked my way up to do business behind doors in frail shacks and then upgraded my status. But I still hated Carlos and wanted to destroy him.'

Vincent pointed to Naina.

'Carlos left India with her, Naina. That changed everything. My dad was so pleased with the idea of Carlos starting a family. He gave Carlos the contacts and the capital to start the empire in Mexico. I was left with paltry Goa and no competition. Bitch, complicated things beyond repair,' he screamed at Naina. She jolted in surprise.

'She doesn't remember that, of course! She has no memory of her first twenty-two years of life,' he continued venting.

'What?' My mouth fell open. My world had just collapsed. It all made sense—why she had been confused and scared of me.

My heart went out to her. She didn't know her past—her memories were wiped out—her time with me was all gone. I felt a sudden lightness in my body and found myself reaching for her.

no country for a dead man

I bent down on my knees and hugged her. She hesitated at first and then awkwardly hugged me. My hands caressed her back, and I felt her heart thumping against my chest. In that second, I realized I had to get her out of there. Vincent had gone mad. I had to find a way out of here.

I understood his entire plan. I was an easy scapegoat, with half of the investigative agencies already hungry for my blood. He never meant for the DEA or Mendes to take Carlos out. Carlos was too personal for him. He would kill Carlos and get his empire, and I would get a bullet in my head.

I was on my own now. I sincerely hoped Richard would believe me if I ever made it back home.

Something was glistening behind Naina. I focused on the object and a wave of hope ran through my spine.

A gun? Jose left it behind...purposely?

I slowly moved my right arm to her side and grabbed the gun.

With new hope and adrenaline rushing down my veins, I swung my arm hitting Vincent's knee with the gun. I knew his knees were in bad shape because I had beaten his knees really badly at the Navy Pier and yesterday in the cab. Surprised, he screamed and fumbled to reach for his gun which he had placed on the other seat because he had got so cocky that he felt he was untouchable.

I swung again and hit his kneecap. Vincent recoiled and lurched forward, holding his knee with both hands. I quickly hit his face—blood spluttered from his mouth. Naina sprung into action. She kicked him hard on the left side of his face.

She yelled at me, 'We have to get out of here.'

'And go where, Adi?' Vincent screamed in pain, holding his knee. 'You can't go anywhere! If you go back to the US, you are a dead man. Listen to me!' He coughed out blood drops on his palm. He pushed himself on the seat with difficulty. 'Richard is dead! I had Terrence kill him. I couldn't leave any loose ends. The information about those accounts you gave me—they were Richard's and Sullivan's. I had 100k dollars transferred in their accounts—the money is drug money with ties to Mendes. Tomorrow's newspapers and news channels will be running their story for weeks. How they tainted the DEA and committed treason against the US with your help.'

My heart sank, I was in no-man's land. I was trapped. I couldn't go back to the US, not without Richard's support and he was dead.

'Adi! I know I screwed you really bad and I apologize for that. All you ever did is help me. Please understand, I had no choice. You are trapped, there's nothing you can do to get out of here alive. So listen to me for the last time. Your work is done. You are free to go anywhere except America and Mexico. I'll let you go. Nobody will ever know about your hacking.'

When I didn't flinch, he pointed to Naina and added, 'Now that I have Carlos's family, he will come begging me. After I'm done with Carlos, I'll let Naina and this boy go too. I'll personally escort them to you wherever you will be in the world,' he offered his hand to me.

'We are all loose ends to you, Vincent!' I was done believing any word coming from his mouth. I screamed and hit his knee again. This time, I wanted to break it, so he could never walk again.

I grabbed his gun and gave it to Naina. She pointed it at Vincent's head. Arjun held onto her waist tightly.

Vincent drew a hunting knife from the inside of his jacket and flung out his arm to attack me with it. The blade missed my neck, but scraped my shoulder.

Naina shouted at him not to move, but he chuckled and paused while I looked at the knife in his hand. He waved it back and forth.

He swung the knife with full force. I threw myself back on the seat, escaping the tip of knife by an inch. As I fell back, I pushed up and kicked him hard in his ribs. He bit his lip in pain. I kicked the hand which held the knife, and it fell next to my feet. I scooped it up, cocked the gun and put it on Vincent's temple.

He thumped the side of the car with his hand wildly. In an instant, all four doors swung open and an army of generously paid men pushed their guns inside. Vincent yelled at them to not shoot. Obviously he hadn't come this far to see his meticulous plan fail.

His men tussled, shouted and roared in anger. They meant pure business and couldn't wait to empty their bullets into my head.

the great escape

'Enough, Vincent! Move!' I yelled, pushing him out the door. The mob of angry gunmen stepped back, making room for us to get out. Vincent exited clumsily. I stepped out behind him. Jose and Phillip looked at us in awe.

'Jose is our man. He's our informant in Mendes's gang. Carlos will be here any minute,' Naina screamed at me. *Finally some news which is in my favour!*

Jose nodded his head and showed us a phone. He had an open line with Carlos.

'Let's get the fuck out of here! Carlos will find us. Phillip, you on our side?' I yelled at Phillip with Vincent's head still clutched between my arm and ribs. Phillip looked at me and then to Jose who translated what I said. He was stunned and changed his loyalties for the second time in five minutes. He struck his strong elbow in the head of the gunmen next to him, and snatched his automatic rifle. The other gunmen immediately reacted and shifted the aim of their guns onto Phillip. I yelled, telling them that I would shoot Vincent if they made a move.

'Phillip, get my dog! Cubby!'

Phillip didn't need any translation for that. He jumped onto his feet and ran in front of the limousine and disappeared behind it. Vincent tried to make a last desperate attempt. 'I'm your only hope, Adi. You will not leave this alive. You are too deep in this shit. Richard is gone, there's nobody friendly waiting for you in Chicago, not even your wife. I'm your only hope. You let me go, and I will let you live.'

Phillip entered the scene with a BMW SUV in style. He whistled and put the window down, and out came Cubby's head from the open window. Cubby barked at me. Our feet sprang into action and we moved cautiously and quickly to the SUV. Vincent's knee gave up and he stumbled, pulling me back. I pulled his hair hard and broke his nose with the gun, 'Vincent! Just shut up.'

Naina pushed Arjun into the back seat of the BMW. I jumped in after her and dragged Vincent to the door, making him stand on the running board of the vehicle. Naina strapped Arjun in the seat belt. We were ready for an high-octane car chase.

Jose ran around the vehicle and took the front seat. Phillip rammed the gas pedal and directed the car out of the gates, leaving Vincent's helpless men behind. Vincent held onto the window for his dear life.

When we were about half a kilometre out of the mansion, I yelled in his ear, 'You are now an enemy of Mexico and the US. If you escape them—Mendes and Carlos will find you. If I'm a dead man, so are you, motherfucker!'

I pushed him off the window, his body flew for a split second and then fell with a loud thud on the moving dirt road. He rolled on the road for a long time before coming to a halt. I stared at him through the dirt clouds and flipped my middle finger at him. It was childish but very satisfying. I felt exhilarated.

'Where are we? Anyone knows? We need to get in touch with the police!' I yelled at Phillip over the raging noise of the speeding car.

'No! We need to get to Carlos,' Naina yelled at Jose. Jose handed her his phone.

'Wait a minute! How did you know Jose was on your side?' I asked, bewildered.

'I handpicked him and planted him in Mendes's gang.'

'You handpicked him. We could have used him all this while! Instead you let me fight with the dogs!'

'Listen James Bond...it's not like we had time to ourselves for chit-chat. When do you suggest I should've hinted at you? In front of André or Mendes?'

She spoke fluent Spanish on the phone. I tried not to watch her, but I couldn't help it and she caught me looking at her. Suddenly she erupted, 'Phillip, take us to the executive airport!'

Phillip took a moment to figure out the route and then steered wildly. I checked behind to see if we were being followed, and we were being chased by at least four cars which were closing the gap really fast.

I unbuckled and pushed Arjun on the floor. Naina tied her hair in a bun, took a rifle from Jose and climbed over the seats to get into the back of the BMW.

'We are in Mexico City! Can you believe the nerve of Mendes? He simply drove us around in circles only to bring us back to my city,' she yelled over the noise.

I followed her into the back of the car. She was poised to shoot at the cars chasing us.

'Shit! Are you serious about this, Naina?' I asked.

'This is Mexico, *Papi*! Here you either kill or die! What's your choice?' she said.

I started to like Selena—the new Naina. She sounded exotic and badass.

'Kill... Definitely kill!' I nodded with a nervous laugh as the SUV cut a corner abruptly. I lost my grip on the headrest, and I slipped and fell on her, my hand on her thigh, my lips an inch away from her.

A typical Hindi movie scene.

One touch, one kiss—that's all it takes to get the ball rolling.

I will not kiss her. No good will ever come from rekindling an old flame.

I pulled myself away from her when the car swung again. I fell on the floor and her head landed on my chest. I lay flat chanting my mantra.

I will not kiss her. No good will ever come from rekindling an old flame.

She lifted her head off my chest and looked straight in my eyes. Her bun came loose and her silky wavy hair blew with the gushing breeze.

I don't know what went through her mind, but she planted her lips on mine. Before I could act, it was over.

'Thanks for saving our lives,' she said.

Phillip yelled at us about the cars getting closer.

Naina positioned herself on one knee, fired continuous shots on the cars in pursuit. The cars swerved out of her aim. Jose looked in his side-view mirror, and they all yelled at each other in Spanish. I felt like I was stuck watching a fast car chase on a Spanish TV channel with no subtitles. She fired a few more shots at the oncoming cars.

We were now cruising smoothly on a concrete city road in the middle of the traffic. In the outskirts of Mexico city traffic was flowing comfortably.

Jose yelled and pointed towards the front. There was a car right in front of us. Two gunmen were getting ready to shoot at us, and Phillip started switching the lanes to shake them off. I yelled at Naina to drop down. Bullets shattered our windshield and pierced through the seats. Luckily we didn't get hit. Phillip pushed the gas pedal and rammed the rear of the car in the front, making the car veer uncontrollably. Then Phillip hit them from the side. A deafening screech echoed in the highway. The side of the front car had got stuck in front of the BMW in a

T-bone position.

I realized it was a good chance to do permanent damage to them. I yelled at Naina to stay down and brace for the impact.

I yelled at Phillip to apply the brakes hard—really hard on my signal. I looked back and saw the car that was chasing us, pick speed.

'STOP!' I screamed.

The BMW's tyres screeched loudly, making smoke clouds. The car that was chasing us didn't expect the sudden stop and it ran into our SUV with a crushing impact. We all shook violently and the front car was thrown five feet in the air. Phillip punched through the falling car, smashing through it. The car's bits and parts flew everywhere. Phillip and Jose laughed nervously in excitement.

We had gained speed again. I looked back through the window as we pulled away from the car in the back. That car's engine or radiator was broke, and it stopped in the middle of the road. As if timed perfectly, a large construction truck coming from behind with speed crushed the disabled car by running over it.

Naina was impressed, but there was no time to bask in glory. A few more cars veered from both the left and right lanes, behind us. Phillip yelled and waved his hands frantically to let everyone know about an oncoming tunnel. He made another hard lane switch and careened the BMW into the tunnel.

Jose and Phillip yelled at each other again. Naina listened to them and after a bit of hesitation she held the gun at shoulder level and aimed at an eighteen-wheeler truck which was going parallel to the BMW. She aimed and busted its front tyres with a flurry of gunshots. The truck's tyres exploded with a loud boom and filled the tunnel with echoing explosion sounds. I felt like I was in the middle of a Hollywood action sequence.

In the past two days I had survived a gunfight, rammed a car into another, faced the fear of claustrophobia in a tiny death box, participated in a dogbite, killed a man and now I was being chased with cars full of gunmen in the streets of Mexico. Something divine told me that I was not going to die in a road crash.

The big truck was carrying milk—it lost its way and veered in the middle of live traffic and slowly started to turn on the side, spilling white milk on the road. Rubber from the tyres flew off in the air and zoomed past our car. The truck driver lost control of the truck and rammed two of Vincent's cars on their side. Both cars got pinned to the sides of the massive moving wheels of the truck. Sparks erupted with metal banging into metal and eventually the cars got sucked in under the wheels and exploded as the truck tore through them. The truck driver managed to slow down miraculously without harming any other vehicle and came to a stop, blocking the entire side of the highway.

Naina did a fist pump, but, just when she thought that the truck had blocked the highway and the other cars behind it, two more of Vincent's cars punched through under the tail section of the truck's trailer.

Suddenly the tunnel's scenario changed and fireballs exploded from the mutilated vehicles.

We still had two more cars on our tail again, they retaliated through their guns and started firing at will. I fell down on top of Naina and yelled at the others to keep their heads low. Cubby was already hugging the floor along with Arjun between the front and middle seats.

They sprayed shots on our vehicle, randomly shattering the glass, throwing a million little shards at us.

Naina screamed in anger and blindly fired at them from

the rear window.

'Stop, stop! You are killing innocent people,' I yelled.

'They are killing my son. We need to kill them,' she yelled back.

'No, we can't kill them. They have more firepower. We need to outrun them. How far to the airport?' I yelled at Phillip.

Naina answered, 'Ten minutes.'

Phillip picked up speed, increasing the distance between Vincent and us. I looked ahead and told myself that I had to do something and find a way out. My eyes saw another big trailer truck in front of us.

'Phillip, get on the right of the truck—stay steady until we get a clear shot. Be very careful. This may be our only shot.'

Turning back to Naina, I told her to fire shots at the truck so the scared driver would speed up. She fired a few shots at the back and the side of the truck. The truck driver took off. We were still inside the tunnel. Phillip was now matching the truck's speed. Vincent's men were in cars which were famous for their powerful engines. They followed us in the middle lane, running parallel to us.

'Keep it steady, Phillip! On my mark Naina, you shoot the front tyres. Jose, you cover fires as if there's no tomorrow.'

'What happened to not killing innocent people?' Naina asked with wide eyes.

'There's no one in front of the truck, and that's why he is going so fast. This is our only chance before we hit the real city traffic,' I said.

I positioned myself in the back seat, and Naina peered outside waiting for the truck's front tyres to come into her frame of vision.

'Now!' Jose started firing indiscriminately at the cars from his window. The tunnel echoed with gunshots. Naina fired and ripped off the threads of all four front tyres with a long flurry of shots, and I blasted the truck's four back tyres at the same time.

Vincent's men got duped by Jose's cover fire.

The tyres of the truck exploded and its trailer tipped over one of Vincent's cars, crushing it. Only one car remained. Phillip floored the pedal and took off like a bullet. I climbed over the seats and rushed to Phillip, looking at the overhead direction signs. Phillip took a hard turn towards the airport.

As our car was turning left at the end of the tunnel, a heavy garbage truck was entering the opposite front lane.

I thought Phillip wouldn't make the left turn and the truck would ram into us.

We are going to die!

But Phillip managed to cut across the rampaging truck by a few inches and now raced towards the ramp. Suddenly, the last of Vincent's cars came out of nowhere and rammed us.

Naina screamed and started shooting until she ran out of ammunition. By that time, she had done enough damage. Thick layers of smoke billowed from the front of Vincent's car and then almost instantly, the front of the car exploded. The hood of the car broke off and flew a few inches above the car and then it self-rammed into the front shield. The broken windshield and explosion shook the driver, the car veered off the lane frantically and then suddenly rolled over in the middle of the highway. The car tumbled and rolled multiple times before coming to a thumping halt.

Jose then took out a pistol from Phillip's waist and threw it at Naina. She not only caught it perfectly, but she also pulled the hammer back and checked the chamber all in one slick move. I stared at her in amazement.

Jose shouted, 'Airport.' In the front, I saw an airplane landing. We were about a mile away from the airport and were speeding on an empty road leading to the airport.

Naina's eyes lit up with hope.

At the same moment, a flurry of bullets ripped through the roof and the interior of our car. I quickly covered Naina and fell on the floor. Many bullets pierced through Jose's head and torso. He fell forward, still strapped to his seat. We lost our tyres, and the vehicle sped like a shaken snake towards a deep ditch.

I quickly pushed half of my body out of the driver's side window and started shooting at something or somebody. As the dust settled, I saw a bright red motorcycle blast through the smoke. Vincent was riding it.

What the hell?

He opened fire. I got mad and I opened the car door on my side and yelled at him on top of my lungs.

'Vincent! C'mon! This is your last chance. Walk away from this!'

'Walk away where, Aditya? This is my life,' he yelled, riding on the bike, watching the road precariously. He smiled at me and then aimed his gun, at me—and then paused, he started to slow down, and the distance between the bike and the car increased. He thought for a quick second, debating between right and wrong. He chose evil again—his lips curved into a shrewd smile and he fixed his gun on me, picking up speed.

'No, Aditya, I'm not going anywhere. I will rule all these bastards!'

He was ready to shoot at me, when from the corner of his eyes he caught a spark in the dark. Someone fired at him. He immediately lost his balance. His bike wobbled.

Vincent flew in the air, but his hand grabbed the opened door of my car. I grabbed him by his jacket and pulled him up with all the strength I had in one hand.

Phillip rammed through the security door of the airport, sending the security guards scrambling.

Naina yelled, 'This is our area. Take us to the hangar.'

Her instructions were cut short when our heads moved in unison following a wave of an unbearable RUPP-RUPP noise overhead.

A glossy helicopter hovered above our heads and Mendes peeked out from it with a gun which looked like a grenade launcher.

Suddenly Mendes fired a grenade at us. It hit the front of our car—Phillip manoeuvred the car to a halt. The airport security started shooting fiercely at the helicopter. Mendes reciprocated in style, taking out their posts in shots one after another.

Wasting no time, Naina held Arjun and jumped out of the mangled car and ran for cover in the hangar. Cubby followed them.

I pushed Vincent's heavy body and we both fell out of the car onto the rocky surface.

'Leave me alone, Aditya. I'm not going to let it go. I lived my entire life hating Carlos, and I just can't let him win.'

'C'mon Vincent... We can make this work, Bro! Let's go...'

'No, Adi, you go save yourself. This is my revenge.'

I looked at him, realizing that he was a lost cause. I spun my neck around and scanned for the nearest safe zone.

I realized I was standing in the middle of an active war zone— bullets were flying past me, the smell of gunpowder was in the air and explosions and screams of people numbed my ears. I had no control on this war any more. I was going to die. I fell on my knees. I saw Naina running away in the distance with her son, and I drifted away into another world.

I stood proudly outside my house, admiring the white and apple-green paint and the dark black driveway. I saw the white

French doors of our house on which hung a welcome sign that Karan had made in the third grade. Giant evergreen cedar trees glowed in the sunlight streaming into our backyard. I stepped inside. A chandelier shimmered, warm light flooded the space.

I felt my body floating in the air and the scene changed. I was in my bedroom. Koyal was gazing in my direction, she smiled. I felt a bump, and I fell on the floor—suddenly the scene shifted. The carpet turned red with blood. The room trembled vigorously and Koyal screamed loudly. The windows rattled and family pictures shook off the wall. My house started collapsing. I reached out for help, extending my arm, but the floor beneath me cracked apart and I floated again and fell on the hard floor.

I was getting sucked into a deep hole and then I felt a touch of a hand on my hand. I looked up and found Naina, Maya and Koyal. They heaved and pulled me up. I felt loved and cared for. They wanted me to live. They wanted me to fight and go on. They had protected me all their lives.

A loud bang and I was brought back to the reality. Mendes's heavily damaged helicopter started to hover erratically. The pilot decided to pull up but the helicopter fell to the ground on its belly with a loud bang. Mendes quickly sprinted out and then charged towards Vincent and me.

Suddenly, the firing stopped. I stood there watching Mendes advancing like a mad bull. He threw his gun on his side. He knew he was in the wrong territory today, but his mission was to kill Vincent before he died himself. He advanced in rage and rammed Vincent in his stomach, lifting him up from the ground and throwing him back on the ground hard, really hard.

He kicked Vincent in his face. Vincent cried in pain. I wanted to help, but I realized I couldn't do anything. Vincent was getting what he deserved. He had ruined so many lives for his greed.

He was my friend, but he had used me all along. He deserved

what Mendes was doing to him.

I despised Vincent, but suddenly something changed in me and I slid out the long rifle from our broken car and snuck up behind Mendes. Mendes lifted his right leg to crush Vincent's face with his big elephant foot when I swung the gun at Mendes's left knee from behind. He fell to the ground, screaming in pain. Suddenly, four bullets hit his chest simultaneously and punctured his torso. He stayed on his bent knees for a few seconds before his body rolled to the side.

I looked in the direction of the shots and saw a manly figure standing with a gun in his raised arm and Naina clinging to him.

That was Carlos.

a new day

I woke up in a bed in a large and opulent bedroom. I had no idea how long I had slept, but my bruised body was still hurting.

I needed to go home.

One nightmare was over, another was waiting—I had to face the US government in Chicago upon my return. I stood under the wide sparkling shower in a spacious bathroom. Its walls were made of large red stones and ample sunlight twinkled through the artistic sky window.

I dressed in tasteful clothes which were put out for me on the bed.

I dressed up and walked out of the room. I should've been happy that a gigantic burden was off my mind. I did not feel the usual sadness in my heart. Naina was contented in her world. I was happy seeing her with her family. I stepped out of the room and entered a lavish marble hall. Breathtaking light fixtures and rich colour statuettes and paintings made it seem like we were in a palace. An attractive housekeeper greeted me and motioned for me to follow her.

In the centre of the walkway I stood facing a tall Holy Mother Mary's marble statue.

The aroma of food hit my nostrils and opened up my senses. My stomach grumbled and I realized how hungry I was.

I arrived at the table full of food, fruits and drinks.

Naina, Carlos and Arjun welcomed me warmly. The woman

left me there and slowly backed away from the scene.

Carlos walked up to me graciously. I extended my hand in anticipation, but he stretched his arms open and embraced me tightly for a few seconds. Then he pulled apart and kissed my cheeks.

Carlos reminded me of Antonio Banderas. He had a stubble, a long tanned face and was wearing aviators, a white flannel shirt and turquoise blue cotton pants. The man oozed *mafia*.

He stepped aside and then Naina walked up to me with her flowing hair. A hypnotic whiff of her perfume arrived before her and played with my heart. Naina looked at me with affection and then slid her soft arms up my chest and knotted them behind me. My arms stayed in the air for a second and then they embraced her. It was a different kind of hug. A friendly one. It felt very nice.

Arjun winked at me and gave me a high five.

The hug and the kiss from Carlos showed that he was a family man and was grateful to me for returning his family back to him. He was nothing like Vincent had described. We sat on the table and dug into the food. They had prepared an Indian breakfast for me and it was delicious. Carlos spoke to me in fluent Hindi, displaying his Indian connection.

They asked me about my family. I told them about Koyal and Karan. Naina listened to my every word with pure admiration.

After the meal, Carlos took Arjun inside. I walked with Naina in her villa's beautiful flowered walkways. She spoke to me with a compassionate voice.

'Aditya, I'm sorry for what I did to you. I don't exactly know what happened between us in India, but I do know in my heart that I meant a lot to you, so much that you didn't hesitate risking your life for me. You could have walked away when I didn't recognize you, but you stayed. You stayed for me, for my son and I'm so thankful to you and so is Carlos.'

We stopped under a gazebo near the luxurious pool filled with sparkling blue water, which splashed and made waves due to the mini waterfalls cascading down from the landscaped rocks. I had a million things on my mind. Naina and I sat in front of each other in silence on two elegant wrought iron chairs. I was waiting for explanations, a lot of them.

She gazed into my eyes and spoke in a tender voice. I knew it was a very difficult situation for both of us.

'If I could, I would wish to have my memory back even for one day. But for now, this is my life. I have chosen to not look into my past. Your Naina died in India fourteen years ago. The one in front of you is Selena. You should also wipe me from your mind and live your life with your family. I hope you found the closure you were looking for.' She put her hand on my hand and comforted me. She leaned forward and kissed me on my cheek and then walked away.

I watched her walking away. I felt I was ready to move on. She looked back at me.

I asked, 'What would you do when you wake up one day and remember our past?'

She said without hesitation, 'That will be the happiest day of my life, Aditya, and I will thank God for giving me my memories back, for completing my life.' She turned back and disappeared behind the big pillars.

I sat there, lost in thoughts. I had so many questions. How had she lost her memory? How did Carlos come into her life? What happened in Bangalore?

In that very moment, I heard Carlos approaching me.

'Our girl has been an enigma for her whole life. I know you have many questions, and you have the right to know everything,' he said. He sat down on an empty chair and breathed a long sigh. 'I thought of this very moment many times in my life—that some day you will show up looking for answers. I guess today all of us have found closure. I met Selena when she was Naina in Delhi, when she was being hunted in Vasant Vihar by her family. They had killed her school boyfriend, and she had left her home. When I met her in a cigar shop in a shopping complex, I had no idea how our fates would intertwine. She was never safe. One day she called me and asked me to take her away from India. I believe that's when she was with you. She left to save you. Her father and brothers were bloodthirsty and kept coming for her. In one of the ugly bloody fights, her father hit her on her head. When she woke up in the hospital, she didn't remember a thing. I was there and we decided to leave India for good. She chose to let the past die. No girl of any age should suffer such things, Aditya...no one deserves that. She was so young and had lost the meaning of family until we built this family bit by bit.'

I closed my heavy eyes for several moments. A wave of emotions came over me. She had such a horrifying past, just like Maya, and I had no clue about it. I owed my life to these strong women in so many ways.

'Vincent was a needy child from the beginning. He had everything, but jealousy darkened his heart. He's gone too far this time, and he will pay for this. He will be handed over to the US government and that will help you in getting back to your home. It's the least I can do. I'm one phone call away if you ever need anything in life.' Carlos patted my shoulders.

it's over

Lost in thoughts, I followed my co-passengers to the immigration area with a pounding heart. This was where my life was going to take one last dramatic turn, where I would be escorted away from the crowd of normal people and would be stamped a smuggler, a drug dealer and a murderer.

My stomach flipped with fear—the fear of losing my life and the family I had tried to save in the last two months. I approached the immigration booth with my passport clutched in my palm.

A commanding female voice resonated in my ears. 'Sir! Please step forward, Sir.'

My feet grew heavy. I looked into the eyes of the young African-American officer—a bit young to be in that powerful seat, judging who enters her country and who doesn't.

I smiled nervously as I stopped in front of the glass. She prepared to ask me her usual questions before her focus shifted from me to a commotion behind me. I turned around and saw an army of airport security marching towards me. Travellers made way for them and, as expected, all eyes turned to me. Memories of the DEA dragging me from my house came back to me.

One of the men in a suit stopped in front of me and flashed his badge, while other men in uniform took away my bag and documents. The man in the suit took me away from the immigration area. We hopped into an electric cart which moved slowly through the empty hallways.

I sat between the two suited men. Nobody said a word. The car stopped in front of a door. They signalled for me to get down and took me inside a small church with long prayer tables.

I looked at the far end and saw a statue of Jesus on a cross. In the middle of the layered tables sat a person I knew. Richard Nelson. I'll be damned. The man who knew everything—my saviour—my Jesus Christ!

Dark clouds of fear scattered away from my mind in the blink of an eye and my face lit up with sudden surge of optimism. I unhooked my arms from the grip of the suited men and quickly stepped forward. I saw that Richard's right leg was plastered and his ribs were heavily bandaged.

Somehow, he had survived Vincent's murder attempt. I needed to know if Richard knew that it was all Vincent. That he had been the mastermind behind all this, that he had played a dirty deep game and set everyone up for his sibling rivalry. He was the one who pushed Nick into Terrence's bad company and who had pushed me to the edge.

I hoped Richard found something useful from the pocket diary I gave him two days ago. I hope he knows Vincent wired 100k dollars to his and Sullivan's accounts to trap all of us. I had no proof of any of those accusations against Vincent. I just simply hoped Richard was smart enough to see through all that bullshit and understand me.

He looked at me. 'You are a free man, Mr Aditya Malhotra, all of your records are cleared as if wiped clean from the slate.'

He smiled. I didn't expect that information so easy and so quickly. It was like someone very powerful had just flipped a switch, changing my life from fucked up to blessed. I stared at him in shock and awe.

'This was never your fight, but you did in two days what

many agencies couldn't do in years. You gave us the best results since Escobar. You took out Mendes—that's just the best news I have heard in my career. The pocket diary you gave me had all of Mendes's contacts of America, and we are busting them down one by one. I know everything. We have Vincent. His ass is going to the prison for a long time, until it disappears from this world. He was delivered at the DEA's doorstep by someone very powerful. I'm guessing Carlos. I have to admit this is the quickest capture. No paperwork and legal battles for jurisdiction and extradition with the Mexican government. He's spilling his guts in this unbelievable web of lies and conspiracy. He's finally doing something good for you. He admitted to killing Soleil, wire-transferring me and Sullivan the money and sending Terrence to kill me. Well, almost killed me, but that asshole was no match for me.' He chuckled and showed me his biceps.

He signalled for his men to step back. Richard leaned in and whispered, 'I'll have the surveillance videos of your hacking expedition expunged.'

I was stunned and looked at him with gratitude.

I cleared my throat and asked, 'What about Carlos?'

He said, 'I don't think Carlos will be a problem any more. You must have changed his heart too. From his message today, I get the feeling that he and I will be friends. After all, he seemed like a decent family man.' He paused and smiled compassionately at me. He nodded at the suited man who gave me my passport.

'So go on now. Your family is waiting for you outside.'

I felt light. I longed to see Koyal. I extended my hand and he shook it firmly.'

'You are a hero, Aditya, and that's what your family knows. You have done nothing wrong. Walk out proud and celebrate your life with them.'

I thanked God and ran for the door. My feet moved slowly at first, then picked up pace. I busted open the door. I started running again and jumped over a cart full of bags.

I caught sight of Karan sprinting towards me through the thick crowd. Behind him, Koyal stood up on a bench and craned her neck to catch a glimpse of me.

My feet didn't stop until I reached my son and wife. I lifted Karan in my arms and opened the other arm to hold Koyal.

We were a family again—this time for real. I had found reasons to live my life in the best way I could.

We walked out of the airport, my heart full of happiness and my eyes fighting hard to keep the tears from rolling down.

a new beginning

Three months later. The first day of spring.

'Do not open your eyes! No cheating, Karan!' Koyal instructed cheerfully. She walked in front of us. I was walking Karan by blindfolding him with my hands. Nick and Maggie walked alongside us with their newborn baby.

'Ta-da!' I exclaimed and removed my hands, allowing Karan to see our new house.

It was a proud moment for all of us. We stood admiring our new house. It was a modest duplex, but it was ours. Painted in white and apple-green, it had a black driveway and white French glass doors on top of which hung the Welcome sign Karan had made in third grade.

The look on Karan's face was priceless. Everyone was excited and happy. He rushed from one room to another, and I felt his heart racing when I held him and showed him the way to the backyard. There was an old oak tree on which I had built a tree house.

'Dad! Is that a tree house?' he asked, dazzled with surprise.

'Not just any tree house. It's a heated room with chairs for you to hang out with your friends and read comics and books. I bet every kid in this block will line up to be your friend, so they could hang out with you in this coolest tree house.

'No TV! No Xbox?' he exclaimed.

His response made everyone laugh.

'You know I'm joking, Dad!' He hugged me quickly and

ran through the soft snow. Koyal and Nick ran after him to help him get on the ladder.

'Congratulations!'

I heard a voice and instantly recognized it. I turned around and smiled seeing Richard in the backyard patio. He was dressed in his usual avatar.

'I'm sorry the door was open, so I showed myself in. I brought a gift!' He chuckled and raised the wrapped box.

We sat in front of the fireplace with the crackling fire giving warmth. Richard swirled the cognac I gave him in the glass.

'I'm happy for you, Adi, you did a good reset on your life. All I'm offering to you is a choice to do better. You have a real talent for it.'

'Before you left for Mexico you asked if I trusted an average Indian engineer for a mission. I didn't sleep at night. Today I'm saying an average engineer with two weeks of training brought down 32 per cent of North America's drug distribution network. Imagine what you can do for this nation with full undercover training to run covert missions.'

He emptied the golden cognac in his mouth and swallowed it. I stared at him with a poker face. I reached over and picked up the warm bottle of Courvoisier cognac and refilled his glass.

'DEA Aditya Malhotra reporting, Sir!' I said with a smile.

acknowledgments

I thank my parents and sister who loves everybody and my friend, my brother Baldev for his continued support in my literary struggle.

Here's what I love: I love sitting at my desk, staring at the blank screen and bringing my imaginary characters to life. I am fortunate to have chosen this path to create a larger-than-life story yet draw nuances from life to add elements of relatability for my dearest family members and that's you—the READER of this book. This book is entirely for your entertainment, this is a book about growing up, and I'm sure many elements about growing up in India will strike an emotional chord with you.

I would also like to express my gratitude to the following: Jyotsna for being my first editor, Dibakar for pushing me to be the writer I should be. And Rupa for publishing me.